# Who
# Holds
# The
# Devil

Michael Dittman

Manta Press, Ltd.
www.mantapress.com
Cover Design by Tim McWhorter
Author Photo by Hemke

First Edition

*Acknowledgements*

*To Amy, my first and best reader; to Mr. B, the Prince of Cats; and to the Carnegie Libraries of Pittsburgh, whose wonders never end.*

Like one that on a lonesome road
Doth walk in fear and dread
and having once turned round, walks on
and turns no more his head:
because he knows a frightful fiend
doth close behind him yet.
- *The Rime of the Ancient Mariner* Samuel Taylor Coleridge


A man sees in the world what he carries in his heart.
-*Faust,* Johann Wolfgang von Goethe

# PROLOGUE

*Pennsylvania, 1875*

The morning promised clear skies on the day that Sam Mohawk's acolytes rebelled against him. At dawn, ten men with axes, scythes, and rope burst through the opening that served as a door to Mohawk's luxurious tent. The eyes of the disciples adjusted to the dim light to find Mohawk lying naked in bed with three of his wives. He didn't bother to move or act surprised. Instead, he simply stretched, like a cat awakening from a nap in a sunbeam. Blood from the events of the previous night crusted his arms, his dark hair, and the sharp lines of his cheekbones.

In just a few minutes, the men broke his jaw and threw him to the floor to kick at his ribs and spine.

"Cover your shame, you whores of the devil," one man spat at the women. The rest of the group closed in to slap and beat the women, berating and threatening them, mocking their nakedness. For their part, the women stood defiant, refusing to cry, and instead, and only after being commanded to do so, rose to put their shifts back on from their crumpled emptiness on the floor. The mob wrapped a gag around Mohawk's mouth; the pain the pressure put on his shattered bones shot through his head and brought him to the edge of unconsciousness. The night before, the rebels discussed cutting out his tongue, but when the moment came, with his bright burning eyes glaring at them, no one raised their knives.

"Save it for later," someone mumbled. The men threw Mohawk, still naked, and the three women, clad only in their shifts, into the back of a hay wagon that waited outside Mohawk's home. Two men with axes stood watch over the captives. With a snap of the reins, the strange parade began its march.

By the time the wagon and its human cargo reached the outskirts of the town of Butler, a small crowd of twenty residents gathered behind it. People, children first, threw rocks at the captives. One boy threw a chipped piece of slate that arced up and caught a guard on the forehead, opening a cut. Blood spilled out, obscuring his sight. He cursed the boy and cleared his vision by shaking his head like a wet dog. Blood splattered on the hay and the captives. Mohawk sniffed the air as blood caught in his hair and his bound hands. He smiled behind the knotted rags and through his broken teeth. The shattered bones of his jaw ground anew against one another. One rebel cuffed the rock-throwing boy on the ear and yelled for those gathering to stop throwing stones. There would be time for that sort of thing soon enough.

The trip through the orchard paths to the place where the hill was cut away into flat lots and the houses of the town sprang up below took only twenty minutes. The wagon creaked to a stop. One of the guards pushed the women off the wagon and onto the path. The crowd stepped forward and kicked them with heavy boots, spat on them, grabbed them by their hair and threw them back to the ground with cries of "whore" and "Jezebel." The women never spoke or cried out, but stared dreamily around as if unaware of what was happening to them. Their silence infuriated the crowd and whipped the onlookers into a fever pitch. The guards threw Mohawk to the ground. He landed heavily on the side of his face, and the crowd moved in immediately. Their rage was organic; it grew and thrived as they fed it more blood and anger. The early morning sun reddened, and the air thickened as the crowd's cries grew louder and their heavy blows landed on

Mohawk. A boy of no more than twelve rushed in towards him and, with a single swipe of a jackknife, lopped off his right ear. Blood gouted and spilled on the dirt. A roar erupted from the crowd, which had grown as bleary-eyed townspeople parted curtains to see the cause of the commotion. Dressing hurriedly, they left their homes and joined the crowd, swelling, then doubling its size. They pushed closer. Thuds sounded as blows from fists, feet, and clubs landed.

One of the men, who had burst through Mohawk's door just an hour earlier, moved forward and looped a rope around his neck. By now, both of Mohawk's ears and his nose had been cut off. The rope sat on his collarbone, slick with blood. A jagged, empty wound bled where his genitals had hung. His left knee bent at an impossible angle. Behind the gag, he still shouted, but no one understood what was being said.

They dragged him through the crowd to one of the black walnut trees that lined the path on which the wagon traveled. The rope was thrown around a thick branch and three men hauled Mohawk off the ground. They looped the loose end of the rope into a knot, tying it off on the trunk. Mohawk's eyes searched the crowd as the men heaved on the rope, lifting him from the ground. His eyes bulged and his bowels loosened. Boys threw rocks while his body swung and his legs kicked. People would later say that he looked right at them, right into their eyes, and they felt as if something had brushed against them.

Then, as quickly as it had come upon them, the crowd's fever of rage passed. Mohawk's wives disappeared while the crowd watched him struggle. The mob wandered off in groups of twos and threes. There was still time enough to complete the morning chores. There were two dozen people there that morning, but afterward, after the fever passed, few would admit to taking part. The town knew, though, and people stayed away from those who Mohawk had recognized, marked, and, they said, cursed. Around lunchtime, a great pillar of smoke arose from the creekside place of the Institute, visible from the town's center. No one made a move to put the blaze out, and by dinner, Mohawk's life's work was nothing more than smoking ash and rubble.

Mohawk hanged from the walnut tree for two days. The second night, someone cut down his body, dragged it a distance from the hanging tree, buried the corpse, and planted an oak sapling on top of the freshly turned earth. The season for planting had passed, but the tree survived and flourished. It grew tall and strong even as the lynching tree withered and died.

Eventually, the town became a city; the orchard cut down, and houses built where fruit once ripened and fell. People were married, lived, and died. Soon, no one spoke of Sam Mohawk and his Institute, at least not in the way they once had. If his name was mentioned at all, it was as a local curiosity, his death a sad reminder of how people "used to" act towards outsiders with ideas that seemed strange. The oak which grew over his grave dominated the neighborhood, which came to be known as Institute Hill, but the memory of how the name came to be faded in time.

Twenty-four men, women, and children looked upon the death of Sam Mohawk. Almost everyone in town looked at the oak tree planted on top of him at some point, especially in the fall when its leaves blossomed reddish-brown and fat acorns that squirrels refused to touch dropped to the bricked street. Almost everyone looked at the way the tree held its colorful leaves deep into the winter. Almost everyone looked, but almost no one allowed themselves to see.

*Pennsylvania, Present Day*

Here, where the grid of the streets has faded to boxes of strip malls and the strip malls to weeded lawns, and the lawns to bars and mobile home courts, there are no streetlights, and the night is completely dark. That night, a front was moving in and the cold wind cut through Matt Garvey as he fumbled with his truck keys. He was drunk and shouldn't be driving. He needed his job on Butler's streets crew, and to be on the streets crew, he needed a CDL. If pulled over by a cop in his current state, the state would pull his license and the city would let him go. He wasn't even sure why he had gone out. It was a Sunday night and Halloween. That week, at work, he had told anyone who listened that only kids and amateurs got drunk on Halloween. But he had been going stir crazy in the house, so he fired up the pickup and drove to Tony & J's, a bar on the side of Butler closest to his house. That way, his plan went, he wouldn't have to drive through the city to get there and back, thus lessening his chances of being picked up by one of the overeager city boys, who, in Matt's estimation, should spend more time rousting the homeless in their jungle camp by the railroad tracks than worrying about working guys who might be one or two over the limit.

The drive was simple, well suited to navigating while drunk. East out Bonniebrook Road, around the golf course, then on Carbon Center Road to his place—a trailer he had put down on three acres of land that his father had split off from the family farm as a graduation present for Matt. That had been twenty years ago. Now his home showed a sagging roofline and smelled of fast-food wrappers and old dog. It was still better than living in the city with everyone on top of each other and junkies breaking into houses and cars all the time.

He was on top of the figure before he could even register what happened. The guy hopped out of the ditch by the State Game Lands like a crippled deer. He dragged one leg behind him and held up his arm to shield his eyes from the truck's headlights.

"Jesus!" Matt yelled, slamming on the brakes. The back end fishtailed, and he smelled hot brakes and burnt tire comingling. He threw the truck into park, breathed deeply, and then jumped out into the pool of light where the man seemed to be caught.

"Buddy, are you trying to get yourself killed?"

The man lowered his arm and Matt started. The man's face was a mass of scars. He was missing an ear and his nose was a hole in his face.

"Jesus," Matt chuckled, recovering. "That's a hell of a costume, buddy. You really got me."

The man made a low moan from the back of his throat. He stooped at the waist and held his head in his hands.

"Are you…" Matt realized that what he was looking at was not a costume, "okay?"

Matt took a step closer.

"Are you hurt, buddy?" he asked, closing the distance. The man moaned deeply again. The sound penetrated Matt. His breathing quickened as adrenaline spurted into his bloodstream.

"Look, let's get you in the car. Why don't I get you to the hospital?"

The man shambled towards the passenger door. Matt followed him, opened the door, and watched how the man pulled all of his weight up with arms, then lifted his leg and dropped into the cab. Matt shut the door, crossed in front of the truck, and got back inside.

"It's a bad night to be out there, like this. Do you, do you got a place to go?" He didn't look at the man but felt his eyes burning into the side of his head.

"How about some music?" Matt clicked on the radio, but all that came through the speakers was a scratching, sizzling noise, like a starling caught in a chimney. The man leaned over to Matt as if about to confide a secret. Matt suddenly felt very sober.

In the city's white pickup the next morning, no one on the crew spoke. The general rule of thumb: Matt was the chief, and when the chief was hungover, it was better for everyone to keep their mouths shut. Finally, Hunter, the new kid, broke the silence.

"You look like shit."

Matt looked at him but didn't speak. Angry red veins shot through his eyes and deep, dark hollows circled them. His skin carried a greasy sheen. Another five minutes passed. Hunter shuffled through the order paperwork.

"You missed the turn. Fleeger Ave. is the first stop this morning."

The rest of the men winced, awaiting Matt's blow-up at Hunter's disrespect. When it didn't come, they relaxed, puzzled.

"Change in plans. We're taking down a tree on Orchard Street first this morning."

"Orchard isn't even on today's sheet," Hunter said.

"Last-minute thing." He turned his head around to the two guys in the crew cab. "To be honest, this one is off the books. It's a favor I promised to an old friend. Anyone got a problem with that?"

The men sat silent. Matt spat a long brown rope of tobacco juice into an empty Mountain Dew bottle.

"All right. Well, I am in your debt then. Hunter, we'll worry about the paperwork later."

# CHAPTER 1

When people talk about a beautiful fall day in the northeastern United States, what they're really talking about is an autumn day that is just like a summer day—warm, sunny, and clear. This concept has never made sense to me. A fall day should be cool with a breeze. There should be clouds moving around, sometimes obscuring the sun, sometimes allowing it to shine through, and other times coloring it a golden sepia as if filtered through a glass of beer. The day should be short, the dark treading on the light's heels, anxious for its business to be done. Animals should run about with important tasks on their minds—fattening up, finding dens, hiding from what they know is coming. People should be subdued, talking in low voices. Dreams from the night before should linger and trouble them late into the morning. Sounds should travel further than they used to and be warped and changed by the nascence of leaves to muffle them. The world should be the world the summer people know, but slightly changed, wavering and unrecognizable at the edges. We should be reminded that we are not the ones at the center of things on a perfect fall day.

That's what a beautiful fall day should look like. That's what the day was like when Sam Mohawk's tree was cut down.

I was still asleep when they started taking down the tree. My street is steeply inclined—in Southwestern Pennsylvania, the cities run up and down the hills like exposed seams of coal and, like those coal seams, they're mostly emptied out, leaving only smoldering pits and abandoned machinery. I watched my neighborhood change even in the eight years I had been there. The houses crept into disrepair. The craftsman bungalow across the street went from being owned by a widowed teacher who yelled at her dogs in the same voice and tone I imagined she once yelled at her husband, to being rented by a young woman who, although inexplicably wearing some variation on a Catholic school girl uniform every time I saw her, would arrive home every night at around three, typically in a car without a muffler, packed with young men. They would all sit on the roof smoking weed and drinking beer. The next morning, she would still be wearing her uniform and walking in the direction of Saint Scholastica High School. I never saw any parents. She disappeared one day, and the owners cleaned out the house with a leaf blower after filling two roll-off dumpsters. It still sits empty.

The neighborhood sank into this state organically over two centuries–the land had once been a lush orchard, much of which had been torn down after a tragic fire at a nearby orphanage and the land then used for housing. But there were still amazing old trees—my back yard was framed in black walnut trees that must have been at least 100 years old. They dropped their leathery fruit each year so that it appeared as if some sort of prehistoric lizard had haphazardly laid eggs.

Across the street from my home, next to the schoolgirl's house, was what I came to know as Sam Mohawk's Oak. The alley that ran beside my house had once been a road delimitating the end of the orchard and the beginning of the town. The road had probably been a native trail before that. The oak stood at what had been an ancient crossroads—now blocked by a piece of guardrail in poor repair. The rest of the road ran down a steep hill to the bottomlands of the town. I have no idea how a horse and carriage had once descended—the old streetcar rails were one block over on a much less steep hill. This place was once a city but now a palimpsest, overwritten in lines and emotions, visible in the right slanted light to the right person who looked hard enough.

That morning, November 1st, the buzz of chainsaws through my house's century-old single pane windows had brought me out of a deep sleep with a start. Annoying. Not leaf blower annoying, but still, not great. Out my window, a team of four men with a city truck and a wood chipper. They had already strapped the tree in the early morning filtered light. The crisscrossed webbing meant to control the rate and direction of the fall made the tree look like a dangerous prisoner chained to the floor during interrogation.

I was off work that day. My client, Walt, the writer for whom I did research, was between books, between ideas, and, between you and me, I worried that this pause was the first sign of the end. Even when I took the job almost twenty years ago, I knew the gig wouldn't last forever—we had nearly twenty-five years between us in age. I don't think that he had ever been in love with writing or with words. Books had been a way of making a living that he had fallen into almost by accident and it had worked out well for him. Thanks to the income from the film deals and the bestsellers, he had no motivation to continue writing. Although I never would have said a word to him, it hadn't passed my attention that I had received a healthy raise at about the same time that chunks of what sounded suspiciously like my prose started ending up in his books. I continued doing the work he sent me and, in the meantime, stored money away as best I could and started thinking about Act II of my life.

Originally, as a young man, I planned to have been a writer. That choice sounds quaint now—as if I had told you that I had longed to be a buggy-whip maker or cobbler. For me, the advent of the internet was a double-edged blade. The expanded communications make it possible for me to work in pajamas three or more days out of the week, but it also makes my skill set less useful. When anyone can publish anything immediately, getting the research right matters a lot less. People make twice my yearly income publishing ebooks that read more like loose collections of ideas scribbled down after a fever dream, then formatted and put online for sale. I imagine working in the self-publishing arm of Amazon must be like managing a vast empire of slum properties. Luckily for me, there are a still a few dinosaurs roaming the Earth: men and women whose names alone on the cover mean a best - seller in pre-order before the audience even knows what the plot is about. Many of these marquee writers are old and don't like to travel or never really got into using the internet in a deep, productive way but still feel a responsibility for getting things right. I work for one of them—a prolific historical detective fiction writer. He, writing under about six different pen names at various times, needs to know what kind of food was served in Regency England or what Appolcia, Florida was like in the 20s or the layout of streets of Newport, Connecticut in 1865. He has more money than he could ever spend and is more interested in the scope of his story than the ground-level details. That's where I come in.

I answered Walt's ad in the Boston *Phoenix* two months before I graduated from college. I met him for coffee and we got along. Two days later, he called to say the job was mine if I wanted it, and we've been a team ever since. The work has always been steady and interesting. The pay isn't great, but it's more than I could make as a writer and enough to keep my head afloat— especially here in the outlying suburbs of Pittsburgh where the cost of living is negligible.

That morning, while watching the city crew go to work, I was trying to decide if I was too old for one of those learn-to-code boot camps that were springing up everywhere like litter revealed after a snow-melting winter thaw. I remember thinking that these guys heaving themselves out of the white pickup parked across the street from my house didn't seem to be as professional as the crews the power companies sent out along rural roadways. These four looked like the normal city crew who splashed hot patch on potholes all summer, only these guys were armed with chain saws instead of shovels. They were, I noticed, avoiding the work part of the job in the manner of city workers worldwide. They talked a bit, blocked the street off, smoked a bit, spit on the ground, and then finally set to work.

They had already spent about an hour re-strapping the tree when one guy finally yanked the cord on his saw and it roared to life. Two guys stood ready with more straps and roping, and another appeared to be the spotter. Another hour or so spent with the sawyer in the truck's bucket taking off smaller limbs. One of the rope guys would peel them off and feed them into the small chipper attached to the hitch behind the truck.

My head throbbed from the noise. Just around the time I was thinking of taking my bike down the alley for a ride, the saw stopped, the bucket lowered, and the sawyer clambered out. The crew took a short break and then the guy who had been in the bucket took his power saw and headed to the base of the oak. The tree stood about 50 or 60 feet high. Why no one thought to take it down in chunks, I still don't know—that's what professionals who I talked to later said was standard practice. Instead, the sawyer went at it, cutting the trunk at the base on the side away from my house and away from the street so that it would fall backwards into my neighbor's lot.

Except it didn't. Even now, after everything that happened, I still have trouble remembering the exact details of this part. There's a blank spot in my memory, like pages torn from a diary. But when I close my eyes, this is the movie that plays on a loop: The tree begins to settle away from the house, then, against all laws of physics, as if it were caught in an unimaginably strong wind or gently pushed by a giant hand, it turns the other way—towards my house, towards the window where I stood watching. The rope guys begin to yell. I see their mouths moving, but I can't hear anything over the machinery noise. The tree continues to fall. It catches a powerline and pulls the wires down. Sparks explode as the wires, free from their insulators and looking for ground, flail wildly. The trunk hits the ground and takes a huge chunk out of the stone wall that sits between my front lawn and the sidewalk. The floor shakes beneath me with the force of the blow. The noise rings in my ears as if I was sitting in the middle of a car crash. The giant oak is rent in two. The wood is split down the middle and twisted like a spiral fracture of the leg. The break reveals a deep hollowed out spot in the middle big enough for a man to crouch. All the electricity in the house has vanished. The normal tone of the room, humming with power and life, is gone, but the gasoline powered truck and chipper outside continued to roar, which is why I, thankfully, can't hear the screams when the powerlines whirl about and lay onto the sawyer. The wires wrap around him like the stinging tentacles of a jellyfish and burn his body into an ashy, hollow thing.

Later, the newspaper said that the man was killed instantly, and I have no reason to doubt its report. What I saw, the spasming of his charred and blackened body, must have simply been reflex. A windswept from the direction of the stump and whirled the woodchips and the smoke and the burnt bacon smell all together and then vanished just as quickly. Men were screaming as equipment was hurriedly shut off. Orange emergency cones were tossed out, closing the street for the rest of the day. I sat, shocked and transfixed for hours and then, even though it was still daylight, took to bed, and slept fitfully. The smell was still there the next day when I woke. It lingered for days, the worst part.

The power crews worked into the night long after the police and ambulances had left. The next morning, the power was back on. A new crew was on the street cleaning up the oak—a professional group, this time with the bright orange equipment. The noise was deafening, and for the second day, I fought off a merciless headache. I went through the motions of the day with a nagging undercurrent of fear and anxiety. I was being irrational, I told myself. After all, in this scenario, I was by far the luckiest element of this horrific little tableau.

Around lunch, someone pounded on my door. One of the crew stood there, her hair stuffed up inside her hardhat, her face glistening with sweat even on this cool cloudy day.

"You the owner?"

"Of what?" I asked, confused.

"This house?" She shook her head a little in exasperation.

"Oh. Yeah. Right. Yes, this is my house."

"There's some damage to your wall."

"Right. I saw that."

"Boss sent me to tell you that someone from the city will be in touch about fixing it."

"Okay. How long will that be?"

"No clue."

"Sorry?"

"Not our job. We're not city. We'll take the tree trunk off, but you'll have to wait for the city to call about the actual repairs."

"Oh. I… Okay."

She turned and left. Talking to her made me feel worse. I couldn't shake the feeling that something terrible was about to happen to me. I would go about the motions of the day, making tea, for example, when a thought would fall into my head. I would imagine it was my body on the ground, sizzling, with my body fat rendering into a pool before catching alight. The thought wouldn't leave, playing over and over in my head. Then a sentence, or even just a few words: *That will be you. That's how you're going to die. Those screams are what you will sound like.* I had been dealing with these attacks of intrusive thoughts for years now. No one knew about them. I had done the research; I knew what I was supposed to do. It never worked. Not engaging with the thoughts was impossible, even though I knew it only made it worse.

I went back upstairs to watch more of their work. It was as if I were in a trance, hearing and seeing myself in the place of the dead worker. When my phone buzzed a few hours later, I could hardly summon the energy to answer it. The voice on the other end was old-man loud. Walt, my client, was used to people listening. He steamrolled ahead in conversation. Even when he asked a question, he wasn't looking for an answer.

"Moody! How goes it?"

"You wouldn't believe me if I told you."

"Listen, I… What the hell is that noise? I can barely hear you. Something wrong with your phone?"

"No… that's what I was talking about—the city was taking a tree down outside…"

"My God—you must be bored if that passes into the unbelievable category for you."

"Yeah, well, like I was saying, they started…"

"Listen, I won't keep you. I just wanted to give you a heads up. I'm going on vacation."

"Oh?"

"Yeah, down to the Turks and Caicos. November in Boston is just getting too cold for my bones."

"Okay. A vacation, huh? Have you ever been on a vacation?"

"My life is a vacation, baby. Do what you love and you'll never work a day in your life."

"So, what you're saying is that you won't have any work for me in the foreseeable future."

"Right."

"How foreseeable?"

"Well, I'll be down there until April. I mean, I'll be in touch, but I thought you might want to know."

"Budget."

"Exactly."

"Okay. Well. Have fun. Send me a postcard."

I had adopted resignation as a coping strategy shortly after my wife had left me. The path of least resistance isn't very scenic, but at least you're never traveling alone.

"Will do, but there's something else."

"Shoot."

"So, I don't want to leave you completely in the lurch, money-wise, you know? Well, there's this guy. A fella I met at a reading. He's the real deal: has a couple of novels under his belt already, teaches up here. Anyhow, he's working on a book set in Pittsburgh, and I gave him your name. Said you're the best researcher around when it comes to local color and all that."

"Well, thanks. What's his name?"

"Um... I want to say James something. Maybe Bill? Anyhow, he'll be calling you, but, just so we're on the same page, when I come back, I get first dibs on you, right?"

"Yeah. Of course."

"Okay, kiddo. Good luck. Talk to you later."

# CHAPTER 2

Two weeks later, I hadn't heard from the mysterious new client or the city about the damage to my wall. Shortly after his call, I had emailed Walt and asked for the new client's name, but I hadn't heard back from him. The longer I waited, the more the anxiety built around the edges of my mind. I started staying in bed longer, listening to my worries bounce off the inside of my skull. I put off leaving the house for groceries and didn't put out the recycling for pick up. I could feel intrusive thoughts nibbling around the edge of my consciousness, looking for a way to get in. I needed a win or at least a feeling of control in some small part of my life, so I mustered the last bit of my willpower, threw on my jacket, and walked downtown to the old city hall to see what was going on with the repairs to my wall.

The city had built a new city hall, a brutal concrete structure, some thirty years ago, but had kept the old Victorian mansion that had served as the old city hall for nearly a century. The sexy stuff, gun permits, court system, and the like, was in the new building where there were metal detectors and security guards and cameras. This concrete palace was the place where the city made it easier for itself to exist. Here, the bureaucrats made sure that their life-support machinery ran smoothly. On the other hand, the old city hall was where citizens went to get help, and the system ran slowly and erratically. I dreaded going there. I had once received a zoning violation in error and correcting it took three months. But I wanted to have my stone wall fixed, and I didn't want to pay for it.

The old city hall entrance was fronted with imposing, ten-foot-tall wooden doors with windows pocked with air bubbles trapped in the ancient glass. An ancient cast iron fire escape wound from the left side of the building to beside the front door. On the first floor hunched a birdcage-style elevator that I wouldn't have stepped foot in for all the repaired stone walls in the world.

An elderly lady sat opposite the elevator at the folding card table that served as the receptionist's desk. To her left was a spinner rack of pamphlets with area attractions; there weren't many. Heavy velvet curtains hung over the windows, and original pocket doors sectioned off what had been parlors and sitting rooms into individual offices. The house had been beautiful at one time, but now it was full of cheap laminate flooring and warehouse store office furniture that sat behind those dusty, dark doors.

The receptionist was having a lively discussion with an old man with a red VFW hat propped on top of his so that the bill was almost vertical. The gist of their conversation seemed to revolve around a grandchild of someone they both knew who had been arrested for drugs. Not an unusual story here; heroin had swept through twenty years ago, filling the void of the lost industrial jobs—the ladder factory, the coke plant. There was a brief respite during which dirt-cheap meth took over, but once grievously wounded soldiers and sailors started coming back from the Middle East, opioids had returned. Men and women, their bodies ravaged by war, would need painkillers for the rest of their lives. The amount the VA docs prescribed didn't always seem like enough, and imports from Mexico meant that heroin was cheaper than it had ever been. At the same time, pharmacological companies and their reps started marketing Oxy to doctors for a wide array of ailments, and kids started finding half-empty and mostly forgotten bottles of it on their parent's or grandparent's medicine cabinet shelves. They, too, ended up looking for a cheaper alternative on the street. Now, heroin laced with fentanyl, and even carfentanil, had taken hold. When reports of fentanyl first started showing up in the news, I had scoffed—who the hell, outside of that Beastie Boys song, smokes elephant tranquilizer? I didn't joke for long. At least two bodies blue with overdose show up every week in the town and outlying rural areas. The constant search for money for drugs means that if you leave your car or house unlocked, you're a fool.

As the two reached a lull in the conversation, the receptionist looked up at me. Shock registered on her features even although she couldn't have helped but to see me there.

"Oh! I'm sorry…"

"Well," the old VFW man said, "I guess I'll be going. Let you get back to work."

"Okay, Dwight, and don't you worry, I'll be praying for you."

The old man nodded, adjusted the suspenders on his jeans as he stood, and walked out the way I had come.

"Well, now," she said, turning toward me. "What can I help you with?"

"I need to talk to someone. About my wall. The wall in front of my house was damaged. By the city. In the… accident a few weeks ago."

"Oh, my honey. That's not good at all, is it? Well, let's see. I guess you'd want to talk to… well… let's start with zoning."

"Zoning?" I already knew that zoning was a place where the mills of the gods had stopped grinding decades ago. "But the wall is already built. I just need to find out how to get it fixed."

"Oh, but I think you'll need a building permit to work on your wall, so…"

"Right, but, see, I don't want to work on it myself. I want the city to fix it."

"Sure honey, but any work will still require a permit. So, Zoning is up the stairs and then walk straight ahead. Or, if you take the elevator…"

"I'll walk," I said and made my way past her to the stairs.

The stairs were narrow with a worn waterfall-style carpet runner. If two people were to try to use the stairs at the same time, one of them would have to back up. Upstairs, the house was even more of a rabbit warren of small rooms with unlabeled closed doors and dead-end hallways. One could get lost up here for days and never be found. I stuck to the directions and walked straight ahead, trying not to spend too much time looking from side to side. The door that the receptionist told me would be Zoning stood straight ahead without the slightest suggestion of what lay behind it. It was not the same door that I remembered from my earlier visits here. Should I knock or just walk through? What if the old lady had been confused, and I walked into the middle of a meeting or an occupied restroom? Grasp the nettle, I thought. I turned the knob and walked through.

The room was bright and seemed too big for the space of the second floor. There was a desk like a bank teller's, long and tall, running most of the width of the room. Windows and natural light filtered through. The room was warm, almost uncomfortably so, and from somewhere, I heard someone hunting and pecking on an old-fashioned electric typewriter.

"Hello?" I called.

"Yes?" a voice sounded from somewhere behind the desk.

"I, uh… the lady at the desk sent me to see you."

A face popped up like a meerkat from behind the long desk.

"Ruby. She sends everyone up here. Poor dear, I don't know if she even remembers that there are other offices here. What can I do for you?"

This woman was old as well, past retirement age, I would have guessed, but she moved quickly and had a commanding voice.

"Well, you see… I have a stone wall in front of my house."

"Where do you live?"

"On Institute Hill."

"Mm-hmmm… The Historical Society will never let you tear it down. Between you and me, I call it the Hysterical Society." She laughed at her joke.

"Oh. No, I don't want to tear it down. I want to have it fixed."

"Oh! Okay. Did you have a contractor in mind? If it's one who does a lot of work in the city, he probably already has the paperwork."

"Well, yes, I'd like the city to fix it for me."

She looked at me puzzled for a moment and then burst out in laughter.

"You had me there for a minute! And I guess you'll want the sewage and water authority to put in a pool for you too, right?" She laughed heartily again.

"No, I mean, they told me. I was told that they would fix it. The wall was damaged. In the accident. A few weeks ago… you know, by the tree." I was desperately trying not to say *where the worker was burnt to death while I watched*. Partially because she might have known him, but mostly because I was working on burying the memory as deeply as I could.

"Oh." She turned quiet. "Poor Matt." She sighed deeply and there was an awkward pause. "Well, yes, this isn't actually the right office. You'll need to go to…" she closed her eyes in thought and sighed, "the City Solicitor maybe. That's where I would start."

"The Solicitor? I should talk to a lawyer to get a wall fixed?"

"I'm sure there's paperwork to be done."

"Okay. Is the Solicitor's office on this floor?"

"Oh no, honey, she's in the new City Hall."

"But could you… ah… no… that's fine. Thanks." I knew

when I had reached a dead end.

"They never should have been there at all, you know."

"Sorry?"

"That crew, the day Matt died. They never should have been there at all."

"Oh? I thought the whole thing looked a little odd. They didn't seem like a tree removal crew."

"Oh, that's not what I mean. Any one of those men had cut down dozens of trees and some bigger than that oak. No, I mean, cutting down the Mohawk tree and at this time of year. I mean, I'm not superstitious, but still…"

"Mohawk tree?"

She screwed her face up in puzzlement again.

"The Mohawk tree, where they hanged Sam Mohawk?"

"What?"

"You're not from around here, are you, Sweetie?"

"Yeah, no, I mean I've lived here for almost ten years."

"And you haven't heard about Sam Mohawk?"

I shook my head "no," and she beckoned me back in closer.

"He was a real bad guy back in the, well, a long time ago, back when where your house was nothing but a forest. He killed some people. Was it his wife? Or… maybe it was a baby… I forget. Anyhow, he killed them, and a bunch of people hanged him in that forest and buried him. That oak that killed Matt grew on top of Mohawk's grave."

"So, a man was lynched forty feet from my front door?" The real estate guy's listing sheet had not mentioned this tidbit.

"Hanged honey. It's only lynching if it's a black person."

"I don't think that's…" She looked at me and slowly nodded her head "yes." "Okay, well that's… amazing."

"You should look it up, honey. This little city has a lot of history."

"O human race, born to fly upward,
wherefore at a little wind dost thou so fall?"
- *The Divine Comedy*, Dante Alighieri

# CHAPTER 3

Sam Mohawk was his third, and final, name. Elias Butler had been his second. Before that, there had been another, Kurt Mueller, given to him by his mother a few days after he was born, which was also a few days before she died. He had another name, one that he had given himself, but he had buried it deep in his soul. His soul, he liked to tell people in moments that called for great theatrics, had been placed inside a needle, then inside an egg, which had been placed inside a beehive, then inside a tree, the location of which he no longer remembered. This story was an old one and not his. In truth, he had lost his soul in Boston during a fire that consumed his work and sent him back to wandering.

He started writing the story of his life at twelve years of age when he left his small Pennsylvania town and his father's backhands and razor strop to join the 13th Pennsylvania Regiment. He had seen a man who looked to be the same age as his father, but slim with longish dark hair and a mustache that drooped at the corners, step onto an apple crate in the middle of the market area and speak.

"Have any of you seen the signs in the heavens? I have. Last night, shortly after the moon rose, a very distinct and bright cross was visible, of which the moon was the center. The arms of the cross extended on either side, apparently about one degree, at the extremity of each arm was an upright column, seen through the clouds."

Farmers and their families had stopped shopping to listen to the man. He wore a Union uniform, the buttons of which had been polished until they gleamed and caught the sun. His eyes were full of fire and passion. The boy had never seen anyone control a crowd as this man did.

"When the moon was about three hours high, the cross and the columns disappeared, and several bright and distinct circles succeeded. At one time, as many as six great circles were visible. From ten to eleven, two circles were displayed, but those were very bright and beautiful, and what to me, seemed most strange, part of the circumference of one ran through the center of the other—a clear and complete belt."

He paused to wipe his face, and one of the gathered men yelled, "So what does it mean?"

The soldier looked out over the crowd and spoke in clear measured tones.

"It means war, by God. And it means victory for the North. My old father told me he saw the same thing before he signed up for the Mexican War. We left them in a state of degradation and ruin and we'll do the same to the rebels. Now, who is with me?"

A cry went up from the crowd as young men made their way to sign up. Kurt Mueller joined them, not out of a political desire or even with dreams of being a hero. He wanted to learn how to control a crowd with his voice as this man had done.

He was made a drummer, and he took the name Elias Butler. Butler was the name of the town in which he had been born. Mrs. Elias had been a kind-hearted woman in that town who, occasionally slipped him still-warm cornbread when he dawdled outside her picket fence.

In the army, there was food, but never enough, and clothes that didn't fit. Often beaten for insubordination, he was once forced to stand on a barrel in the middle of camp for an entire day for distracting a guard. This brand of brutality was better than the life he had left. He got along well with the other soldiers and was given a dead man's rifle, cut down to fit him, which he used to great accomplishment. Butler never again saw the soldier who had done the speaking that morning in the market.

Late one night, a little over two years from the day that he joined, and a week after the horrors of The Battle of Spotsylvania, he burnt his blood and brain spattered uniform. He snuck out of camp and settled into drifting. He worked as a farmhand for a few years, traveling from job to job. He found work as an assistant to a photographer who taught him to read and write. He was brilliant, the man had told him, a quick learner. The old man treated him like a son and one night, as bitter repayment, Butler cleaned out the cashbox and left. He ran through the money and then, near Chambersburg, following a crowd of excited looking farmers, found his calling as he watched a man selling fake patent medicine to people in real pain. He spent his last dollars on a large suitcase, empty brown bottles, and a quantity of grain alcohol, opium, molasses, and senna. He prospered and moved from a suitcase to a trunk to a wagon in short time. He ran small scams on the side and found that he had become as good a grifter as he had been a killer. He was a genius at spinning the tale of Doctor Morse who had lived among the Mohawk Indians for three years, learned their secrets, and then returned to civilization with an esoteric knowledge of liver pills. Every time he stood on the back of his wagon, he was reminded of that soldier who had changed his life.

One early summer night, in a tavern between Erie, Pennsylvania, and Buffalo, New York, Butler overheard two local teamsters discussing their financial fortune from hauling eccentric out-of-towners up the way to Lilydale. Butler joined the two men at their table, bought them each an ale, and listened to their stories of the wealthy who arrived by train and then set off to visit Lilydale. The town had sprung up like mushrooms after the rain, they told Butler, and women and men wearing expensive clothes and hauling traveling trunks all came to hear word from beyond. Lilydale was a town of spiritualists. Where there are desperate people, Butler thought, there is money to be made.

The next morning, Butler steered his wagon away from the road to Buffalo and followed the directions the men had given him. He set up camp a few miles outside of Lilydale so that people making their way from the station would see and hear him first: wooly little sheep waiting for the shears. One evening after making a fine amount of coin hawking liver pills to wealthy neurasthenics, he made his way into the town itself and sat in on a seance. It was lonely moving from town to town and he often sought out an evening's entertainment where he could find it. In the streets of Lilydale, he saw wealthy and grieving parents attempting to contact their children who had not come back from the War of Southern Rebellion. His knowledge of the war combined with his gift for reading marks made this new field perfect for him.

He and ten others were ushered into the parlor of a small home. They shifted in their seats while the medium sat taking them all in. Emma Moses was a small woman with a round face and cold eyes. She dressed in black with hair tightly coiled on top of her head. She possessed a disarming overbite and long thin, agile fingers. Her assistants fussed in the background, receiving whispered orders from her in their ears. The workers laid a small hand drum, a banjo, and an assortment of harness bells in the middle of the table.

With everyone seated, the woman asked them to join hands, warning them not to break the circle no matter what happened. Butler, who had fortified himself with a good deal of rum, grinned at the woman. Emma Moses did not smile back.

The assistants lowered the lights and, in the dark, Butler heard them open and close the door to signify that they had left the room. There was a silence. The woman to the left of Butler had dry brittle hands and the man to his right such soft skin that

Butler wondered if he had ever even seen a shovel. The room stunk of tallow candles, strong tobacco, and lily of the valley eau de toilette. The sound of the group's breathing settled into one rhythm and that noise, combined with the summer's evening heat, lulled them.

The deep thump of a drum broke the silence. Someone gasped. Moses whispered, "Don't break the circle," and the hands on either side of Butler tightened.

"Spirits," Moses called to the room, "are you here?"

The banjo strummed.

That crafty old cow, Butler thought. He had already marked her assistants when he first arrived, circulating among guests, appearing to make small talk, but, in reality, gathering information that Moses would use later while relaying messages from the spirits. Now, he realized she had somehow freed her hands and was making the noise. Or had she another set of instruments under the table which she was manipulating with her feet? She had already been sitting when we came in, Butler thought, and the tablecloth draped all the way to the floor.

With the rum courage slipping through his veins, Butler broke his grasp on his neighbor's hands and darted for Moses' seat. He dropped to his knees and reached under the table where he found a bare ankle and the body of a banjo.

"Strike a light!" Butler yelled. A moment later, Butler found himself on his back with a pain around his eye. She may not have been much of a spiritualist, Butler thought as he lay dazed, a thin trickle of blood seeping from the ridge of his eyebrow, but she kicked like a mule.

# CHAPTER 4

Even though I had kindled an irrational hope on my walk back from the old city hall, there was no crew working to put my wall right when I made it home. I was out of breath from climbing the steep hill that led up to my house and stood hunched at the foot of my front stairs trying to catch my breath when my phone rang. The screen revealed a 617 number: a Boston number I didn't recognize. I ignored it, convinced that it was a robocall about a non-existent expiring warranty on my car when I remembered the new client.

"Hello?" I gasped into the phone.

"Hi. Could I speak to Aaron Moody, please?"

"Speaking." The sweat between my face and the glass of the phone made it slippery and hard to hold. I needed to get more exercise.

"Oh. Hi. My name is Nick. Nick Porter?"

"Hi," I said still breathless.

"Did I catch you at a bad time?"

"No... not at all. I was just... on the treadmill." Stupid. Why lie? Why not just admit, *No, I'm out of breath because I walked up a hill. It wasn't that steep, but I was carrying my children, you know, middle age and creeping anxiety, on my back.*

"Let me shut it off here." I sat down on my front steps. The damage from the oak, now just a three-foot-high stump, laid out in front of me like the ruins of a child's building blocks. "There we go. Phew. Okay. Thanks. What I can do for you, Mr. Porter?"

"It's Nick, please. So, I got your name from Walt. I'm looking for someone to do some research about Pittsburgh for me, and he recommended you."

Walt had finally returned my email with the new client's name. I had done some due diligence on Nick Porter. He was in his 30s and liked to have his picture taken. He came from money and showed up at benefits as often as readings. He had written a novel, a thinly veiled roman-à-clef, about a group of college seniors in Portland, Maine, who worked in a bookstore, swapped beds, and faced impending graduation and the adult world. The book had earned him profiles in the *New York Times* magazine and *Buzzfeed* and a plum teaching position in one of Boston's finest MFA programs. That had been five years ago, and while he still showed up at openings, other than some essays and cultural criticism, he had not written since.

"That's great. Yeah. He told me you might be calling. What kind of work did you have in mind?"

"Well, the same sort of stuff you do for Walt. I'd fly down and do it myself, but I'm on a tight schedule. My sabbatical doesn't start until the end of next semester, that is to say, spring semester, and I want to have everything ready so I can jump right in and have it all done by the end of summer."

"Eight months. Is it a large project?"

"It's no great magnum opus or anything. Just a detective novel that I want to set in post-World War II Pittsburgh."

"Why not just set it in Boston since you're right there?"

"Well, my agent thinks it might be more advantageous to set it in Pittsburgh. The city is really hot right now, you know. It'll be good for PR. Murder in the Most Livable City? Stuff like that."

"Uh-huh. So, you'll be looking for what? Crime reports, neighborhood stories?"

"Yeah… local color, maps, routes to get characters from one place to another. I'd like to throw a little of what was really going on in Pittsburgh during that time."

"Race relations?"

"Sure. Steel mills, sports, the whole thing. Walt said you did some amazingly thorough reports. You're a heck of a writer yourself, I hear. Walt said you were great about including big chunks of prose, kind of… what was the term he used?"

"Priming the ol' pump?"

"That's it. What a character, huh?"

Had Walt told him that I kept my mouth shut when my writing turned up in his books?

"So, you're looking for a high level of detail, more than just bulleted lists and photocopied city directories?"

"Right. Right. So, I was thinking that I could send you the proposal over to get a better idea of the plot…"

He had Walt's habit of talking over me, but none of the old man's charm.

"That would be helpful."

"And then you could just go for it. It'll be a short-term sort of thing, of course. A month or two at most, I imagine."

"Okay."

"Okay, so you're interested?"

"Sure." I needed money coming in.

"Well, that's great! I'll send the storyline over today."

"Do you want me to send over my boilerplate contract?"

"Oh… right. I guess we should talk terms."

"Same deal as Walt. $75 per hour, plus expenses like photocopying, mileage, parking, all broken out with receipts and documentation. In return, you get the full report written up and a non-disclosure agreement from me."

"$75. Huh. Wow. I guess I was thinking more like $50."

"Yeah, it's not really negotiable." The sweat was drying, and

I was cooling off. I wanted to go back inside. "It's the same deal I worked out with Walt. You could get a grad student from Pitt or CMU for $50. Heck, probably $25, but I've been doing this type of work for a long time. I'm fast and efficient, thorough, and discreet." I paused, letting the last word set in. I was never this assertive with Walt, but sitting there, looking at the ruins of the tree, I felt a thrill, as if I was standing at the edge of a building and looking down. "Did Walt tell you about *Key West Cockfight*?"

"Yeah."

"And…" I was treading lightly here. I really did have an NDA with Walt.

"He told me he hasn't ever actually been to Key West. Or Florida."

"But the book won the PAPA award for writing about Florida. The judges said that rarely had the history and feel of Florida been captured in such a way by a non-native. You will not get that level of detail…" I paused. What had come over me? Why was I selling so hard to someone I didn't like? How badly did I need this money? Bad enough. "… that level of detail, all spelled out in clear easy-to-read prose, from a guy who's also TAing an Intro to Comp course with 250 students."

"Okay, okay. Fair enough. Send the contract over and I'll have my lawyer look at it. If everything looks good, I'll sign it and send it back."

My distrust of Porter grew. It's hard enough to trust lawyers and even more difficult to trust guys who have lawyers.

"Sounds good," I said. "Looking forward to seeing the proposal."

"Talk to you soon."

The phone went dead. I wiped the slick screen on my shirt and tucked it back in my pocket before walking around back to the deck.

Most people buy the story put forth by Google and the

others. Everything has been digitized and is only a search away. I'm not saying that I miss the days of pouring through microfilm just to get a look at something simple like two lines from a fifty-year-old *New York Times* article, but to be honest, it was good for business when people thought they had already found everything worthwhile after two or three runs through a search engine using a basic keyword search. I looked like a magician when I showed up with information that they hadn't seen before.

The truth is, there's a lot of stuff out there, fantastic stuff, interesting stuff that lies beneath those low hanging fruit that any kid could find for you. There are vast uncatalogued archives all over the world. Eastern Europe? Asia? The amount of stuff just sitting in museums and archives unlabeled is mind-blowing. Even here in the States. Walt had underwritten a lot of research trips over the years. Every town bigger than 500 people seems to have a historical society with a little museum set in the oldest house. They collect information and artifacts like hoarders, and none of them have the money, time, or knowledge to even keep a simple catalogue, let alone digitize it. If you can talk them into letting you dig around, more often than not, they just showed you the basement with endless bankers' boxes, gave you a vague idea of where they thought the material might be, and then showed up again to roust you when they were ready to lock up.

So, when I show up with some great information, not the stuff that's shared on Facebook a million times or incorporated into "20 Odd Things You Won't Believe About Your State" written by a new college graduate who just moved to your state from 500 miles away, then I look like a wizard. There's no genius to it, of course, just slow, plodding, methodical work. The work most people hate to do. The work I find to be like Zen mediation or panning for gold. Nick wouldn't see any of the really good stuff, though. I'd cherry-pick one or two things that wouldn't show up on the first three pages of a google search and incorporate them.

Something told me he'd be suitably impressed.

"Mrrrrwwwwwww." A strident annoyed meow assaulted me as I turned the corner.

"B! How long have you been there?"

Mr. B stood on the railing deck eight feet above the concrete drive below. A small cat with black and grey tiger stripes, enormous paws, and a tail that was preternaturally poofed. He was vocal in everything, expected food and affection, and was a master jumper and climber. He was not my cat, but spent most of his days with me. He had shown up one afternoon two years ago after my wife left, while I worked in the yard. I heard a cat yelling and when I turned around, he was on the railing, sassing me. He didn't run when I approached. Instead, he followed me and walked through my door into the kitchen like he owned the place. I fed him canned tuna, after which he hopped up on my couch and fell asleep for several hours. I thought he was lost. He was not. Turned out, he lived a block away with a middle-aged bodybuilder and his mastiff. But Mr. B spent most of his days here and even some nights in the winter. Often, he was the closest thing I had to human contact.

"C'mon, dummy." I walked up on the deck and he jumped down. "Want some grub?"

We walked into the kitchen, and I dug out the kibble. I had just poured the food into his bowl when I smelled a noxious burning scent. I slammed the bag onto the counter and spun around to check the oven. As I turned, dizziness overtook me. A fog drizzled into the periphery of my vision. Mr. B looked up, puzzled by his kibble as I sank to the floor, overwhelmed by nausea.

"Hey, buddy, I…"

The cat and my kitchen island grew and then faded in and out of focus. Two figures appeared, translucent and super-imposed on the walls of the kitchen like a double exposure caught on film. The burning smell got worse and I could feel bile at the back of my throat.

A man, short and dark with intense burning eyes and a thick mustache punctuating a florid face, was screaming at the other figure who had grown smaller as I watched. It was a child. A boy. He wore ragged pants and a simple white shirt. His face and hands were filthy. The room bloomed with the smell of sweat and unwashed clothes.

*You whoreson. I won't be disrespected by the likes of you.*

*Please, I was tired.* The smaller figure raised his hands in an attempt to protect himself. Both figures faded in and out of sight.

*What have I told you, Kurt? When it is harvest time, you pick!* the larger of the two shouted.

The smaller one twisted his body away, trying to provide a smaller target as the larger one pulled back his hand. I saw what I thought was a belt, before realizing it was a leather razor strop in his hand. The father brought it down, aiming for the boy's back, but the boy's twisting meant that he received the blow on the thin skin of his rib cage. He screamed in pain, and I could see red blossoming under the white of his shirt.

*My own son! I have given you everything. Everything!*

The strop continued to come down with force, like an ax cutting wood for kindling.

*And I find you asleep in the orchard.*

The boy had given up now. He collapsed beside me on the ground. His wide eyes stared in terror and seemed to meet mine. He closed them for a moment, then opened them a slit and smiled at me. He knew I was there, watching.

The last slash caught the boy across the face and opened a gaping wound like a gill. The boy's blood splashed onto my face. I tasted warm copper in my mouth, and before I could scream myself, I passed out.

When I came to, there was a trail of watery yellow puke down the front of my shirt. Mr. B lay curled beside my head on the cold tile. When I stirred, he looked up at me quizzically.

"C'mon, buddy," I said, pulling myself up with the lip of the marble counter. Mr. B stretched his back, ignored my motioning towards the door, and hopped onto the couch. I let him stay and even managed to change my shirt before I drove myself to the hospital.

# CHAPTER 5

The morning after disrupting the séance, Butler sold his medicine business lock, stock, and barrel to the son of a dry goods store owner who was looking to see the world. Relying on both greased palms and thinly veiled threats of supernatural retribution, Emma Moses flexed her influence following Butler's performance at the séance. The Lilydale council banned him and his patent medicine from the city limits, and that decision was fine by him. He had a new focus for business and began a slow trip up through the Burned Over District, where the fire and brimstone of those earlier preachers followed by the rapping and knuckle-popping of the Fox Sisters turned over fertile soil.

By 1871, he had grown into a handsome man of twenty-one with a keen mind. He was tall and thin with delicate hands and shining brown eyes. His mustache was trim and his hair lay on his head under a macassar sheen. He used his youth and good looks as an entrée in the spiritualist circles where he now found himself. He sat in on other spiritualist's meetings and séances, watching how they prepared the marks. He plied them with drink and flattery and walked away with their secrets, improving on them, continuing to hone his craft on his way up through the Finger Lakes. By the time he arrived in Boston six months later, winter had settled in and he had become a top-notch spiritualist. He had a knack for the work, and if he were honest with himself, he loved the attention. Soon finding a modest apartment in Allston, he set about making a lucrative living pretending to contact dead boys for grieving parents. He would have died an amoral and happy man had he not had the misfortune of meeting someone who actually possessed the powers and abilities to which Butler was only a pretender.

One cool spring night, after a highly lucrative séance in which three dead soldiers expressed their love for their wealthy mothers from beyond the veil, Elias Butler made more in one night than he had in the previous month. More importantly, those men and women would tell their friends. He was ensconced in the Green Dragon drinking the third ale of the evening when a man slid into the seat opposite him. The man was tall and thin with dark skin, burning eyes, a fearsome goatee, and hair parted down the middle. He wore an egg-shaped charm in his lapel.

"Quite the show tonight," the man said. He offered his hand, "Doctor P. B. Randolph."

Elias began to rise from his seat. "Elias Butler." He shook the man's hand and stood as he spoke. "You might not realize this sir, but 'show', well, the term is offensive. I practice the art of communicating with the dead – necrophony." Butler believed himself to be the originator of the term and had been working to popularize it whenever given a chance. As he spoke, he slipped into the rhythm of his banter, "… had a deep connection since birth, a silver cord if you will, that connects me to the spirits. I have honed my skills in India with the Hindoo, in Tibet with the…"

Randolph smiled as if Butler were a child who, though intelligent, was speaking nonsense. "Mr. Butler, I know who you are. And, unlike you, I have been to India. And Africa. And Europe. And places you only talk about in your shows."

"Sir, I must object to your suggestion that I…"

"I've talked to the dead, Mr. Butler, and, unlike you, I can control not only the living but the dead as well. And those creatures which are neither alive nor dead: creatures that would drive your penny-ante patrons screaming mad from their own drawing rooms." His gaze held Butler. The stare paralyzed him. *He's a mesmerist*, Butler thought with a chill of excitement. Here was a skill that he read about and wanted very much to learn. He could, he thought, use it to great effect in his shows. Butler pushed hard against the gaze like struggling to awake from a deep dream state.

"Sir," Butler choked out, "I see now that we are brothers, if not in skin, then in deed. But surely, there are enough people in need of spectral condolence that we need not be rivals."

"I have no interest in stealing your clients, Mr. Butler. On the contrary, I am here to make you an offer. The dross labor I do to fill my purse as a trance medium has allowed me to understand that while many of us lift tables and summon spectral horns, there are a very few among us who have real gifts, or at least the potential for great gifts. I think, Mr. Butler, that you are one of those people. I have been watching you and I have seen an aura about you. So, what I am offering you, sir, is the chance to see the world from my vantage point."

For the next two years, Butler worked under Randolph's tutorage. In payment for instruction, Butler turned over thirty percent of his earnings from his readings and seances which grew in popularity among the Boston elite. Randolph instructed him in the rituals of what he called "sex magick". The women, and even a few men, of Boston flocked to Randolph and Butler. But Butler was greedy.

Randolph himself possessed powers of mesmerism the like of which Butler had never seen before. With a quick glance, he drew the will of his customers away like tapping a maple tree for sap. But, for all of Randolph's talk of speaking to monsters beyond comprehension, he spent much of his time reclining on overstuffed pillows, giving forth long lectures on the importance of coitus. Randolph's library was well-stocked, but much of it the older man had declared off-limits to Butler. When Butler would attempt to steer the conversation back to his learning how to move to powers beyond conducting simple séances for pay, Randolph, while exhaling billows of acrid hashish smoke, would warn Butler away from reading those books, speaking vaguely of things that he had seen that would torment him forever. Butler began to see himself as being little more than an apprentice, following the man around during the day, tending to his errands, and then turning over the takings from his evening performances.

Randolph may have kept his books closed to Butler, but he was open with his friends. Practitioners of all sorts of magic, as well as civilians, were familiar guests at the dinner table. At night, a panoply of languages ricocheted over the turtle soup. People were willing to pay any sum to join Randolph and his friends as they dawdled over sherry. One night, a short white man joined them at dinner. He was thin with sharp cheekbones. He wore the same egg-shaped lapel pin on his jacket. Randolph greeted the man warmly.

"Butler," he said, "come and meet the good professor. L.W. this young man is Elias Butler. He's a striver and a top-notch earner. Butler, allow me to introduce to you my good friend Professor Lauron William de Laurence."

"I've heard about you," de Laurence said peering into Butler's eyes. "Call me L.W." He turned to Randolph. "I think you're right. This one does seem to have a bit of talent about him."

"Shall we dine?" Randolph asked, ignoring de Laurence's comment.

Over dinner, Randolph drank and dominated the conversation while Butler carefully watched de Laurence. He had heard of this man as well. de Laurence had developed a reputation as a bit of a clown: outlandishly dressed, stealing the writings of other practitioners and presenting them as his own, and hosting outrageous orgies with participants decorated as Indians or

Africans. The man seated across from Butler was no fool though. His eyes were sharp, and he drank sparingly as he took everything in and gave little back.

The men retired to Randolph's library for brandy and cigars. Randolph packed an enormous hookah full of hashish for his own enjoyment. Within twenty minutes, he was engaged in a monologue about the race of men who lived on the Earth before Adam. Butler had heard the tale many times before, but at least it was better than Randolph's explicit anti-onanism lecture.

Before long, Randolph dozed off in his overstuffed chair and de Laurence stood.

"Don't judge him too harshly, my friend," said de Laurence. "He really is a brilliant man and a good man. He did much for abolition before the war and for the free Negro now. A credit to his people, but who among us could live under the threat of genocide and extinction and not need to release the pressure?"

"You are not the man I took you to be, Professor."

"Please, it's L.W. You, on the other hand, Mr. Butler, are what I had hoped you to be." Randolph handed Butler his card. "Come by my atelier. I may be able to help you quench your thirst."

He turned back as he stood with his hand on the doorknob. "This evening has been a pleasure, Mr. Butler. I hope to see you again soon."

# CHAPTER 6

"Not a stroke, no." the doctor at the ER ignored me in favor of his paperwork as he spoke. "You said you were doing some exercise right before?"

"Well… kind of… I was walking," I said, sitting up, crinkling the paper beneath me.

"Well, I would chalk this episode up to blood pressure. You know, when people stand up too fast and get dizzy? That's called orthostatic hypotension. You were probably a little dehydrated from the workout…"

"I was just walking."

"Uh-huh- a little dehydrated and stood up too fast and, well, down you went. Still, though, you should see your primary care doctor to make sure nothing else is going on."

"Thanks," I said. On the way out, I had to sign some release papers. I didn't study them closely, dreading what would inevitably come next.

"Do you have insurance?"

She knew I didn't. I told them as much on my way in through teeth clenched against nausea.

"I do not."

"Okay. How did you want to pay today?"

"Can I get billed?"

The woman, cheerful up to this point, suddenly looked tired.

"Yes. We have payment plans available too, of course. And if you like, you could talk to one of our financial consultants to…"

"I just want to go home."

"All right, Mr. Moody. One more signature and you're on your way."

Returning from the hospital and opening the door into the kitchen proved a test of faith. I entered the house like I was wading into an icy lake: a toe first, then the rest of the body. Anticipating the shock. But nothing appeared. No attacks or visitations or whatever the hell it was that happened to me earlier. Looking through to the living room, I saw Mr. B still curled up on the couch. Soft snores rose from his direction; his chest rising and falling. I felt exhausted; there is not stronger soporific than watching a cat sleep.

Mr. B woke when I closed the kitchen door. He followed me upstairs into the bedroom, and, after I collapsed, jumped up and curled into the small of my back. His heat slipped through the blankets. The streetlights outside glowed through the window. A dread that was becoming familiar settled like an ache behind my eyes. I tried not to toss and jostle the cat so that at least one of us could sleep.

What had happened to me? Even the MRIs didn't convince me I wasn't dying. When that boy from the vision smiled at me, he seemed so real. So intense. Some people, even people I knew and respected, would have immediately started talking about the supernatural and the visitation of spirits. At the time, nothing could have seemed more ridiculous. The hooves drumming a migraine in my head were horses, not zebras. I refused to even admit the possibility of the supernatural. It wasn't even worth considering.

The last thing I heard before drifting off to sleep was Mr. B's owner walking the street in front of my house calling for his pet. Ordinarily, I would have rousted the cat and brought him out.

I hated the idea of people aimlessly walking the streets, lost, searching for someone they loved. But tonight, I wanted another living thing beside me.

I sung of Chaos and Eternal Night,
Taught by the heav'nly Muse to venture down
The dark descent, and up to reascend...
- *Paradise Lost*, John Milton

# CHAPTER 7

*Here's the thing,* Alek thought when he woke up. *Here's the thing about magic and junk. You start using them both, thinking they'll make you feel better. You think this is something that will help. But, of course, you're wrong. They both help themselves to whatever you have to offer until you're hollowed out like a husk in a web.*

He felt hot and feverish—the sheets were damp and the lack of spit in his mouth made swallowing difficult. His legs ached, and he had no idea of the time. Heavy blue curtains covered the windows and, with the walls painted light blue, there was the sensation of being underwater. He was still in the clothes he wore on last night's walk, and on the walk the night before that, and possibly the night before that. Recollection was difficult.

Years ago, after coming home from the hospital, he found that his father had covered all the mirrors in black fabric. Even then, through the thickness of his morphine haze, the gesture seemed over-dramatic. He knew what he looked like. There had been mirrors at the hospital. One by one and over the course of months, Alek's father had taken the cloths from the mirrors, except for the one in Alek's room. He left the decision on when to remove that one to Alek. The dark gauze still hung there.

Alek remembered little from the hospital stay. The trauma and the drugs had chewed a great hole in his memory. People had been, he thought, kind to him.

He remembered what happened before the hospital. He

remembered Susan with her one good arm, somehow dragging him out to her car after everything had gone so wrong. Leaving him there in the back seat, she ran back and gathered everything into her bag. She returned, having taken the time to lock the bag in the trunk, while he laid there in agony, his skin feeling like it was still on fire. She drove with her one arm while the other flopped and twitched like a fish waiting to be gutted.

"Here's what we're going to do. We're going to tell people we were goofing off. That we..." she gritted her teeth against the pain, "that we were being stupid and we climbed up a pole, a utility pole, just for kicks. And we must have touched a wire by mistake. Okay. Got it? Say it back to me."

Alek only screamed back. By the time the hospital staff lifted him out of the car, his weeping skin had stuck to the upholstery and there was a peeling noise, like tearing open an orange.

He was in the hospital for two weeks and on a morphine pump the whole time. He clicked it repeatedly as if worrying a string of rosary beads, even after it stopped delivering. His father came to see him when he wasn't at work. They watched re-runs of *Law and Order* on TV and didn't speak. His father didn't know what to say to the ruined mess that had once been his son, and Alek was too high on most occasions to do more than moan and mumble.

His entire face remained wrapped for weeks. The accident had cost Alek one eye, both ears, and most of his nose. His mouth was an open hole ringed with thick keloids of scar tissue. His right foot curved and bent like a fist. His toes were gone. He could still walk, though with a limp while wearing special shoes.

He couldn't remember if Susan had visited him. His father said that she had, but he had no recollection of her being there. He remembered the voice as his most constant companion.

After the accident, the voice never left. It sometimes tormented him, describing what new tortures his mother was undergoing in Hell. Imaginative and wicked, it never repeated the same scenario twice. *Well*, the voice would say when he begged it to stop, *you wanted to know, right? I'm just helping you out. You know you pushed her to it, right?* The only thing that quieted it, even for a small amount of time, was heroin.

Alek met a soldier his age in physical therapy. A stream of molten copper from the core of an IED had hit the ex-infantryman in Iraq. When Alek told him that the cost of the Oxy was draining the family's resources, while at the same time doing less and less for his pain, the man introduced him to his dealer and injecting heroin. Now, his life revolved around the drug. He would buy a little extra sometimes, thinking that he would stash it away in case of a dry spell, but that idea never worked. Sooner rather than later, he would sigh, look at the tiny glassine bag, and then cook up the extra, telling himself that he would save some back the next time. He still got maintenance oxycodone from his doctor for his injuries. Always would, he assumed.

His father tried to make Alek's life as easy as possible; always made sure Alek's disability checks got cashed. He turned the money over to him and never asked his son where he walked at night. His father was a baker and left for work around four am each morning, just when Alek was coming back in. Alek walked at night. No one stared at him then. He walked up and down cold and lonely country roads. He talked back to the voice, yelled and screamed at it and no one shied away from the guttural noises, the kind a rabbit makes before it dies in the mouth of a fox. He walked to Antonio's house to see if he could score. If it was cold, Antonio would invite him in. They would drink beer and watch TV. If Antonio had friends over, he might be cruel to Alek, cursing him out and making fun of him. But if he was alone, they would sit and Antonio would talk about his own childhood. Antonio told him he had been a great high school baseball pitcher, probably would have been drafted straight after graduation if the coach hadn't destroyed his rotator cuff with fastball after fastball. As Antonio nodded out, he would continue talking about how everything, the girls, the respect, all of it, disappeared then, so why bother finishing school? Besides, he mumbled, it was the doctor's fault for giving him those pills in the first place.

Alek would make sure his friend was breathing, then gather up his coat and go back out to walk. Sometimes, people would slow to pick him up, but when they caught sight of him in the red glow of brake lights, the car would speed off, spitting gravel in his face. Other times, people, groups of young people who had heard of the Burnt Man, would wait and pick him up. Sometimes they gave him rides back into town. Sometimes they would drive deep into the woods and make him get out of the car there and try to find his way home. Once it had taken him two days. A group of men, boys really, took all of his clothes and left him to walk home shivering and naked. He had almost completed the journey home, but someone in a house along the road heard him yelling and called the police. He sat in a prison uniform inside a holding cell for six hours until the cops figured out his real name and called his father to pick him up.

But always, always there was the voice: taunting him, cursing him. Sometimes, it would be kind to him, telling him things would be ok. Someday he would find a sweet woman who didn't care about his looks who would take care of him; Beast had found his Beauty hadn't he? Then the voice would turn and use the false hope it had created as a hammer to drive him back into the ground. It would feed him just enough to make sure he was still starving. It reminded him, like picking at scabs.

That's what it had been doing this morning as he arrived home, passing his dad on his way to work. Making sure the room's curtains were closed, Alek got the cigar box from under his bed. His rig was there. The clumsy clubs of his hands shook as he made preparations. The voice had steadily grown stronger and more strident over the past month. If he waited until the voice reached its crescendo, he would be unable to do even simple things like tie off. He would be at its mercy until it tired of him.

*That bitch.*

Susan, he thought. Her name is Susan, and she was my friend.

*Friend?* The voice thundered. *Friend? Where is she now then? Now, when you really need a friend.*

She suffered too.

*Suffered?* The voice chucked like sandpaper on a headstone. *Suffered. Aww… her little arm got a boo-boo. Look at you. No, for Chrissake, on second thought, don't! You're fucking disgusting, aren't you? She gets to go on with her life and you're, well, you're this. And the kicker is, it was all her idea anyhow!*

No, that's not true. It was my idea. She was helping me.

*Phew. Boy, you are a sucker, aren't you? The way I remember it, she wanted to show off how powerful she was and dragged you along by your pecker. You know she doesn't even like guys, right? You never even stood a chance with her. She turned you into a monster and you were never going to get laid anyhow. And, my gods, you're never going to get laid again, that's for sure. You know, I can't even remember, did I burn your cock off too?*

Alek had good veins. That phrase was something he remembered a pretty nurse telling him when she was changing his IV lines in the hospital. So, I'm a little lucky, he thought. He pressed the plunger, then replaced his kit into the box, shoved it under the bed, and laid down.

*That's it, huh?* the voice asked. *That's okay. I'll be here when you wake up. You know what I was thinking would be fun? We should go out during the day sometime. Walk around downtown a little. Get some vitamin D from the old sun. You've been looking awfully pale these days.*

As sleep claimed him, the scratching chuckle faded into white noise.

# CHAPTER 8

Mr. B woke me at dawn the next morning by licking my hair. I tried to ignore him for as long as possible, but there's no snooze button on a cat. Downstairs, he ate his kibble and then stood at the door. When I opened it, he dashed down the street, assuredly to cage a second breakfast from his owner. The prodigal son returned. It reminded me of an old joke: two people are talking. One says, "We had this cat when I was a kid. He would disappear for weeks at a time, then show back up, looking healthier and happier than when he left. We couldn't figure out what was going on. One night we followed him. Turned out that he had a whole other family on the other side of town!" The other replies, "Hey! Just like my dad!"

I spent the morning drinking coffee, fussing over a poem that I had been trying to write for a week, and studiously avoiding the kitchen. Nick's synopsis and the contract had shown up in my inbox late the night before. His idea was strictly by the numbers— a lost daughter of a wealthy man, a private investigator, and a lot of shady types doing business in the shadows of what was then the booming steel economy. In the end, the hero finds the girl, they have a night of passion and the PI finds out the rich client had inflicted cruel physical abuse on the woman and her mom. PI has a code of honor, however, and brings the woman back to her dad at which point, the woman pulls a gun that she had pocketed while the PI was asleep and kills her dad, then herself. Cops show up, PI realizes he will never know true love.

Not great stuff, but easily written, and easily slotted into post-war Pittsburgh because of the generic nature of the story: gather some stuff about the jazz scene in the Hill District, some of the sleaze downtown, the crime families in the suburbs, early morning among the fruit truck drivers making deliveries to the Strip. Nick really could bang this out in eight months I thought, maybe even with enough time left over to write up an idea for the inevitable sequel.

The pay was what we agreed upon and the deadline was ambitious, but deadlines were made to be broken. I signed my name on the printout, rescanned it, and sent it off. I spent an hour sketching out some rough ideas for research and color, trying to figure out how to get the feel of a time that I had never known. In the 40s, Pittsburgh had been twice the size as it was when I first came here. Back then, there was filth filling the skies and lots of money floating around. Now it was all driverless cars and robotic surgery startups. I cleaned up my ideas, turned them into an outline, and sent them off, too. Clients liked to get something right away. A little gift like this made them feel special and important. I logged ninety minutes in my time tracker and went to grab a shower and dress.

I needed to get out of the house. I could feel my chest tighten every time I even thought about going to the kitchen. I started with the task I dreaded the most: I would stop to see the City Solicitor. Afterward, I would head down to the Main Branch of the Carnegie Library in Pittsburgh's Oakland neighborhood. Nick's job would not be hard, and I could have started on the internet from home, but I wanted a safe place, filled with other people.

The new courthouse had the glass doors one would associate with schools and prisons; they worked to funnel the supplicants and those about to be punished into three separate lines for the metal detectors. I emptied my pockets into the plastic bowl and started through the arch.

"Uh-unh," the guard said, stopping me.

I hadn't heard an alarm go off.

"Oh, it might be my pants, the buttons are metal."

"You got a knife in your bowl," he said, nodding to the offending object.

"Yeah, that's my pocket knife." I had been carrying knives since I was a boy—one never failed to come in handy. This one was barely a knife, though. It was an old multi-tool: a Gerber Artifact, a model that the company doesn't even make anymore. The Artifact was a constant companion in my front pants pocket. The black powdercoating on the tool had worn to a beautiful patina in places and the design was exceptional. One end was flattened to be used as a small pry bar and notched to strip wire or pull nails. I had never tried either, but it worked great in pulling staples out of manuscripts. Below the pry bar, a bottle opener. At the other end was a tiny screwdriver head, a hole for a keychain, and an Xacto blade. When it was dull, the blade could be easily replaced rather than worrying about sharpening. I had cut myself when replacing the blade and was pretty sure some of the gunk on the fold-out joint was my own dried blood. The size of an old-time church key bottle opener, I used the tool every day. I found its weight, the solidity of it, in my pocket comforting. I worried it like a talisman or flipped it in my fingers when bored or thinking. I had even used the screwdriver end to dig dirt out from beneath my nails. Killing or even harming anyone with it would have taken hours, maybe days—death by a thousand tiny cuts.

"Can't take it in."

"Okay. Can I leave it here and get it on my way out?

"Nope."

"There's nothing to it. What if I took the blade out?"

"What are you going to do with the blade then?"

"Throw it away?"

"Huh-uh. Not here."

"What am I supposed to do?"

"Can't help you, friend."

I stomped back outside, found a boxwood to the side, and dropped the tool under it.

"Welcome back," the guard said. This time I sailed through.

The Office of City Solicitor wasn't listed on the directory. The Information Desk was, however, and I walked over to the woman working there. They must keep them here, I thought, until they lose it, then ship them over to that sad folding card table in the old city hall.

"Hi!" I said, mustering cheer. "I'm looking for the City Solicitor, but I see she's not listed on the directory."

"That's right." She didn't bother to look up at me.

I felt the muscles in my neck tighten.

"So, could you help me find her?"

"She doesn't have an office here. Hasn't for years. She keeps a private practice and office—only comes here for the board meetings."

"Ha. Of course. Listen, maybe you could help me. A couple of weeks ago, a tree came down on the stone wall in front of my house—I live by the hospital on Institute Hill?"

"Okay," she said, clearly uninterested.

"So, I wanted to get it fixed."

"Sounds like an insurance problem to me."

"Yes. Yes, it does. But here's the thing. City workers brought the tree down. One was killed?"

Her eyes widened with realization.

"A tragic accident to be sure," I continued, "but someone at the scene, someone from the clean-up, assured me that the city would repair the wall. And when I went to Old City Hall, they told me to come here and ask the solicitor."

"Well, I don't know why they would have told you that. Terri wouldn't have anything to do with something like that."

"So, who should I talk to then?" I was leaning on the desk at this point. My headache throbbed at the edges of my temples.

"Hmmm…. Sounds like a Streets and Public Improvement issue."

"Okay. Now we're getting somewhere. On what floor could I find them?"

"Oh, they're in the Old City Hall. You'll have to go down there."

"Of course. Of course, I will. Thank you so much for all of your help."

"Mmmmm…."

On the way out, I stopped to get my tool. It was gone. Someone had taken it in the fifteen minutes I was inside. I wasn't that surprised.

"I just want my damn wall fixed," I mumbled to myself as I pulled out of the parking garage and headed down Route 8. There was no way I was ready to jump back into the cesspool maelstrom that the city hall visits had become. Interstate 79 would have been a faster drive, but I always went down Route 8 and had become used to its visual landmarks: The Succop-Audubon park, then the golf course, the creeping sprawl of Pittsburgh and the concurrent uptick in traffic, Gibsonia with its strip malls and houses from the 1950s when the little town was as far out as the suburbs extended, the Fitzsimmons Metal Company, the railroad tunnel, the Crazy Goat Coffee Shack, then around the turn onto 28 with Millvale below and the Shaler Water Works on the right, the zeotropic public art on the retaining walls that keep Troy Hill from collapsing into the highway, then across the Vets Bridge, climbing the hill with Uptown on one side and the river on the other, then a turn onto Forbes Avenue, and finally a right into the museum and library parking lot. The familiarity was comforting. Sometimes at night when I couldn't sleep, I would play the drive out in my head, visualizing each landmark. The mental exercise kept the intrusive thoughts at bay and lulled me like a meditation.

Carnegie's offer to municipal libraries was a simple one—I'll pay for the buildings, but you have to provide the site and the funds to run them. Being a businessman, he added stipulations, one of which was the open stack systems. Instead of patrons deciding what book they wanted and then asking a librarian to retrieve it for them as was customary, in Carnegie's libraries the patrons were free to browse the shelves. With that simple change, a diminutive robber baron Scotsman changed my life forever.

I have spent a great deal of my life in libraries. I find them, even in cities where they are largely populated by the homeless, to be quiet and safe. They are warm in the winter and cool in the summer and have accessible water fountains and restrooms. But beyond all the creature comforts were the glorious worlds that opened for me in the libraries of my small-town youth. I learned about science and medicine, explorers and monsters, and sex and death in those books. In the same way that a child from another time might have had a treehouse or a secret playhouse in the woods, I had libraries as a shelter and a place where, though surrounded by people, I felt an individual. Without them, I never would have thought that I could become a writer. Even as a child, I dreamed of walking into a library and seeing my name on a book on the shelves. When that didn't work out, I still took solace in working, sometimes almost living in the library as I helped Walt and others do their work. Especially Walt. I may not have my name on those books, but my words lived inside most of them.

The Carnegie in Oakland is as unlike the small-town library of my youth as Walt's life was from mine. As a boy, I was impressed that our town's library had an elevator. Here, I climbed up flights of marble steps worn in places from hundreds of thousands of feet. Frescos of gods and goddesses in robes of gold leaf looked down at me from the stairway walls. Great oak double doors opened into the main reading room.

Here, the huge barreled ceiling of the library had once been skylights. Blacked out with paint during World War II, by the time people realized they should be restored, heating and cooling ducts had been run beneath the glass, making restoration impossible.

The awe of the murals and the bookmatched marble wainscoting transitioned into the new sections, tall windows looking out on courtyards and open airy spaces that resembled a technology company's headquarters, or, when I was feeling less charitable, a forward-thinking hospital renovation. Past these sections were the stacks, rooms that looked like no one had tended to them after the 1970s—a riotous sort of neglect with antique marble water fountains framed by drywall, painted with the sort of cream-colored paint that came in giant buckets at a very low price. The floors were segments of thick glass placed to let light better circulate and frosted for privacy. I always felt a bit like I was walking through the clouds as the light seeped from both above and below. At the far side of the room sat the original radiators with window nooks above them. Patrons luxuriated like spoiled housecats here in the winter and on cold, rainy, fall days. One section of windows overlooked the interior of the Carnegie Museum of Natural History. Below the readers, the entire cavernous space served as a diorama where fossilized tyrannosaurs stalked the bones of long-dead diplodocuses through a forest of plastic greenery.

I headed upstairs. The path was one I could have walked blindfolded: up the grooved marble stairs, a right, fifty-two steps, then another right through a doorway and up some stairs. Signs encouraged patrons to climb the stairs and learn about Pennsylvania history, but the overall feel is that, once you start up the stairs, you're headed somewhere that is off-limits. A collection of ladders rested beside a narrow staircase. Reaching the landing halfway up to the uppermost floor, there was evidence of old windows, their frames partially hidden by drywall and stair risers, the glass blacked out. I've never figured out why or what the windows look out upon, but the library itself can feel labyrinthine. After all these years, the library map I carry in my head is still incomplete. More than once, I've wound up turned around when walking with my nose in a book. The basement has the characteristics of an extra-dimensional maze and passthroughs to the connected museums and lecture halls exist behind unmarked doors. There are large sections of space in the library where I know, from walls and windows, that something has to exist, but I'm not sure what. I have a reoccurring dream where I find hidden rooms in the library—rooms that change and shift in location and contents as patrons walk past them never noticing.

At the second landing, a sharp right and I arrive—the Pennsylvania Department. Typically, the main room is occupied by a handful of researchers like myself, genealogists mostly. Today, they glanced at me as I walked in. One nodded hello. A couple are regulars who recognize each other's faces, but there isn't a lot of chit-chat. That's fine with me. I love libraries and want them to be accessible to everyone. I also want them to be quiet and nearly empty when I'm there working. I prefer the ambient hum and *thip-thip-thip* of microfilm machines winding to small talk. The room itself is open and spacious with fluorescent lights hanging from the ceiling. I rarely left a research day without a splitting headache. There are long tables, each with four seats featuring the finest leatherette upholstery. People claimed these tables for their work, notebooks, laptops, and books spread out, glasses pushed up on heads, reading, mumbling, and searching with the occasional smile as a particularly useful or juicy fact surfaced—prospectors panning for gold with their pans and shovels.

If I continued up a half flight from the main room of the

Pennsylvania Department, and then turned left, there is a smaller reading room - an even quieter place with a tall table. I often dragged my materials up here to work if I want to stretch my back or if there was a cougher in the main area. On the back wall hangs a solid looking oak door. A sign claims the door leads to the Conservation Department, although I had seen no one come in or out or even heard movement beyond. The room's other door leads to a single-occupancy restroom. The privacy of the restroom makes it a good place if you feel unwell or if, say, your wife has recently left you and you need to sit and cry for ten minutes.

The main room was always full of familiar faces. The people weren't friends, but we saw each other enough to exchange nods or waves. The librarian was the only person to whom I regularly spoke. Dinah was a constant presence in the research area. Of medium height with a mellow brown complexion, she wore funky cat eyeglasses. She was plain enough overall that they fit into her look rather than seeming like an affectation. Stickers and pins covered her ID lanyard which always seemed in her way. I feared I would find her body in the stacks one day, her neck snapped after the lanyard caught on a title as she plowed through the shelves at her usual rapid speed chasing down a 19th-century cemetery record or a reference to a distant Frick relative in an old copy of the *Pittsburgh Press*.

She was whip-smart and a better researcher than I, but she seemed to like an audience. For some of us, just finding the information, hoarding it away like a chipmunk gathering acorns for winter, was enough. Or, in my case, presenting it like a magician to an audience. Perhaps more aptly, like a farmer bringing livestock to a sausage maker. Dinah, however, was enthralled by the process and the explanation of how she got from point A to point B and wanted people to know. With her love of showing her work as she made progress towards a solution, she would have made an excellent mathematician.

We were friendly, the way two people who work a regular job in an office might act towards each other. One day, after I came back from the upper room to get more resources, my eyes swollen and red, booze on my breath from lunch, she asked me if everything was okay. My tears welled up again, and she took me by the elbow into her office and there, I'm still embarrassed to say, I told her the story of my wife leaving me. She didn't say anything. She offered no advice, but I wonder if behind the sympathetic eyes she wondered what the best way to research how to reset a broken man was.

Since that day, she has been cheery and a little flirty in a harmless sort of way. She invited me out for a drink not long after I wound up in her office. I had demurred; my life was still too raw at that point. When she asked again, I made more excuses. I didn't want to make coming to the library awkward. We remained chatty and close, and I always sought her out when making my way up the stairs to the Department.

Although most of the records had long since been digitized, the room still had card catalogs and locked map drawers and rows of file cabinets full of microfilm and fiche. I've been to lots of libraries with their vinegary smell of old film, but strangely, this room was always scentless. Even the researchers who, as solitary introverts sometimes passed on the social niceties of hygiene, seemed ghostly and non-present: no smell, not even shampoo or an unfortunate choice of cologne. Ghosts looking up other ghosts in the endless daisy chain of time. I sometimes thought that an afterlife like this wouldn't be so bad: a perpetual Sunday afternoon in a research room in a library, quiet, hushed, diffused light pouring in, surrounding us shadows in search of that one answer that would change everything.

# CHAPTER 9

Butler showed up at de Laurence's a few days later. New construction stood empty next to derelict row houses. It was a neighborhood, Butler thought, that was either on the way up or on the way down. He picked his way around the piles of dung and oyster shells that littered the sidewalk in front of a stylish milliner's shop. Stopping in front of a building constructed of cut stone, Butler checked the address once again. He knocked on the heavy oak door with heavy black hinges. de Laurence himself answered the door and led Butler up three flights of narrow stairs to the top floor. The ceiling was made of cleverly curtained skylights. de Laurence showed him the pulley system and the thick black curtains that could quickly turn day into night, or de Laurence said, provide privacy at any time. The floor was a simple pine worn smooth by time. The brickwork had been whitewashed, although not recently. Stacks of books sat everywhere alongside boxes of candles and chalk. On a far wall, shelves filled with jars, all labeled with de Laurence's spidery handwriting, stood waiting. The air of the room held a smoky, burnt, sweet smell like ripe fruit roasting over a fire. Butler quickly traced it back to the incense braziers that hung from the ceiling beams.

"A lot to take in, isn't it? Will you have some tea?"

Butler's head snapped back to de Laurence who had taken a seat near the stairs.

"It's very... impressive," Butler managed. "Randolph doesn't have any of this. I've read, of course, of the accruements people like us require, but this…"

"It's a lifetime's work," de Laurence said, waving his hand about the room. "The silliness of the seances pays for all of this. It's expensive keeping two places in the city, but…"

"Of course, of course," Butler said settling in a chair opposite him and accepting the proffered tea. "Does… does Randolph know about this place?"

de Laurence laughed, throwing his head back and slapping his knee. Butler feared for the balance of the man's tea saucer.

"Know? Good god, man, at least half of these treasures were found by him." de Laurence stood and wandered to one of the bookshelves. "He wasn't always such a… what's the word they use now? Ah… a hophead. Yes, I think that's it. He wasn't always a hophead. He was, as I said the other night, a great man. An accordingly great thirst for knowledge."

"Pardon me, sir, but that's rather hard to believe. He keeps his books away from me as a mother hides sweets from her child."

"Ah, I don't doubt it in the least. He favors you greatly you know. Told me that he thinks of you as a son. You see, sir," he turned to face Butler, "that's precisely why he keeps you from things. You are not the first substitute son he has taken under his wing. But you are the only one still on this plane."

"I'm not sure I understand."

"Then let this be your first lesson in true magic. There is always an exchange. The infernal are extreme capitalists. No one walks away with goods and services for free. And the bigger the purchase, the dearer the price. Do you see?"

Butler nodded his head.

"I don't mean to scare you, sir. You do have the seeds of an exceptional talent in you. Would you like to try something?"

de Laurence and Butler spent the rest of the afternoon hunched over the floor. de Laurence had opened *The Key of Solomon* for him, a text that Randolph had expressly forbidden. The older man showed Butler how the runes and sigils needed to be created on the floor and brought forth bowls and knives to be laid out. By dinner time, they were in their shirtsleeves and sweat had accumulated on Butler's forehead from the sheer emotional effort of it all. They stood back and took in their work.

"It's like an altar," Butler said.

"No," de Laurence said. "That's something I might tell the clients at my other house to help sell the mystery. This, my boy, is like a laboratory or an engineer's desk."

That night, as Butler watched, de Laurence summoned a minor entity. It looked no more than a will o wisp, but de Laurence had been adamant that Butler respect it and realize that even such a small creature could destroy his soul without a moment's exertion and wished to do nothing less.

When Butler returned to Randolph's early that morning, the man remained where he had fallen asleep in his overstuffed chair. His pipe drooped from the side of his mouth, the sharp smell of hashish still heavy in the room. Soon, Butler became a regular visitor and a keen student to de Laurence. Randolph may have been able to convince curious Boston virgins to join in orgies, but Butler was drawn to de Laurence's darker talents and knowledge of summonings and magic circles.

In the end, there was no dramatic confrontation, no sudden epiphany that the two men and their goals had grown incompatible. One night, Butler sat sipping a brandy in the library, perusing an incomplete translation of an Egyptian text listening as Randolph snorted and farted in his drugged sleep like an old dog, a thin line of snot drooling from his nostril to encrust his mustache. At that moment, Butler realized he had learned as much from Randolph as he ever would. The next day, he wrote an anonymous letter to the husband of one of Randolph's sex magick acolytes detailing his wife's adventures and the time and location of the next meeting. The husband was gentleman enough to allow Randolph to pack a few belongings, but ruffian enough to hold him at pistol point while he did so.

Butler moved his few possessions into de Laurence's home and began greedily consuming the man's library. A few weeks later, he received a brief note written in Randolph's hand, in care of de Laurence. Randolph had found a house in New Orleans and was settling into a lucrative séance business there in a building near the French Market. He could look out at Dutch Alley and clients could make the journey to his salon under the pretense of shopping. More importantly, he found the mores of the city to be a bit more permissive. The letter wasn't purely social, however as it concluded:

*My dear boy. I know that it was you who set me on this journey. It may seem nonsense to you, but I really do not feel any ill will towards you. The student always resents the master; that's how the arrangement has worked since the Jinn rode the winds before Adam was even an idea. I also am aware of and understand your relationship with de Laurence. And so, I must warn you. de Laurence may not be who or what he seems. He and I were once very close, and we both trod the same path towards knowledge—the one which I have left but which he continues. He has opened many doors uninvited. There is a ledger to magic, and while mine has been redeemed, I fear that his is still deeply in arrears.*

*You will always have a home here with me in New Orleans, should you need or desire one.*

*I remain yours-*
*Paschal Randolph*

# CHAPTER 10

I spent most of the morning photocopying and annotating maps of Pittsburgh, showing how Nick's characters would have gotten from the Hill District to the Mexican War Streets and back, making sure to note which street names had changed and when. I went back through the directories and dug up the names of bars and restaurants and a barbershop. Nick liked that sort of authenticity. Dinah suggested including some tidbits about the Amato family's gambling rackets which also seemed like the sort of thing that would make Nick's day. She spent an hour helping me chase down some court records. Unlike me, she had clever, fast hands with the microfilm. When we were done, I had more than enough to keep Nick quiet for a while.

"Thanks for all your help today."

"Anytime," said Dinah. "It was good to see you again. We were starting to think you had given up on us. Gone off to write that novel you used to talk about."

"Haha… No. That's… ah, well. The follies of youth, you know."

"Well…"

"Hey, listen, before I go. You don't happen to have anything about Butler County, do you?"

She gave me a puzzled grin.

"We have a plethora of resources from our neighbor to the north. What exactly are you looking for?"

"Well... there was this guy named Sam Mohawk."

"Mohawk? Well, if you're after ghost stories, have I told you about The Judge?"

The Judge was one of her favorite stories, and I had heard it many times. The sheer joy she took in telling the story was clear. Each time she relayed it, she added a detail or two. I crossed my arms and leaned back into my seat as she started telling it again.

"This library, the very one in which we're standing right now, opened in 1895. There was a judge who liked to come here. He would show up almost every day, walking among the stacks, perusing the old books, asking the librarians questions about authors and for book recommendations. One day, in the early 1900s, he hung himself in the stacks. No one ever knew why. He hadn't seemed sad; he hadn't lost money or been disgraced. The librarian came in and found his body. Rigor mortis had already passed, but his eyes were bugged and filled with blood—the whites turned near completely red and his tongue lolling purple and obscene. The ambulance men arrived and hauled off the body. There was no notice in the paper, of course, not like today where news people would have been swarming about. The staff was shaken, but figured that was the end of a sad story. Who knows what goes on in the hearts of men anyhow?"

"Then, it started happening. Mysterious writing began to appear in the library. Now, of course, any library has its issues with graffitos, even back in the 19th century, but the writing wasn't at shoulder height like you would expect. No, it was on the ceiling. On these high ceilings where someone would need a ladder to write anything. The words appeared repeatedly, exactly where the noose had hung. The color of the ink changes from time to time, but the words are always the same."

She took a deep breath as she approached the kicker. Eavesdropping patrons leaned in a little more.

"Sentio Est Hic..."

Here I joined her in unison: "Latin for 'The Judge is Here.'"

We both laughed.

"All right, all right, fine. You've heard that one before?" she pouted.

"Maybe once or twice," I smiled back at her.

"You really know how to ruin a story."

"It's all in how you tell it," I replied.

"Jerk," she smiled back at me. "So, why Mohawk? Is your boss writing horror now?"

"What do you mean?"

"Well, old Sam's story isn't a secret. Sets up a cult. Makes his followers toil for his gain, eventually they get fed up and lynch him. Only lynching in Butler County if I remember correctly."

"That sounds like my guy. No, it's for me. Just a personal project."

"I knew you were working on something of your own. Good for you!"

"Well, ah, thanks."

"Want me to print out the finding aid for you?"

"Yeah, that would be great. Thanks."

Dinah brought back the double-sided printout. I spent the rest of the afternoon going through newspaper clippings, maps of Mohawk's Institute Farm, oral histories from people who had lived there, and even a few photographs of the aftermath of the lynching. I made photocopies when I could and took photos when I couldn't.

"Thanks again, Dinah," I said when finished. Outside, the sky had darkened. The library would be closing in thirty minutes, and I hated to be the patron who kept the workers late.

"No problem. You know, if you're interested in Sam, you should go to the Institute Farm site; I mean, if you haven't been there already."

"The site? Where is it?"

"In your neck of the woods. I was there once. Years ago. If I remember, it's past the hospital and down a dead-end road. There was a sign, I think, but this was fifteen or twenty years ago. On a Girl Scout trip of all things. What were they thinking?"

The way Dinah described it meant that Mohawk's farm was just a few miles from my home. Maybe not even that far.

"I mean, imagine taking twenty-three tweens to the site of a cult farm and then…"

"You've been a huge help today."

She snapped back into business mode.

"No problem. The farm site might have some more records. It's run by one of the colleges up there."

"Oh, okay."

"You better get moving on this Mohawk book though. Before someone else beats you to it."

"Why do you say that?"

"Someone else was in last week looking at the Mohawk information. That's how it goes, right? Nobody touches a subject for decades and then bang, everybody wants a piece."

"Someone was here, looking up Mohawk?" This couldn't be a coincidence.

"That's right. Young woman, early 20s. Said she was doing research too. I don't know if she's the real deal though. Here's the thing, we got to talking about the ghost stories that float around the old Institute—you know all the stuff kids tell each other at sleepovers—and she says that she actually works at a witchcraft store. I guess, technically she called it a metaphysical retail outlet, but tomato, tomato. Here, hold on."

Dinah walked back to her desk and opened a drawer.

"Got it. She left me her card. Asked me to get in touch with her if I thought of anything else. Said it was urgent. Ah to be young again when digging through archives was a matter of urgency, huh?" She offered the card.

"Oh, uh. Hold on, I'll take a photo of it and you can hold on to it." I dug for my phone.

"That's okay. You can have it. I won't go out of my way to help your competitor, and if I need to get ahold of her with dramatic new revelations, I'd be emailing you first, anyway."

"Hey, thanks." I looked at the card.

THE ELEMENTAL CRAFT
415 BROAD ST
SEWICKLEY PA 15143
(412) 741-2257

On the back was a name in neat looping script: *Evanora LaCosta*

"Maybe you two could work together or something. Research always goes faster with more eyes."

"Yeah. I don't know. I'm used to working by myself. But thanks. Maybe I will give her a call." I hoisted my bag onto my shoulder.

"Listen, again, just thanks so much for everything. I really appreciate it."

"Again. It's not a problem." She smiled. "Don't be a stranger for so long next time. You know... my offer for a drink still stands."

"Oh, yeah. It's just that..."

"Okay. Fine. Get out of here before we both end up embarrassed."

# CHAPTER 11

From where he was on his bed, Alek could hear the raindrops sizzling on the roof. The temperature had been dropping all day with a cutting wind coming from the south. As the afternoon wore on, the rain threatened but held off until dusk. That's my luck, Alek thought, and picked at a scab on his arm. His skin had begun to itch again. His habit no longer got him high, not really. It got him to normal, to a place where he could function and think and sleep. And if he could sleep, then the voice inside of his head would have to sleep too.

*Now why would you want me to be quiet,* the voice said. *I'm your only friend these days, aren't I? What shall we talk about today? How you almost had an acting career before that bitch melted your face off? I know! How about what your mother's up to in Hell?*

He pulled on his boots and a jacket. His father had dozed off in front of the television again with a glass of bourbon beside him. On the screen, an old man with suspiciously lustrous hair was talking about the Steelers. Alek left a note: Out for a walk. Look for me when you see me. He propped the paper beside his dad's glass and closed the door as quietly as he could.

With the wind and the rain, the walk to Antonio's was a long and cold one. The voice kept up a constant monologue in Alek's head, sometimes explaining how hideous he was or detailing the infernal torture the voice insisted was being visited on his mother at that very instant. Ironically, the worst was when the voice mumbled. Alek couldn't hear what the voice said which somehow made it all the worse. Sometimes the mumbling sounded like it was carrying on another conversation with a third person. Or thing.

Antonio's trailer was the only home on a dead-end dirt road. At one point, there had been a farm across from Antonio's place, but now only a single crumbling outbuilding remained. Ivy crept up the wood of its splintering grey siding. Light and water dropped in through the tin roof where rust had eaten holes. Wild rose bushes had taken over the fields. In the spring, the air was so thickly perfumed that Alek felt dizzy and nauseous from the sweet air. Now, in the late fall, only the brambles remained, looping like barbed wire across trenches.

*I used to farm. Did you know that Alek? Now, I know you're thinking what did I grow, but that's the wrong question. What you should ask is what did I harvest? Ah-ha-ha-ha.* The laugh was dry and nasal.

Alek pounded on the trailer's cheap white aluminum door. Antonio kept weird hours; Alek was never sure if he would be home or not.

"Shit!" Alek heard from inside. "Who is it?"

"Alek." His voice was loud and thick like his tongue had swollen to fill his mouth. His lips, mostly composed of keloids, refused to move properly.

*Oh, my gods!* The voice in his head laughed hysterically. *Did you hear that? Imagine that voice on the stage. Ladies and gentlemen, I give you The Elephant Man!*

"Who the fuck?" The door jerked open. "Oh, hey, Alek. C'mon in man." Antonio shivered in the night air. "Fuck man, you got to be freezing. Sorry I didn't hear you at first. I was just chilling with the tv and some drinks."

Antonio walked back in and collapsed on the couch. "Take your coat off and grab yourself a beer man. In fact," he said, shaking the near empty can in his hand, "grab me one too, okay?"

The trailer's door opened into the living room. There was a sickly-sweet smell to the entire house—of slowly rotting wood and of garbage left out too long. To the left were the bedrooms and bathroom, to the right the kitchen where, on the far wall, under a row of crank-operated louver windows, sat a scarred kitchen table pockmarked with cigarette burns and covered with taco wrappers and empty convenience store cups. The once white refrigerator was now flecked with rust that had eaten through the enamel and leaked into long stains down the front.

Alek dropped his coat in front of the door and ran his hand through his soaking hair as he walked into the kitchen. He found some fast-food napkins on the counter beside the sink and used them to dry his hair and face, then opened the fridge. He brought two cans of beer back to the couch, pressing the cold containers to his chest so as not to drop them with his club-like hands. He brought the beers back to Antonio who took and opened both of them before handing one back. Alek nodded his thanks as he sat down and used both hands to bring the beer to his mouth. A thin rivulet ran out the side of his mouth.

"Jesus, dude," Antonio said shaking his head and gently laughing, "like you weren't soaked enough already? So, is this a business or social visit?"

Alek shrugged his shoulders. "A little of both."

"Okay, so chill for a while." The room reeked of marijuana. "I was just taking the edge off. When you pounded on that door, I thought I was going to hit the roof," he said laughing.

They sat for nearly an hour. Antonio did almost all the talking about women, about the guys he bought his drugs from, about how everyone seemed angrier than usual, hateful even. All the while, Alek tried not to focus on the voice gibbering a steady stream of obscenities and bile into his ear. Soon, he was no longer following the thread of Antonio's monologue. He stood up and walked to the bathroom. His skin was crawling, like a thousand centipedes making their way across his body, burrowing their way inside his track marks. He retched, but there was nothing to vomit. He ran water and splashed it on his face. For a moment, when he opened his eyes, his old face was in the mirror. Chiseled jaw, bright clear blue eyes, a sprinkling of dark stubble across his cheeks. Then just as quickly, it was gone, replaced by his new face, his real face with patches of hair like a chemo patient and thick red knots of scars.

*Ha ha ha ha ha! Oh, that one never gets old, does it?*

"Hey, grab me another beer, will you?" Antonio shouted. Leaving the bathroom, Alek made his way into the kitchen and opened the refrigerator. He grabbed a tallboy of Steel Reserve.

*Hey*, the voice said, *you know what would be fun?*

Alek felt a burning sensation in his right hand. Strength and dexterity flowed back into it. He clenched and unclenched his fist, trying to drive away the pins and needles. It felt as if he'd slept with his arm trapped underneath. He opened a drawer and pulled out a pair of scissors.

*No, not those...*

He put the scissors back and pulled out a cheap, six-inch chef's knife.

*There we go*, he heard. *You need the right tool for the job.*

"Make sure you get something for yourself too," Antonio called from the couch. As last words go, Alek thought they weren't that great.

*Butchering is always so much harder than you think it will be*, said the voice. *There's all that lifting and shifting of dead weight.*

Alek cleaned himself as best as he could in the trailer's bathroom sink. His clothes would have to be burned.

*Maybe next time.* He closed his eyes against the voice's words. *I said, maybe next time, there could be a little more suffering. He went awful quick. Still, I'm not complaining. You did a nice job. I feel better already.*

Antonio's body lay naked on the floor. Blood pooled beneath him. There was a wide spray against the living room wall where Alek buried the knife into the side of Antonio's neck. The couch was soaked. Alek spent hours under the voice's direction carving symbols into the meat of Antonio's body. He'd cut out his tongue at the root. The room stank of blood.

"Be quiet," Alek said under his breath to his image in the mirror.

*I can hear you. Be as quiet as you like, little mouse, but I'm the one in charge here. I'm helping you. Remember, you're just my hands. Speaking of such...*

Alek's hands turned clumsy again. Bringing them into fists stretched the skin and caused pain.

*Aw, did you think I was going to let you keep them this time? Look at the bright side, you're a face only a mother would love, but all those scars mean no fingerprints. Oops, did I say 'mother' again?*

Alek made his way into Antonio's bedroom and hooked his crippled hands into the drawer pull on the bedside table. He opened the cigar box inside and grabbed a bundle of glassine bags filled with heroin, each one stamped with a pentagram and the logo BAPHOMET underneath the image. When he tucked them into his jacket pocket, his hand brushed on something cold and wet: Antonio's tongue. Vomit rose in the back of his throat. He pulled the tongue out and placed it in the cigar box. He closed the box, placed it in the drawer, and left the house. If he walked quickly, he would get home before dawn, but after his father left. He could finally get some rest.

# CHAPTER 12

Butler was a quick study and de Laurence was liberal with his resources. Butler still performed seances and other spectacles with a share of the earnings going to de Laurence, but on off days and late into the night, Butler read copies of the grimoires that had been strictly off-limits with Randolph. He drew circles under the careful eye of his instructor and spread salt that no demon could cross. He stood in the shadows mouthing incantations along with de Laurence as his patron casually made deals with beings that had previously existed only in Butler's worst nightmares. He saw de Laurence reap the benefits of these deals. He possessed money and women and the power to control the thoughts and actions of man. Butler saw blood spilled into bowls that quickly boiled away from some unseen heat.

While de Laurence was at his seances, open only to the highest levels of Boston Brahmin society, Butler secretly practiced his own summonings with the most minor of creatures. He knew, from his readings, that the flattery and praise these beings heaped upon him, the promises that he would be greater than de Laurence, were only trickery, yet he longed for a grander evocation than these translucent shimmers of cold light that brought whispers of promises that he knew they were too minor to fulfill. de Laurence's books suggested that a greater sacrifice was needed in order to bring a stronger creature to this plane.

de Laurence was furious when he came home to find Butler

seated in a protective chalk circle having summoned an imp no larger than a toddler. A pair of bloody poultry shears lay on the floor. Butler cradled his left hand, the front of his shirt soaked in blood. The topmost joint of his little finger lay smoldering, the flesh slowly being consumed by an unseen mouth, in a brass bowl. The end of his ring finger hung loosely by a shred of skin and tendon. Butler's face was a sickly greenish pale, and he struggled to keep his eyes from rolling deep back into their sockets. Rot and decrepitude filled the air.

de Laurence heard the imp's voice slither through the room like a piece of baling wire brought slowly over slate. The creature was explaining that it was just a herald for a much stronger entity who was pleased with Butler's offering. de Laurence's chest constricted with rage and fear. The older man roared a few words, and the creature disintegrated with a low sucking sound leaving a small pile of ash in the circle.

"L.W.," Butler started.

The hand hit Butler's cheek with the force of a blacksmith bringing down his hammer. Butler fell back on the floor and his eyes blurred with the sudden additional shock and pain.

"I told you," de Laurence said, raising his hand again, "you are only to accompany me on summonings." The sound of the backhand connecting with the flesh of Butler's cheek echoed against the high ceilings. "You have no idea what damage you could do." Spit flew from his mouth. de Laurence swung again and Butler flinched away. One of de Laurence's rings caught the ridge of Butler's eyebrow and blood-splattered, then flowed. de Laurence stood straight, slightly out of breath. "Consider it a monument to my charity that I don't dismiss you outright." He grabbed Butler's hand roughly, and the younger man jerked with the sharp pain. "You fool," de Laurence's voice had grown quiet. "Those will turn gangrenous if we leave them like that. The rest of that ring finger will have to come off." He dropped Butler's hand

and made for the door. "I shall call the surgeon." He stormed from the room. Butler fell to the floor.

Some of the blood from Butler's face landed in the summoning bowl now laying on its side inside the circle. Butler lay on the ground heaved with wracking breaths. *So like a father, isn't he?* A whispered voice so quiet as to be almost inaudible, the timbre so like Butler's own voice that he wondered if it was merely his thoughts. *So hypocritical, so vainglorious, when, in truth, do you need him at all?* The last words trailed off as the last of the blood sizzled off and Butler felt sure that he must have imagined the entire episode.

The surgeon was an old man and a drunk. Butler recognized his type from the war. The type of man who measured his success by the stack of severed limbs outside of the operating tent. He took off the hanging tip of the ring finger in a matter of seconds and without anesthetic. The doctor saved Butler's hand, and maybe his life, but the young man's humiliation festered like a pus-filled sore. Randolph may have been a sad old hophead, but he had respected Butler. To be struck like that, like a child. And didn't Butler know almost as much as de Laurence now anyhow? All he needed was the time, the experience and that was why de Laurence was hamstringing him. He knew that Butler was stronger and better than him. Slowing his studies, Butler came to believe, was the way that de Laurence was keeping control of him. He didn't speak to his master for ten days. He nursed his wound and plotted and schemed and then showed up one night for dinner, appropriately contrite.

de Laurence acknowledged Butler's presence with a nod.

"I want to say," Butler began as he sat.

"It was for your own good," de Laurence interrupted. "There are things, compacts, agreements, between our world and theirs that must be followed and obeyed. If you don't know the rules, you will be taken advantage of. Imagine yourself in an Arab bazaar trying to buy a camel. You have no idea of the customs or the currency or even what you should purchase. You would end up with your throat slit. So, it is when dealing with the Far Countries."

"I understand," said Butler and hung his head contritely. "And I agree. You are correct. And I appreciate your concern and care."

de Laurence smiled, and they began eating. Butler waited until close to the end of the meal and then spoke again. "I have… well, that is to say, I felt bad about the rift between us, and as a means towards recompense, I spent my time thinking about my actions and coming up with a suggestion that might serve as a sort of apology."

de Laurence cocked an eyebrow. "Go ahead."

"I think," Butler said. "I think we should start a school, an esoteric institute."

# CHAPTER 13

In the morning, I typed up my notes for Nick and sent them off. I made another cup of tea and settled down with my Mohawk information. To contemporary eyes, the story didn't seem that unusual overall. Tragic, sure, but supernatural? Evil? I wasn't sold. Mohawk had appeared in the city of Butler out of nowhere one day. Soon afterward, he was spotted in town explaining that he was starting a new community of believers at what he called the Institute Farm. He claimed to have taken the name Sam Mohawk after being visited by a spiritual presence one night in a cave in the New Hampshire woods. Those who followed him would find the true secrets of the world. He used a lot of vague phrases: Celestial Beings, the Clockworks of The Beyond, so it's hard, at least from the newspaper accounts to tell exactly what he was selling. A local farmer deeded him seventy-five acres on what was the outskirts of town today, but what would have been forests at the time. Today, railroad tracks ran along the creek that would have powered the mill that he built, but during Mohawk's time, it would have been pristine. In short time, he had built that mill and a number of other buildings and cleared ground for a huge fruit orchard. The work was too much for one man with a small crew of amateurs to have completed, but all the accounts said that it seemed to go up overnight.

The handbills that he printed advertised hard work, a simple diet, a worshipful attitude, and celibacy as the cornerstones of the

Institute. That last part, celibacy, apparently was a "do as I say and not as I do" sort of tenet. From the more sensational the accounts, I was able to assume that Mohawk chose women who joined to be his "spiritual" wives. The group built an orphanage that was supposed to house kids, lots of kids, whose parents had died or just couldn't take care of them anymore. Then, inexplicably, Mohawk had been ambushed and lynched—the crowd led by a dozen or so of his acolytes. On the same day, the orphanage and most of the other buildings and tents of the Institute burned to the ground. A scholarly article that I found suggested that his followers rebelled after finding that Mohawk had begun adding some of the young orphan women, girls, really to his bed, but the evidence was scant.

Some bones, although the reports were unable to give a clear number, ("charnel pit" was a term that was bandied about) were found in the ashes. No one was willing to say for sure if the remains were those of people who had died in the fire or if they were those of the missing orphans. The former acolytes went their own way and the Institute cult was largely forgotten. Today a small three-acre lot of the former site is owned and operated by Slippery Rock University, a state school thirty minutes north of the ruins. I decided to visit Mohawk's old home.

The site was close enough to walk, the weather was cool and grey, and I needed the exercise, so I set out on foot and regretted the decision almost immediately. Only a mile and a half away, Google Maps told me that the trip would take twenty minutes. It took me closer to forty minutes, and sweat dripped in my underarms after the first ten. When had I gotten so old?

The yards and sidewalks were deserted of people, but stray cats were everywhere. I counted eight in the first mile before the sidewalks ran out by the hospital complex. They lounged on cement porches or under cars or strutted with purpose down the street. A big black cat walked in front of me for a half-block then sat and watched me go. The animals were so much of a fabric of the city, that I didn't notice them anymore even when looking right at them. Occasionally, someone would write a letter to the editor or try and form a committee to do something about the number of cats wandering the streets, but the hubbub all faded quickly. The city, it seemed on most days, belonged to them. I didn't mind. At least cats didn't break into cars or overdose in coffee shop bathrooms.

When I got to the hospital and the sidewalks stopped, I walked on the road surface. The potholes were even bigger seeing them outside of the vantage point of a car. The edges of the blacktop crumbled on the sides and trash was everywhere; Chik-Fil-A wrappers and endless beer cans. The litterbugs of Butler had a predisposition for Steel Reserve tallboys.

The Connoquenessing Creek ran to my right. The water sounded pretty and looked clear, but just a few years ago, it was one of the most polluted waterways in America, just behind the Mississippi. Heavy industry used it as an open sewer and left the contamination as a gift even after the jobs were long gone. Around a bend, I saw the sign I was looking for. Exposure to the Pennsylvania winters had worn the paint into a crackled map:

The Old Institute Mill
1883
Operated by Slippery Rock University

The driveway wound into a curve. Around it, to the left, I saw an area fenced in by a four-foot-tall stone wall topped with carved stone spires. Age and pollution had stained the stones with black streaks, but the undertaking must have been incredible at the time. The stones were cut and polished smooth, each one three feet long. On the far side stood a 12-foot-high gate with a massive stone serving as a rotating gate. Just off to the right of the mill stood a small outbuilding. A wooden sign in front of the building identified it as the smokehouse. As I drew closer to the mill, the sound of water filled the air.

The mill was smaller than I imagined it would be. A stone staircase lead down to the ruined dam and the creek. The building resembled a barn with wooden siding all around, grey and pickled-looking from a hundred and fifty years of snow and sun. A door to the side stood open with a "Come In! We're Open!" message on a chalkboard propped beside it.

Inside, the space was cool and dim. Light filtered through the gaps in the siding. A desk had been placed to the left with the requisite display rack of pamphlets for area attractions. A millstone six feet in diameter sat on the floor, with grooves deeply etched into its face. A small collection of gifts and souvenirs stood for sale on shelving that looked ready to collapse at any moment.

"Oh! Hi! Welcome!"

A young woman came down the roped-off stairs that led to the second floor. She had long hair on top that flopped down over the shorn sides and back. She wore heavy oversized black-framed glasses and was chunky and unformed as if she were trapped in adolescence and hadn't yet grown into an adult body. Her eyes were bright and quick and a smile flashed across her face as if she had just been surprised with an unexpected gift.

"I didn't hear you come in. I was upstairs doing inventory."

"Hi," I said.

"So, is this your first time at the Institute Mill?"

"Um… yes."

"Okay, so my name is Kara. I'm a volunteer docent here at the mill and I'm also a sophomore at Slippery Rock. History major."

"Okay," I said.

There was an awkward pause.

"So, did you want a tour? It's free."

"No… I think I'm just going to look around right now."

"Okay," she said, shrugging. "Well, I'll be at the desk if you need anything."

"Thanks. Hey, what is that thing outside?"

She looked puzzled. "Which thing?"

"The thing with all the stones."

Oh! That's the Institute cemetery. It's super cool. Do you want to go look at it?"

"Um… maybe when I'm done here?"

"Great!" she settled back down and started to flip through her phone.

A layer of dust clung to everything in the mill. Hard to avoid with years of chaff and dirt rubbed into the boards and the gaps in the construction letting in the environment. The first floor was basically a large open room. The interpretive plaques set around the room explained that the mill had been built with a speed never before seen in the area. Townspeople claimed that the Institute residents worked on it around the clock with fires burning all night long. Unlike other mills, it didn't take in grain from the outside and only served the community here. The mill had been operational only a few weeks before the fire. When the Institute burned, although the mill structure survived, the dam was destroyed (some said sabotaged according to the text) and the area was left to ruin.

"So," I said, returning to the desk after making my circuit. "Sabotaged, huh?"

She put her phone down and her eyes gleamed.

"Crazy, right? How much do you know about the Institute?"

"A little," I said. "but mostly just…"

"The ghost stuff," she finished, nodding her head.

"Well, not really, I mean."

"No, don't worry about it. We don't get a ton of visitors, but most of the ones that we do are only interested in talking about the ghost stuff. It's cool. At least you're not one of the guys who shows up and wants to know more about the sex stuff."

"Yeah…" I said.

"Oh, no. You're not one of the sex stuff people, are you?"

"No! No, no. God no. I'm… Yeah, the ghost stuff."

"Oh, thank God. Thought I had really stepped in it for a second there. Okay, well, Mohawk, and this is all off the record, I'd get in trouble if I don't stick to the script, so are we cool?"

I nodded my head.

"Well, Mohawk was a real piece of work. He got lynched. You know that, right?"

"Yeah."

"So, he was a real nutball, and there are all sorts of references at the time to black masses and the devil showing up here and that's how everything got built so quickly. I mean it is really impressive right? The city council even delivered a letter to the Institute requesting that they leave immediately. I would have liked to have seen how that went over.

"Anyhow, so, I don't know, like cults everywhere, he pushed somebody too far, probably, sure, because of the open marriage, no-one-has-sex-except-for-me policy and they drove him into town and killed him. And now, the place is supposed to be haunted."

"Is it? Haunted, I mean?"

"Yeah, I don't really believe in that stuff…"

"Me neither," I said quickly. She looked at me quizzically for a moment, then continued.

"Okay. But, power of suggestion and all that. Sure, some spooky stuff happens when you're locking up and it's later at night. Some ghost hunter people come by about once a year and make a big pronouncement about how 'active' the place here is. And, of course, there are the kids."

"Oh."

Kara rolled her eyes. "It's the biggest pain about working here. Kids are always breaking in or trying to break in. The director told me once, like way before my time, that he came in on a Monday and it looked like an honest to God Black Mass had been held here, all sorts of marks on the floor and scorching from fires. Took them more than a week to clean up and the weird smell from the incense or whatever? The place took like six months before it smelled right."

"Wow," I said, "that must have been a pain."

An awkward pause hung in the air between us. I avoided her eyes and made a show of looking at the beams of the mill. She broke the silence.

"So... do you want to see the cemetery?"

"Sure."

"Oh, I'm supposed to remind you that we have a gift shop here for your gift buying needs." She swept her hand towards the rickety shelves that I had noticed on my way in. Gamely, I walked over and checked out the inventory. There were some postcards that looked unironically vintage and tchotchkes like small pewter replicas of the mill.

"Ummm.... I'm good."

She shrugged.

"I don't think anyone has ever bought anything, but I have to ask."

"Sure," I said.

"Okay," she said, grabbing her jacket, "let's go look at the cemetery."

"So," she started as we approached. The tone of her voice changed as she began to recall her script. "You'll notice that there are no headstones in the cemetery. Mohawk told his followers that their names would be unimportant in the next world, but you will notice if you look closely at the wall surrounding the burial ground that there are small carvings in the rock that ring the entire structure. We still haven't figure out what they are. However, some of them do look similar to ones in old magic books, grimoires." She pronounced the word with an over-enthusiastic French accent. "But, to complicate the question, we don't know if Mohawk's followers carved them or superstitious people did it afterward."

I looked closer and there they were. No more than three inches high, a grouping of pentagrams, headless figures with what looked like triangles for wings. Circles incised inside of each other and more. They repeated all the way around the wall like a chanted phrase.

"… trying to convince my boss to make tee-shirts with the symbols or at least prints, but he says we don't want to encourage the kooks. But I'm thinking, they're already coming, so why not make some money from them? I'm sorry, that sounds terrible, doesn't it?" Kara was back off-script and her voice was brighter and happier.

"No, no," I said, "pragmatic is the word. How many people are buried in there?"

"Good question! Short answer, we don't know. Someone with ground-penetrating radar came sometime, in maybe the 80s? Anyhow, there are a lot of bones down there, but they're all sort of jumbled. It's actually more like a mass grave, but we are absolutely forbidden from using that term, but it is what it is, right?"

"Mm hmm…" I stopped examining the markings and moved to the gate.

"So, this," Kara said, walking up beside me and slapping the massive slab of rock that made up the gate, "is maybe the coolest thing here. It's a solid piece, weighing more than a ton that serves as a gate. It's perfectly balanced. It looks way too big to move, but it just takes a little push," she reached out and gave it a shove. The gate, which had been partially opened, obediently and smoothly closed. "It's incredible. I don't know how they did it. Here, you give it a try."

I stepped up and reached my hand out to push the gate. As I applied pressure, an aura settled over my vision and everything glowed for a moment.

I was away from Kara and the rest of the present day. Now, I was looking into the graveyard where a pit had been dug. Torches had been placed in the ground around the hole, illuminating the scene. Two men worked pulling bodies out of the back of a wagon. Another man, tall and with the beard of a Civil War general, stood to the side. His body appeared to twitch, move, his features stretching out of place and then oozing back together: two faces sharing the same place in a double exposure. One face human with glittering eyes and the other monstrous with offset eyes and an open mouth with a lolling wet, swollen tongue. The bodies that had been pitched in were horribly disfigured, gutted, and in the flicker of the pitch, I could see that one had what looked like bite marks tearing away its cheeks.

*Oh, the face,* I felt rather than heard a voice in the bones behind my ears, *the face has the sweetest meat of all, those round plump cheeks.*

I woke up on my back with the sun burrowing into my eyes. I blinked, then squeezed my eyelids against the light. My head was throbbing.

"Oh, my God! You're up," Kara was on her knees beside me, gently shaking me. "Are you okay?"

I tried to sit up and felt vomit rise in the back of my mouth. I laid back down.

"Yeah, I think. What…?"

"I have no idea! You reached out, touched the gate stone, then fell down, like you were dead. I seriously thought you were dead. And I left my phone in the mill so I didn't know if I should go back or stay…"

"No. I'm… I'm okay."

"I shook you," she looked guilty, "but then I thought, 'Oh my God, I don't think you're supposed to shake unconscious people', so I stopped. I hope I didn't hurt you."

"I think that's with a spinal injury. No, I'm, I'm good." I managed to sit up this time. "I have, maybe, I think, I have migraines."

"Migraines that make you pass out?"

"Sometimes."

"That doesn't sound good. You should see a doctor."

"Yeah, I did. Can you, ah, help me up?" I threw an arm around her and she helped me to my feet. She smelled like cinnamon gum, and I panicked for a minute, *was a weird smell a symptom of a stroke?*

"Does my face look all right?" I asked, panicking more than a little.

"Uh. Yeah, I guess. I mean you didn't cut yourself."

"Is it drooping? Can you understand the words I am saying?"

"Yes. Why are you asking me these things? Are you sure you're okay?"

"Yeah. I think I'll just go home."

Relieved, I leaned heavily against the cemetery wall and felt a static charge move up my spine. Kara saw me flinch.

"Do you want me to call someone? I don't know if you should."

"No, it's fine. I don't live that far away."

"Okay," she said. "Look, not to be a jerk or anything, but you're not going to sue, right?"

"No. I'm not going to sue."

"So, then, maybe we don't have to mention this to my boss or to the college?"

"Sure. No problem," I still saw halos around everything. Kara sounded far away.

"Thanks," she said, "I really appreciate it. It's just that. I need this internship to go well. Especially after the last one."

I nodded my head, and she helped me away from the wall.

"Well, um... bye? Thanks for coming. Come back anytime."

"Thanks," I said, "I'll do that."

The walk home was long and slow. I mean, it must have been. I don't remember it.

# CHAPTER 14

de Laurence found Butler's idea for a school, an occult lyceum, an institute of hidden knowledge, to be enticing. The location would be a large building near Beacon Hill. The lower floors would be open to the public where a staff of spiritualist charlatans would lead lectures about palmistry, and phrenology, and provide seances and spirit photography. Butler would oversee it all while de Laurence spent his time on the upper floors sharing the true occult practices with the wealthy and curious. They would save money on upkeep by having one building instead of two. Butler had neglected to mention that once de Laurence was gone, he would take sole possession of the institution.

With de Laurence's blessing, Butler hired contractors and builders. He still kept his busy schedule of seances and, in secret, increased his study in de Laurence's library. The three floors of the building, surrounding a glass ceiling courtyard filled with flowers and herbs went up quickly. Architectural remnants, bits of gothic statuary and Arabic tile, filled the first floor and a collection of stained glass bled colored light into the rooms. It was just eight months after construction had begun that Butler made another suggestion: a grand summoning for a grand opening. de Laurence would invite his wealthiest clients to see him bring forth a creature the likes of which none of them had seen before. After such a show, the wealthy dilettantes' money would come pouring into de Laurence and the school. de Laurence agreed with some reluctance. He worried because the stronger creatures, he had told Butler, constantly sought access to our plane. When they were here, they didn't enjoy being trifled with.

The night of the summoning, Butler spared no expense in the trappings that the wealthy customers would be expecting. He had learned the value of showmanship from de Laurence while sneering at it in private. That night, topless women with their heads shrouded in peaked black masks stood at the four corners of the expansive room holding torches. Butler and de Laurence spent the day scribing the magic circles on the marble floor with chalk. Butler marked closely where de Laurence secreted the books when they were done copying the patterns. As Butler increased in knowledge and power, his mentor had become like an old woman jealously guarding his recipes by leaving out tiny bits of information. *Randolph was wiser than I gave him credit. The time had come*, Butler wrote in his journal while he hatched his plan to remove de Laurence, *that the student should exceed the teacher*. de Laurence had one more bit of usefulness left in him—*even an old hen*, Butler had scratched across the page, *can still provide a feast for those who hunger*.

The hall filled with the wealthy and wine was passed all around. A thrill filled the air: faces were flushed and breathing heavily. The room filled with heat and humidity and the smell of bodies pressed together. Finally, de Laurence began the ritual.

He wore his robes and skullcap that Butler had come to find ridiculous. He took his place in the protective glyphs and began his incantation. Butler stood behind him and off to the side. He mouthed the words soundlessly along with de Laurence. The old man retrieved a long knife from his robes and a rabbit from the small cage that had been set in place hours earlier. The animal's screams reverberated in the hall, and de Laurence silenced them with the knife, slitting the animal's throat open. Hot blood gouted into the bowl. de Laurence placed the dead animal to the side and then cut a deep slit in his own arm, wincing, but never faltering in the chant as the two bloods mixed in the bowl. The air shimmered and grew thicker like newly set gelatin. The co-mingled blood sizzled and boiled and the smell of rotting meat filled the room. A noise like the edge of a whirlwind filled the air. Butler could see de Laurence's mouth still moving, but heard nothing but the growing sound of the storm. The sheer pressure of the noise against his sinuses and ears made Butler feel as if he was holding his head inches away from a passing freight train. He moved closer to de Laurence.

Inside the circle, mist and what looked like tongues of pale flame, licked all around the enclosed area. Shapes formed then melted: a bull's head bellowing in rage; a horned creature with no eyes and a giant, slobbering unhinged jaw; a squid with stingers at the end of its tentacles which lashed against the invisible walls that kept it contained, its giant beak working, opening and closing with a mawkish wet noise. Men and women fainted and fell to the floor. Wine glasses shattered. Servants ran from the room. Butler moved behind and even closer to de Laurence. With a single, smooth motion, he shoved him. The man's left foot struggled for purchase once and broke the protective chalk line as he fell into the circle, next to the creature.

The room exploded. Butler stood stock still, unable to move. He watched as the squid thing jabbed a stinger deep into de Laurence's guts with a noise like the tearing of parchment. It pulled him from his feet and, with another tentacle, began flaying the flesh from his face as a hungry man would slice the peel from an apple. Butler could hear de Laurence's voice now. He was cursing Butler in a deep guttural voice which continued until the monster reached in and deftly plucked out his tongue by the roots. Butler realized that one of the creature's saucer-sized eyes, completely black, soulless, had been watching him the whole time de Laurence was being skinned. The gaze drew him in further. The roar in his ears increased and his vision began to tunnel. The last thing he saw was the creature stepping outside of the circle where it had been broken and the demon's pale fire filling every nook of the room.

When he awoke, Butler found himself in the empty hall. He was surrounded by ash but was largely unharmed. A terrible smell filled the shell of the building. The hall was empty, but he slowly realized that he was not alone. He went through the next few days with the increasing feeling he was being watched.

He fled Boston as quickly as possible. Everything in the lyceum was gone. All of de Laurence's precious books burnt to ash. Butler was able to save a change of clothes and a few of his notebooks from his old room in Allston which he had kept as a bolthole. The day after the fire, the newspapers had already begun to hint that dark matters were at hand at the source of the blaze. He trusted that the Brahmans who had escaped before the "accident" would stifle the story in its cradle, but he was not so sure that they wouldn't do the same to him to keep the events hidden. He boarded a New York City-bound train without looking back.

His face was still raw like a sunburn from the fire. Sometimes he swore that the smell of burning flesh had lodged itself in his nostrils. Eating was impossible. He feared that he would have stayed awake for days if he didn't have his laudanum.

The voice sat in the back of his head. Sometimes he visualized it curled into a tight nautilus shell of patterned conformity embedded in the bone just behind his ear. The first time he heard the voice he had been on the train from Boston to Manhattan. He had been watching the trees click like a zoetrope outside his window when a pressure started to build inside his skull.

*It's our time now, my boy*, it whispered. *No more parlor tricks,* the voice guffawed. *Sex magick? Hilarious. Little boys flipping their cocks on the table to see whose is biggest and calling themselves wicked for their game.* That laugh again. *My little mouse, we will show the world what it means to be wicked.*

The landscape outside his window melted and his head flooded with images that were as real as if he were experiencing them first hand. Bodies exposed and mutilated. Burning animals and children, their eyes melting and smearing down the flesh of their faces. A screaming that keened into a high wailing tenor and all of it underlaid by the noise of a million cicadas *chk-chk-chk*ing as they burrowed beneath the skin not to eat their way back out for seventeen years.

Butler woke two days later in Bellevue. When the nurse asked his name, he blurted out the first thing that came to mind. "Samuel Mohawk," he said and the beast's voice inside him roared in laughter. Two days later he was released having been told that he had suffered a fit, perhaps brought on by an excess of laudanum following his experience at the fire. His doctor, a bright young man with a calm voice, advised Elias to recuperate somewhere quiet and to leave the city if at all possible.

*Leave the city for somewhere quiet? What a wonderful idea*, said the voice. *I've always wanted to see where we grew up.*

The trip from New York City to Butler, Pennsylvania took more than a month. The newly christened Mohawk avoided the trains and traveled by foot, hitching rides on wagons whenever he could. Farmers and salesmen, and not a few con artists recognizing one of their own, were often desperate for company. At first, he sought out the solace of companionship away from the pitchy night in the jungles of tramps and other forgotten men and women.

He kept to himself after he woke covered in the blood of a man with whom he had shared a fire and rabbit stew the night before. Mohawk had run out of laudanum and the voice kept him up long after his traveling companion had fallen off into deep snores.

*Do you remember that Reb you bayoneted at Gettysburg and how he screamed like a pig at slaughter? How high and child-like his voice was? How he begged for his mama to come and stitch his belly back up? Or that boy, what was his name? Oh, that's right: Samuel? Aha ha ha ha ha ha! You stole his name, didn't you? That's a wicked thing to do to a friend. You and he were friends, remember? You were going to go out West and be drovers after the war, weren't you? Of course, Samuel ended up with half of his brains splattered across your face at the Battle of the Wilderness, so he probably wouldn't have made much of a cowboy.* The voice laughed silkily. *You know, I still see him once in a while here in Hell. He's lost a lot of his piss and vinegar, but I'll bet he remembers you…*

Mohawk's fork was still clenched in his hand when he woke, an unidentifiable soft body part balanced at the end of the tines. The voice in his head roared in laughter while Mohawk vomited, then built the fire back up and dragged his companion's body into it in an attempt to hide the cause of death.

*Your first time and already thinking about hiding the evidence. Oh wait, this isn't your first time at all, is it? It's just like the bishop said to the actress, You're a natural at this!*

# CHAPTER 15

My blackout at the Institute Mill shook me deeply. For a week, I spent most of my time lying in bed and looking at the ceiling. I wanted to know what was going on with me, but at the same time, I didn't want to find out the truth. As long as a doctor didn't tell me that I had a brain tumor, I could still pass the hallucinations off as middle age or blood pressure problems. I didn't bathe and got up only to use the bathroom and see if Mr. B was ready to come in or go out. Thanksgiving came and went. I wouldn't have even noticed if I hadn't flipped on the television that morning and seen a bloated Snoopy and Superman floating through New York City. Mr. B and I split a can of tuna that night for our feast and watched old *Midsummer Murders* on Netflix.

Finally, I managed to roust myself. I showered, shaved, and dressed. I fortified myself with two cups of Earl Grey Breakfast tea and began emotionally preparing myself for another visit to Old City Hall. Before I could get any further into my day, my phone vibrated in my pocket. As I fished it out, I realized that it was Nick from Boston. I sighed and answered.

"Aaron?"

"Hi, Nick."

"Been a while, buddy. I was starting to think that maybe you had fished out on me."

"No, no. Did you get the info I sent over?"

"Yeah, yeah, just looking at it now. That's why I called."

"Everything okay? I thought you'd like the gambling ring stuff."

"Yeah, no, that's great. The whole thing is great."

"But?"

"Ah, well. It's just that, I guess when I talked to Walt... I guess, I was just looking for material that plugged a little more directly into the plotline."

"It's all solid stuff, Nick. I don't want to tell you your business." This conversation was an occupational hazard. A client with a vague expectation would sometimes sound like he was asking for advice on how to incorporate the research into the plot, especially color stuff. But I learned that if you made a direct suggestion, the writer would get defensive: the old "Who's writing this book, you or me?" argument. Walt and I had actually gone through it a few times before he had enough cash and reputation socked away that he no longer cared who was doing the writing as long as his name was on the cover and his face was in the magazine.

"But you're going to," he said. There it was.

"No, no, no... look, like I told you on our first call, I've been doing this for a long time. From experience, I can tell you that your synopsis has a solid plot ..."

"Right."

"But it's not buried in Pittsburgh. You could drop the story into any city and it would still work. So, all you need are some details, make sure the names are all right so that the online community doesn't spend all of its time nitpicking."

"Right. I get that. But look. I have an idea."

"Uh-huh,"

"Walt said that sometimes you would do little, I don't know, let's call them mock-ups. Where you would use his character and show how the information fits in. He said you did that for him in *Key West Cockfight*. And some of the other later ones."

Bastards. Both of them. Walt had set me up with a hack who was looking for a ghostwriter. He would protest if I called him on it. I could hear his gravely old man voice now: *Moody, kid, I did it for you. You're going to need the money and a new whale of a client. It might be a shit sandwich, but you still gotta eat, buddy.*

"Aaron? You there?"

"Yeah, I'm here." The rough of it was that the Walt voice was right. I did need the money. I just didn't know how much more of my self-respect I was willing to sell. Walt and I had a give and take. He was lazy, sure, but he was still a hell of a writer who had forty-plus years of understanding how a story went together. "OK, yeah. I'll, ah, I'll put together 5,000 words or so."

"Just a mock-up. That's all I'm saying."

"Right. I'll put together a 5,000-word mock-up and send it on to you."

"Remember, I'm on a tight deadline."

"Uh-huh. okay. Well, then, I guess I better get to work."

"Thanks, Aaron. I'm super happy that we're on the same page."

The line went dead, and I sighed again. I really didn't like this guy. I grabbed a jacket and made my way out the door to walk to Old City Hall. I kept my head up and earbuds in my pocket. I hadn't seen Mr. B since our meal a few days ago and, even though he wasn't officially my cat, I worried about him. Addicts and stray cats from outside the neighborhood would wander the streets looking for easy marks and handouts. I had seen more of both kinds of predators lately.

I hadn't made it more than a half-block down the very start of the hill on which my neighborhood stood before my thighs started complaining about the downhill pitch. What did it mean when going downhill was as difficult as going uphill? My wife moved to another state after she left me. One night, in a dark place, I googled her address. Her new home was in a neighborhood that was flat and suburban. She was right; she had always been the wiser of the two of us.

Out of habit, I glanced behind me to take one last look at the house. Anxiety sometimes grabbed me by the back of the neck and whispered disaster scenarios that forced me to go back and check that ovens and coffee machines were off and that doors were shut and locked. Over my shoulder, I could see my crumbling wall and the blackened stump. Tension dripped its way into the space between my shoulders, and I started box breathing. Seven counts in, hold the breath for seven counts, release it for seven counts.

Turning back downhill, I saw a guy who was probably younger than I, but looked twenty years older because of his rheumy eyes, stubbly hair, and lack of teeth, coming up the hill towards me. I stopped and pretended to check something on my phone hoping he would just walk past. Out of my periphery, I saw him slow his pace as he approached. I sighed deeply, not one for confrontation.

The man stopped dead in front of me. He wore a tee-shirt and sores and scabs cratered his arms. Thin red lines ran from his wrists all the way under the sleeves.

"Excuse me, sir."

"Yeah?"

"Now, hear me out. I'm not asking for a handout…"

"Okay."

The man snapped his arm out and caught me around the bicep. His grip was like an iron band. When I was a boy, my dad used to grab me like that when he was angry. The fingertips dug deep beneath the bicep digging their way between the meat and the bone. The pain shot up my arm and into my head.

"Hey! What the hell? Let me go!"

"It's too late for that." The man's voice had changed. The eyes thick with mucus stared directly into my own. His breath was fetid, rotten, like the guts of roadkill spilled out on a summer street.

"It's too late for that. He's out now. He was weak, but he's getting stronger. And he doesn't like you. Birds who dip their beaks in get them snapped off." His fingers tightened more. All I could feel was the pain; the edges of my vision started to darken.

"He has The Burnt Man now. And he's teaching him." The junkie started twisting his whole hand into my arm. My knees went shaky and gave way from the pain. I fell, kneeling, onto the sidewalk and as I did, was ripped from his grasp.

"Gods bless you, Sir. You and yours who will be ours."

He walked off, whistling a song. I was there, on my hands and knees, for minutes. Cars drove by, one honked and the driver yelled something unintelligible. A woman and child heading down the hill towards me crossed the street. They must have thought I was drunk or high. Or, they thought that I was dying of a heart attack and didn't want to get involved. My arm was numb and useless. I pulled myself to my feet, hunched over with my hands on my knees and took deep ragged breaths. A car slowed and parked. I heard a car door shut, but didn't look up. A woman came up beside me with a gentle voice.

"Hey. You okay?"

"Yeah... I just... I..."

I gulped in air, and realizing I was on the edge of tears, wanted to go home. I wanted to go back inside of the house and never leave again. I had books, I had tea. Hell, I had Amazon Prime. I could order everything I needed and be safe. From all this.

"All I want is to get my wall fixed. Why does this have to be so difficult?"

"Okay. Okay. Deep breaths. It's going to be all right. I'm a nurse. Is there someone I should call? I have Narcan in the car if you need it."

"No…" I took a deep breath and straightened up. "No. I'm okay. Just… just one of those days I guess." I sniffled and felt like an embarrassed child. "Thank you. For stopping. All those people, they just ignored me. I could have been dying."

"Take it from me. I see all kinds of people at work. And they're all terrible."

We laughed together.

"Are you sure you're alright?" she asked again.

"Yeah, yeah, I'm fine. I'm just going to catch my breath."

"Okay. If you're sure." She paused at her car door before leaving. "Good luck with your wall."

I waved thanks and stood there for a few more minutes. I closed my eyes and focused on fighting the panic and pain away with deep breaths.

*Mgaoi?*

I opened my eyes. Mr. B stood on the neighbor's fence staring at me from eye level.

"B," I said. "Oh, it is so good to see you, little brother."

I picked him up and hugged him. He squirmed but purred, then used his front paws to push himself away from my chest. I put him back down.

"What's going on with me, buddy? What am I going to do?"

He wound himself around my legs in tight looping infinity signs covering my jeans with his fur. Then he looked up at me and started to saunter down the hill. He got about five feet in front of me and then turned back.

*Mgaoi* he said in his squeaky voice.

"Downward and onward, huh buddy? Once more into the breach, is that it?"

He continued down the hill.

"Okay, buddy. You're probably right. Too much isolation

probably isn't good for me." I looked back at the stump. "Especially not right now."

Mr. B walked to the end of the block with me, but when I made the right-hand turn to go downtown, he jumped back onto a neighbor's low stone wall and started walking uphill back towards my house. He didn't look back.

"See you later, buddy," I mumbled and kept walking. The numbness in my arm had turned into a deep ache, but I could breathe again. The air was cool and crisp and I didn't meet eyes with a single person all the way to Old City Hall.

VFW Hat Guy was back sitting with the receptionist when I made it through the doors.

"… now, you know, I park on the street. No garage you see, well, I mean, no one has garages in my neighborhood. We all park on the street."

"Oh, yes," the receptionist answered. "Well, that's right, isn't it? Now, Harlan and I, we never had a garage. He always wanted one, but he had a little workshop in the basement and that was just fine for what he needed."

"That's right," said VFW Hat. I stood waiting at the reception desk card table. "But here's the thing. Those damn junkies, excuse my language," the receptionist nodded for him to continue. "The other night, those damn junkies, they got into my car."

"Broke the lock!" the receptionist exclaimed.

"Well, no. You see, I had forgotten to lock it. Well, hell, you didn't use to have to. Not just ten years ago."

"Did they steal it?"

"No, no. The cops think they slept in it. There was a terrible mess, you know, in the back seat. Now, who would do something like that? Even animals don't mess where they sleep."

The receptionist shook her head and clucked her tongue.

"Ruined. I don't know that I'll ever be able to sell it for

anything now. And here's the other thing. I had my pistol in there, in the glove box, and damned if they didn't take it as well. And the cops told me there was nothing I could do if I didn't report it stolen," his voice was winding up now. He was in high dudgeon. "But I'll be damned if I'll do that, because that's how they keep track of how many guns you have and where they are."

"Ahem…" I cleared my throat. They turned slowly to face me. "Hi. I don't mean to interrupt."

"Well, I guess I should be getting out of here anyhow." VFW Hat got to his feet from the velvet upholstered seat cushion.

"Well, good luck with your car," I said. He glared at me, as if angry that I had acknowledged that I couldn't help but hear his story, and shuffled out.

"Yes, now young man, what can I do for you today?"

"I'm looking for Streets and Public Improvement."

"You'll go up the stairs. It's the first door on your right."

"Thanks," I said.

"You're very welcome." She began rearranging the travel pamphlets on her desk.

The first door on the right was unmarked. I was beginning to think that none of the doors in the Old City Hall were marked. The absence of signage might have been laziness or budgetary, or maybe the workers switched places every so often. Maybe the old lady downstairs rose like the Mad Hatter and bellowed "Switch places!" and then a mad scrum of flying papers in triplicate and staplers whirling around only to land in a new, unmarked office. How, I wondered, did this place even come close to being allowed under the ADA? I turned the brass doorknob with more confidence than I had during my last visit, wincing at the pain in my arm which soared from a dull throb.

That confidence immediately drained out of me when I realized I was facing the same woman who I had talked to in Zoning.

"Yes? May I help you?" she asked.

"I, ah… I'm sorry. I was looking for Streets and Public Improvement."

"That's us," she said cheerfully.

"But, you… I mean I talked to you in Zoning, like, a week, a few weeks ago."

"Ooh… right. I remember you. That's right, honey. I was transferred out of Zoning into here. Ours is not to question why, right, ours is but to do or die."

*Ours is but to do and die*, I corrected the quotation in my head.

"Ah… so… okay," I took a breath. "You might remember, I was here to find out when the city was going to fix my wall."

"I do remember. And I told you to go to the City Solicitor."

"And they told me to go to Streets and Public Improvement, and, so, here I am."

"New City Hall sent you here?"

"Umm-hmmm," I nodded.

"Well, doesn't that just figure?"

She leaned in conspiratorially, and I could smell the coffee on her breath. "You didn't hear it from me, but I think that solicitor avoids all the work she can. Lawyers! Too busy swimming in their heated in-ground pools full of money to help anyone."

I shrugged and tried to smile like a normal human as I felt frustration tightening my chest. I just wanted my wall to be fixed. I just wanted things to get back to normal.

"Well, okay, what was that address again?"

"113 Orchard," I said.

"Not yours, honey, where was the tree?"

"I don't know that the tree had a street address. I never saw squirrels get mail there or anything."

She failed to see the humor in my joke.

"I'll just look up Orchard St. then, hmmm?"

She walked over to a row of file cabinets that were five feet high and took up an entire twelve-foot wall. From what I could see through an open doorway, they continued into the next room.

"You say it was this year?" she shouted over her shoulder.

"That's right," I shouted back. "November 1."

She hauled out a manila file folder stretched to bursting and put it on the desktop between us.

"The records aren't digitized?" I asked.

"Oh, well. Maybe at the New City Hall, with their fancy computers and metal detectors and those little coffee machines that use the pods, but not here. We don't have the budget for that sort of thing."

She paged through the five-inch-thick stack. Time seemed to thicken and slow. I watched the dust motes float through the sunbeams that shot in through gaps in the curtain. The worker sighed. She had reached the bottom of the stack. She glanced at me to make sure I understood just how much work this task was, then started through the stack again, faster this time. She reached the bottom, mumbled to herself, slammed her palm flat against the stack and looked up at me.

"Wulp," she said, "I don't know what to tell you."

"What do you mean?"

"There's no work order here."

"Well, you know that the tree was taken down. You said you knew the guy who died."

"Oh, I know that Matt died. I went to his funeral. And I'll tell you that not many of my co-workers could be bothered to do the same. But what I'm saying is that there was no order filed here to have that tree cut down."

"So, where is it?"

"I couldn't tell you."

"Why wouldn't it be here?"

"No idea."

"So, what, they were just driving around and decided to cut

it down?"

"I have work orders for two other small tree removals that day, but nothing in that neighborhood."

"Okay, so that's fine. Here's the deal. I'm not worried that the city lost the paperwork about a job where a guy died in front of my house. I'm freaked out, but I'm not worried. With all due respect, I'm sure it's not the first time that paperwork has been lost."

She stiffened.

"But here's the deal. I don't really care about any of that. All I want is to get my wall fixed."

"Well," she said shrugging her shoulders and wrapping the folder back around her stack and carrying it back to the open cabinet. "I can tell you that's not going to happen since there's no proof that the city actually cut down the tree."

"A man died! What more proof do you need?"

"Finding form 234cA in triplicate would be a nice start."

Getting angry with bureaucrats, I have found, never has the desired effect. I turned and walked to the door.

"Thank you for your help. I hope you have a good day." I didn't allow a hint of sarcasm to creep into my voice, but my chest was tight and my stomach roiled. My hands shook as I reached for the door. I was close to having one of my panic attacks.

"Hope in one hand and spit in the other," I heard her say as the door closed behind me.

I leaned against the wall, trying to control my breathing. In through the nose, hold the breath, out through the mouth, hold the breath with the lungs empty, then repeat. Focus on lowering the heartbeat. Slowly, I felt like I could move again. I leaned heavily on the banister on my way down and past the receptionist.

"Did you get what you needed?" she asked cheerfully.

"No. No, ma'am, I did not. What I got was the runaround, and I didn't like it one bit."

"Oh my," she said, shaking her head.

"And," I added as I leaned heavily on the chair where the VFW Man had sat, his butt impressions still visible in the velvet, "I have no idea where to go next."

"Well," she said, "I guess the last resort is to make a public appeal during a city council meeting."

"Yeah," I said, "I really, really don't want to do that. All I want is to get my wall fixed."

"Well," she said, pausing in her shuffling of brochures and casting a look behind her shoulder. "There's always the other department."

"The other department?"

"The one downstairs… in the basement?"

"The basement here?"

She nodded her head.

"I didn't even know there was anything in the basement. What department is it?

"The Basement Department."

"The department in the basemen, it's called 'The Basement Department'?"

She nodded her head.

"Okay. And how do I get to the basement?"

She pointed at the rickety birdcage elevator.

"Really?"

She shook her head yes again. I sighed and took a step towards it. "Oh, but they're not in now. They don't keep banker's hours. "

"So, what am I supposed to do?" I asked exasperated.

"I'll tell you what. You're such a nice young man. You remind me a lot of my Harlan. You give me your cell phone telephone number and I'll call you when I see them come in."

"Really?"

She nodded her white hair, delighted. "It'll be our little

secret."

I scribbled my number down with the pen and pad she proffered.

"Thanks for this. Really."

"Oh, it's my pleasure," she said.

I pounded out Nick's 5,000 words over the course of the next two days. Writers like him who avoid the work of writing—the butt in the chair part—confuse me. That work is the fun part, the reward after the hard slog of research. In terse prose, I piloted his PI through a conversation in a dive bar in McKees Rocks to call in an old favor in order to get some information from a solider from the Amato family and then picked up another section where the protagonist was going door to door among the Victorian homes on the Mexican War Streets looking for the sister of the femme fatale. The story needed some work, so I threw in a little backstory on the PI to give him more of a rounded character. Then I ended with a few pages that brought in a suggestion of a sub-plot with some numbers runners who were working both sides with the cops and the mobsters.

The writing wasn't bad. I wasn't sure that anyone really cared about noir anymore, so I was trying to steer it into more of a thriller feel. I was testing Nick. I figured he would either take umbrage and terminate our relationship, or he would get the pages, change a few words, and congratulate himself on a job well done. I bet on the latter, clicked "send", and tried to get Nick and his story out of my head.

There was enough of a chill outside that I felt justified in lighting a fire. Once built, it burned slowly, sending pops and snaps up the chimney. The house smelled pleasantly of smoke. It reminded me of a high school girlfriend. Her family had a huge fireplace in their open plan home. In the winter, she smelled like a smoked gouda, which I told her I found endearing. She found the image less than charming. I collapsed on the couch and Mr. B hopped up beside me. He had been waiting, curled in a tiny ball of fur, on the chair outside on the deck when I came home, and had marched through the door as soon as it was opened. I arranged a fleece blanket around him, he relaxed, and I dozed off just after his breathing became slow and rhythmic.

I started awake. The November sun was mostly gone, but it was impossible to tell the time. The fire burned low and illuminated the room in flickers. Mr. B was awake and standing on all fours. He had backed up tight against me on the couch—his movement having what awakened me. His ears were perked, his tail bottle-brushed, and his whiskers protruded with the panache of a Victorian statesman.

"What's up, little brother?" I mumbled dazed and groggy.

Then I heard it: a scratching on the door. Or, was it further outside? This neighborhood was full of squirrels, especially this time of year before the snow started to sit on the ground. They ran around endlessly, collecting black walnuts that fell by the bushel. The squirrels had become clever enough over the generations that they would leave the walnuts that fell into the alley, waiting for passing cars to crush the hard shells and reveal the sweet meat. But they had never scratched at the house before.

The scratching grew louder and began to move from place to place. The noise, and whatever was causing it, was definitely in the walls and not outside of them. Mr. B issued a low growl.

"It's okay, buddy. Just some squirrels."

But the noise grew louder and louder. It seemed to come from both outside walls now, running back and forth like a glissando being played. Still, it grew louder. My mouth dried and my body refused to move. The noise was transferring itself to inside my head. I felt the scratching inside my sinuses. Mr. B turned his head and looked at me with wide eyes, then turned to the walls and hissed a chittering, ugly noise that I had never heard him, or any other cat for that matter, make.

Then, the noise in the walls vanished. My head sagged loosely down on my neck as if a puppeteer had released its puppet. A wave of nausea swept over me. Spit gushed into my mouth, but I found that I couldn't swallow and it drooled out. A deep pain settled in my stomach and doubled me over.

A pounding on my front door shook the house. Mr. B looked towards the door and then back at me. His tail shrank to a normal size and his eyes were clear. My pain was gone. How long had I been on the floor? B sat on his haunches and began cleaning his paws daintily. The pounding sounded again. Making my way unsteadily to the interior foyer door, I cursed the cut leaded glass that my wife had loved so much. There was no clear way to see what or who was at the door. I wiped my mouth, took a breath to try and quell the nausea, and opened the door. It was Jerry, Mr. B's owner. He smiled and waved through the front and storm doors. I opened them.

"Hey, Aaron! How's it going? Sorry to drop in this late."

"No, it's ah. What time is it?"

"Just after 10. Were you sleeping? Jeez, I'm sorry."

I had no idea what Jerry did as a vocation. His avocation was lifting weights. He wasn't much taller than I and probably 15 years older, but he was solid. In the summer, he wore cut off tee-shirts and running shorts as he walked his mastiff in the neighborhood. He was big. The kind of big I didn't want to make angry. If he had been 20, his devotion to his musculature would have been interesting. In his 50s, it was fascinating; a man in that sort of shape in late middle age. He had always been exceedingly friendly to me. Much friendlier than I would have been to someone who had proven himself to be a serial catnapper.

"No… no. I just dozed off in front of the fire."

"Oh yeah. Good weather for it, huh?"

"Yeah… yeah."

"Well, you probably guessed why I'm here. Is Rosey here?" Rosey was the name he had given Mr. B. I had known the cat for six months before I met the owner. The cat was Mr. B to me and would remain as such. Rosey was a ridiculous, undignified name for a cat of this caliber.

"Yeah. He was asleep on the couch with me."

"Rosey," Jerry called. The cat didn't come.

"I'll get him. He's probably still asleep. C'mon in."

Mr. B was not asleep, but he had moved to cleaning his ears.

"C'mon, buddy. The big man is here." He gave a *mgaio* as I picked him up. He squirmed. He was not pleased.

"Awww. There he is," Jerry said. "I really appreciate you watching out for him."

"It's no problem," I said. "He's a great cat."

"He sure is," he said as I handed the squirming cat over to him. "Did I ever tell you how I found him?"

He had, many times, but there was no sense in stopping him. Besides, the memory of the scratching still crawled inside my head, and I welcomed any distraction.

"No, I don't think so."

"Well. Jenny, that's my girlfriend, I think you met her." I hadn't. "Jenny was out in an abandoned quarry. She likes to look for pretty rocks, fossils, things like that? Anyhow, she was out by Living Treasures on 422?"

Living Treasures was a throwback to the old roadside animal exhibits of another century when idiosyncratically punctuated billboards reading "Snake Pit Two Miles Ahead!!!" and "Slow Down OR You'll Miss THE amazing Dancing bear" dotted the roads. A time before the Humane Society and certainly before PETA. Just driving past the park depressed me with its wire fences strung out through the trees caging in mangy buffalos and forlorn zebus. The place reminded me of an animal POW camp.

"Uh-huh," I replied.

"Well, she's out there, digging around and she hears this meow and ol' Rosey walks right up to her! Well, she gathers him up and takes him home. But you can see how unusual he is. Have you ever seen another cat with a coat like this?"

He was right. Mr. B's coat was beautiful. His coat was thick and luxurious and a sort of brown mackerel tabby with a grey field. Jerry was right: he looked like a tiny jungle cat. The cat was beautiful and clever, but I knew what was coming.

"So, what we think is that he was some sort of exotic cat that escaped from Living Treasurers."

"Wow! Really?"

"Yup."

"He's one of a kind to be sure."

"Yeah. We actually don't like to let him out, but we have this other cat. Now he gets along great with the dog, but the other cat, he pushes Rosey around. And Rosey is no fighter."

That much was true. Mr. B was, in my estimation, much more of a flaneur or a boulevardier. He avoided the other neighborhood cats. He was unlike the huge ginger cat, the size of a bobcat, that I saw prowling the yards of Institute Hill. That guy took every chance he got to attack the other neighborhood cats, even the one that looked like his brother. If it were possible for cats to have mental issues, I had long ago pegged that orange guy as a sociopath. Mr. B was different. He watched everything. If he could have spoken, I imagined that he knew and could share all the secrets of the city. He was amazingly agile and an incredible jumper. And very wary. Not nervous, but constantly watching and listening: alert and aware.

Mr. B was struggling with renewed energy in Jerry's hands. "Well, looks like this guy is ready to go home."

"I gave him kibble at six."

"Oh, okay. Great. Thanks. Well, I'll see you around."

"Absolutely."

Mr. B looked back at me over Jerry's shoulder. As the man and beast descended the steps, still partially cordoned with police tape now fading from the sun, I closed the doors.

# CHAPTER 16

In the morning, I dug out the business card that Dinah had given me at the library and called Evanora LaCosta. The line rang four times before someone answered. I had expected the call to go to voice mail: a witchcraft store opening at nine seemed odd. Shouldn't they be sleeping in after dancing widdershins around a bonfire all night?

"Elemental Craft," a measured, even cheerful voice on the other end answered.

"Good morning. Could I speak to Evanora LaCosta please?"

"She's not in until two. Is there something I could help you with?"

"No, that's okay. I'll try back then."

I left the house at two, in the hopes that I could catch Evanora without waiting around. Although Sewickley is closer to Butler than downtown Pittsburgh, mileage-wise, getting there takes much longer. Because of the geography, the hills, rivers, and valleys, the drive is circuitous. First, the interstate, then winding roads up and down the foothills that mark the end of the Appalachian plain, then through deep gorges and dark valleys strung with native grapevines. Wild brook trout still hid in some of these streams which seemed hard to believe given the area's endless industrial degradation. There were still wild places here: places that I had hiked to or camped in. Places where, at night, a shiver went up the back of the spine as the unquestionable feeling of being watched settled deep into the lizard part of the brain. But today, in the bright fall afternoon sunlight, everything seemed to be well-manicured. Sewickley had more than its share of beautiful multi-million-dollar homes and many more than its share of horse farms. Retired professional Pittsburgh athletes settled here. The downtown featured boutique and antique stores and fancy restaurants. At the edges of the small downtown, however, old Pittsburgh clung on with submarine sandwich shops and bars with Iron City Beer neon in the glass block windows.

I parked by the library. I had an entire card catalogue of libraries in my head. In fact, I knew most of the small towns around here by their libraries. This one was well stocked and well kept in a classic building, full of nooks and alcoves with strong Wi-Fi, clean restrooms, and plenty of on-street free parking. Unlike my beloved Oakland Carnegie, this one was no industrialist's' gift. Just about the time Mohawk was setting up shop in Butler, a mysterious boat had made its way up the Ohio River to Sewickley in the dead of winter. Kegs of whiskey stood on board with drinks being sold for a pittance. The young men and women, flouting social conventions, swarmed the boat, dancing and drinking for three days straight. On the third day, an argument between two men, one black and one white, broke out. A knife was pulled and when a woman stepped between the two combatants, she was stabbed and killed instantly. In a panic, both men fled and word, regardless of the truth, quickly spread that a black man had killed a white girl. The story grew until it was a virginal white girl who had come to fetch her brother from the clutches of demon drink and then was seized upon, raped, and killed by a gang of African-

Americans. The resulting riot burnt much of the city to the ground. The African-American population was decimated. Those left alive moved as quickly as they could. Even today it was rare to see a non-white face in the town. The boat disappeared during the night of the riot. When some of the unrepentant went to wash the smoke from their throats, they found the boat and its pilot gone, presumably with the girl's body still on board, along with more than a few of the townspeople who decided life on a traveling whiskey riverboat didn't sound bad at all. In response, the town fathers called for a library to be established. "The consequent riot and disorder led some, in the interest in the welfare of young men, to think that such things would not be, had we a place for proper and rational amusement and self-improvement." read the charter that hung in the library. A billiards parlor probably would have better served their stated purpose, but it had worked out well for me.

By three, when I arrived and parked, the sunlight was already slanted and heading towards dusk in another two hours. I made my way two blocks up to The Elemental Craft.

Evanora's workplace sat between a book store and a bike shop. The window displays featured more candles of all sorts and purposes than I could have burned in a lifetime, along with bound bunches of palo santo and sage. The bell that hung above the door chimed as I walked in. The walls of the small shop were exposed brick and the thick scent of incense hung in the air. Aboriginal-style artwork hung on the walls and stacks of tee shirts filled a table. Paper flyers advertising spiritual house cleansings and psychic readings were pinned to a corkboard.

A woman in her twenties of medium height and dark straight hair, wearing jeans and a long red sweater, stood explaining a house cleansing to a woman old enough to be her mother. She didn't look like a witch, I thought. I had been expecting Evanora to be more ethereal, someone with more scarves and maybe a flowing caftan. The young woman had her blue eyes locked into those of the other woman who occasionally nodded her head.

"Every house has its own spirit, right? There are all sorts of cultures that understand these creatures as house spirits or house deities: the domovoy, the brownie, anito, or the gashin, but what all these human stories are really trying to explain is the idea that houses have their own animus and we dwell inside of that spirit. Now, we Americans ignore that spirit and can't figure out why we feel uncomfortable or sad in our own homes. Do you know what I mean?"

She reached out and touched the older woman's hand and smiled. The woman smiled back, hanging on the saleswoman's every word.

"So, with the house cleansing, it's a chance to reset everything, to calm the house's spirit back down and to start the relationship over. It's like the IT guys say, right? 'Did you try turning it off and turning it back on?'"

They both laughed.

"The cleansing is a simple thing, but unlike your computer, the process does require some expertise," she paused for a moment and then continued.

Sealing the deal. It was like watching a mix of *Hocus-Pocus* and *Glengarry Glen Ross*. Potions, I thought, are for closers.

"So, why don't we head back to the counter and I'll help you to get a couple of sessions set up?" The older woman allowed herself to be led back. I pretended to be examining the selection of books: *Modern Sex Magick*, *Witch's Altar*, *The Secret Key of Conjure*, *Practical Candle Burning Ceremonies*. I couldn't believe that I had come all the way here to deal with a wacko—a lonely young woman making a living from fleecing gullible soccer moms. I was thinking seriously about leaving when the noise of the bell made me look up. The older woman was leaving. She had a simple smile on her face as if she had woken up to feel the warmth of the sun on a chilly morning.

"Blessed be!" the young woman called after her. "What can I help you with today?" she said as she turned to me.

"That was some sales job," I said.

"Well, we are here to help people through their journey in life."

I noticed for the first time that her left arm didn't move. It hung stiff against her body. The sweater sleeves were long, but where the arm was visible, the skin was parchment translucent with a network of knotted veins crisscrossing the top. The nails were yellow and ridged and shaped into points. Her knuckles were the size of golf balls swollen and painful and red. She noticed my stare but didn't acknowledge it or pull the sleeve down to hide her hand.

"I'm looking for someone."

"Well… love magic is tricky."

"That's not… I'm… That's not what I mean. I'm trying to locate someone. I don't know where she is."

"Okay. So, I have some candles that you could use in a finding ceremony. Or, maybe a crystal for scrying?"

"No, nothing like that. I'm looking for someone who works here." I dug the card out of my pocket and held it out. "Evanora LaCosta?"

"That's me," she said. "Were you referred by a friend? When I work on special cases as a consultant, I do it outside of the regular business hours here."

"Uh… kind of. Someone at the Oakland Carnegie told me that we share a common interest."

"Okay," she said.

"Sam Mohawk?"

"Oh," she said. There was a long pause. Now, she tugged her sleeve down over her hand. Her stare made me uncomfortable, and I broke it to shuffle aimlessly through the flyers on the counter. Finally, I spoke.

"So, are you one of those ghost hunters, what do you call yourselves, paranormal investigators?"

"Ah, no," she said smiling. "I'm not. And I'm going to go out on a limb and say you're not a student of the occult yourself?"

"That would be fair to say," I said.

"So why are *you* researching Mohawk?"

"It's my job. I'm a researcher."

"How does that work?"

"Well, people hire me, writers usually, writers hire me to help find information. Add some facts or color to their writing."

"So, you're an assistant to someone who's writing about Mohawk. Do you know what their interest is?"

"No. I mean, no, I'm not doing this research for a client."

"You're a very confusing man, Mr...?"

"Moody. Aaron Moody." I reached to shake her hand. She looked at me and let my hand hang there for a second. I brought it back to the table.

"So, here's what I have so far," said Evanora. "You're a research assistant without a client, researching a subject in which you don't believe. Is that about right?" She shook her head. "You are an impressive example of cognitive dissonance, Mr. Moody."

"I live next to... across the street from my house was where, is where Mohawk was buried. And the city cut down his, the tree, and so, I... just wanted to find out more about him."

"You live next to the tree?" She leaned forward suddenly interested.

"Yeah, and...?"

"And were you there when that man died?"

"The city worker? Yeah. But I don't want to talk about it. It was horrible."

The incense smell was heavier than ever.

"And have odd things, things you can't explain, started happening to you? And that's why you're here?"

"No, I mean, kind of." She was uncomfortably intense. "Look, this is stupid. I should have known that this trip was a bad idea. I don't even believe in all of this," I swept my hand towards the stack of tee shirts, "'Support Your Local Coven' woo-woo… stuff. I just thought that maybe, if we were researching the same subject, we could share ideas. But maybe, we're just looking for two different things."

"I'm not so sure we are," said Evanora.

"What do you mean?"

"Well, let's share. What have you found so far?"

"Basic stuff. The mill, the farm, the orphanage, the cult-y part," I grimaced. "The lynching."

"And what about the other 'stuff'?"

"The sex stuff?" I asked thinking of Kara's disgust.

"No," Evanora said icily, "not the 'sex stuff.'"

"Oh. The ghost-y bits. A little, I guess. Sure, I mean, there's some odd stuff that surrounds the story."

"Okay, so explain The Marked to me," she said with a smirk.

"The marked what?"

"You're really not much of a researcher, are you? This is what you do for a living?"

"Don't be snide. What are you talking about?"

"I'll bet you go hungry a lot of nights, depending on this skill to put food on the table."

I glared.

"The Marked," she said. "Those who stood at Mohawk's end. Those who betrayed him and those whom he marked for destruction in his final moments."

"I don't know what you're talking about. There was nothing about that in the files."

"I know something you don't know," she sing-songed back to me.

"Fine. Be a child," I turned to walk out.

"John Butterfass. Jeb Goodrich. Isaiah Garvey."

"What?"

"Three out of the twelve marked. Look them up."

"Where did you find their names?"

"Oh. I have my ways." She wrote something on the back of a tarot reading flyer, pinning the paper to the counter with her ruined arm.

"Seriously, was it something you found in a special collection? Something at the State Archives?"

"They talked to me. Mr. Moody. That's the thing about souls in Hell; they're desperate to tell their stories. If they don't, they forget who they were. Here," she thrust the paper out to me. "See what you can find, oh great researcher."

"We are each our own devil,
and we make this world our Hell."
- *The Duchess of Padua*, Oscar Wilde

# CHAPTER 17

The man who named himself Sam Mohawk turned up in the city of Butler, the place he had left as a child, on a cold spring morning. He had stolen a man's luggage at the Jamestown, New York, train station, and the money he'd received from pawning the stranger's belongings had tied him over. Now though, he found himself arriving back home in much the same way he had left: penniless, cold, and with a deep mixture of foreboding and excitement.

He went to work right away. Butler was no Boston. Smoke and fumes from the glass and steel industry filled the air. The creek running through town bobbed and roiled with raw sewage and dead horses and cows as a rule rather than an exception. This place was not one where he could sell the wealth and prosperity bit and it was too parochial for the bourgeois naughtiness of sex magick.

He began preaching the End Times routine. As a patent medicine man, he had run into this brand of charlatan often enough—sometimes they even believed what they were selling. As a rule, the wilder of the eye and the scragglier of beard, the more likely that they too had been selling magic elixirs a few months prior. But in a town this conservative and this wary of outsiders, the sackcloth and ashes bit would be too strong of a sell. He'd be run out on a rail by nighttime.

He took to speaking next to the granary where the farmers came to buy supplies or sell eggs once a week. He spoke when there was a crowd and when the lot was nearly empty. He wore his only suit and kept his nails clean and his beard trimmed.

"Woe to those who wish to see the day of the Lord!" The voice coming from Mohawk rang clear in the cool morning air. "Already the elect are being gathered together before the tribulation. I have been sent to seek out the elect ones and to bring them together before the tribulation so that they might not see the great confusion which is coming upon the unrighteous world.

"Soon, the abominable dragon shall appear and the fornicators and liars will flee to the mountains and caves, will drink the blood of beasts, and will trust no one. The world will be deluged by war, natural disasters, panic, plagues, and fear.

"Truly, I say to you, this time is at hand. I offer you, beloved, I offer you peace and a home and salvation. Leave your things behind. Gold, silver, and jewels are no more than the cobblestones in the streets. I have been sent as a prophet to call faithful witnesses."

The words flowed freely from Mohawk. He spoke of the unfairness, the inequity between the rich and the poor, and how it was now time to embrace, here on Earth, the idea that in the next world, there would be no money to divide them. He told them that by working together, as a family, they could usher in the New Kingdom here on Earth.

Most days, he felt like nothing more than a puppet. He would take his stance and begin speaking in the same cadence that he had when selling his miracle cures. But then, by the third or fourth sentence left his mouth, the voice took over. He would hear it a microsecond before the words themselves poured out in his own voice. Then people stopped. Then people listened, drawn into his voice, their eyes glazing and unable to break away. He found himself in a state outside himself. He could almost look down upon the man speaking the words about true brotherhood and not recognize himself.

Once he noticed an old woman with hair the color of steel who paused and stared intensely back at him. Her eyes narrowed, and she held out her right palm with her pinkie and ring fingers folded. With her left hand, she curled her fingers into a fist with the thumb sticking out between the middle and index fingers. Her mouth chewed words soundlessly. The voice that was speaking through him choked and sputtered. The spell was broken and people resumed going about their errands. He was still coughing as he watched the woman walk away with a grim look on her face. That afternoon, when he was done speaking for the day, the voice fell silent for hours.

As he walked back to his fire ring and bedroll on the outskirts of town, his body sagged visibly like a marionette being let slack. He had set up camp in a fallow field far enough away from others that his smoke would go unnoticed. He slept under an old army tent that he had taken from the possessions of a drover he killed one night in the woods of Central Pennsylvania. It could have been the same one under which he slept during the war, except this one smelled even more strongly of mildew. In the mornings, he walked upstream to try to find the clearest part of the creek to draw his water and wash his face. At night, he slept deeply and always dreamt of the cold blue flame of the Boston fire.

By the end of the first week, a wealthy farmer mucked through his fields and found Mohawk sitting outside his tent in front of the cold coals of a dead fire. Mohawk stiffened, expecting an eviction. Instead, the old man looked him in the eyes, nodded, and invited him to dinner.

"I, and others, have been listening to what you've been saying, brother," the man said as his wife dished out creamed potatoes and peas. "There are a number of us who are seeking a simpler, more Christian life like the one of which you speak. I wanted you to come to dinner tonight to meet my family and to ask you a question. How can we help? How can we be part of this new kingdom?"

*We need land.* Mohawk heard the voice leaving his mouth. *We need land and tithe.*

# CHAPTER 18

Evanora's challenge had bruised my pride. For the following two days, I hunched over my laptop scrolling through endless pages of digitized newspapers from the region and more than a few personal journals and letters from the time and place, trying to find mention of the names with which she had challenged me, or anything at all to do with "The Marked." The days and nights blended, and I stopped only for trips to the bathroom and to boil water for tea. My search might have been obsessive, but it stopped me from thinking about what was going on inside my head. The more focused I was on research the less I felt the bubble of anxiety beneath my sternum. The hallucinations stayed at bay while I was digging.

Finally, on Thursday afternoon, I stopped to rub my eyes. Outside the sun was dipping below the houses on the other side of the street. Although it was barely three, dusk was already gathering underneath the thick cloud cover. Organizing and typing up my notes took another forty-five minutes:

### John Butterfass

John Butterfass had been a farmer on a twelve-acre plot just to the north of Butler for twenty years. One of the older acolytes, Butterfass was 40 when Mohawk established the Institute. After hearing Mohawk speak at a gathering downtown, he sold his farm and moved his family to the Institute, donating the proceeds to Mohawk. He was employed as a farm laborer there.

After Mohawk's death, Butterfass found work on local farms and orchards but barely made a living. His wife died soon after giving birth to a son who also died. Townspeople interviewed by the *Pittsburg Post* after his death said that for weeks following the death of his wife and child, Butterfass, while sitting in a bar, drinking deeply and often, would complain about the scratching in the walls that followed him from place to place. The other patrons claimed not to hear such a scratching which drove Butterfass into "apoplectic fits."

Two years after taking part in the lynching, on what was by all accounts a beautiful spring day, Butterfass laid down in front of the team of draft horses with which he had been plowing. The implement they pulled cleaved him in two as cleanly as it broke the plane of the dirt.

When police examined the shack where he had lived his last days, they found one of his daughters smothered in her bed. The other was never found. On the wall, Butterfass had written "We Are The Marked. God Save Us." Police believed the words to have been written in blood, but they were unable to determine to whom or to what the blood had belonged.

### Jeb Goodrich

Jeb Goodrich had been a handyman. A small note in the *Butler Citizen* suggested that he had gotten into some trouble downtown in an argument over a horse shortly after he returned from a stint in the Calvary in the West during the Indian Wars. The judge appears to have released him into the recognizance of Sam Mohawk and the Institute.

Although he was only at the Institute for a short time, he seemed to have inspired confidence and moved quickly into Mohawk's inner circle. During his time there, he appears to have met and secretly married, against Mohawk's decrees of acolyte celibacy, another Institute worker, a washerwoman named Sarah Goodfellow.

After the Orphanage burned, Jeb and Sarah moved back in town. There's no mention of them after that for years until they show up again, this time on the front page of *The Citizen*. The neighbors had noticed a rotting meat smell coming from the house for days, and, finally, the police investigated. They found Jeb sitting at their dining room table surrounded by his wife and three daughters-all murdered. Jeb had severed their heads and then reattached them to different bodies. He was still alive, but dying, after taking a straight razor to his face to peel most of the skin away. He managed through the ragged hole that had been his mouth to explain to the police, that he had done it so that "When the gods come back, they won't be able to recognize my family and they'll be spared." He died of sepsis a week later. Morphine, the paper notes, did not appear to lessen his torment.

### Isaiah Garvey

Isaiah Garvey had only lived at the Institute for three months before Mohawk's murder. An unmarried man, he had been arrested for vagrancy in the city and, like Goodrich, released into the Institute's recognizance. His work at the Institute is unclear, but he was young, strong, uneducated, and, by all accounts, handsome.

After the Institute burned, Garvey found employment at the Standard Plate Glass Factory. His co-workers said that he kept to himself, but his health and strength seemed to diminish over the few weeks during which he was employed. He lost weight and dark depths circled his dull eyes. He began to lash out at his co-workers and mumble to himself. More than once he was reprimanded for sleeping on the job. He claimed that he was not sleeping, but that he was hiding his face because he couldn't stand to see what was inside the glass. His supervisor later told the police that he thought Garvey had turned to drink or laudanum and had warned him that he was on his last chance.

One morning, shortly after the start of day whistle, Garvey began shrieking that he was being looked at from inside the glass and that the "fearsome visage would not abandon him." Garvey threw himself through a large plate. Although grievously injured, he was still alive, until he plunged shards of glass deeply into each eye. Police investigated his room at Mrs. Shirey's boarding house and found that he had covered all reflective surfaces with black cloth. Mrs. Shirey told police that Garvey had stopped taking his meals at the house after she refused to set the table with wooden, rather than metal, flatware.

I was packing up my laptop and notebooks when I realized that I still had a little more research to do. An internet search of "Evanora LaCosta" revealed that she may have been right. Maybe I wasn't much of a researcher after all. "Evanora" was the name of the Wicked Witch of the East, and "LaCosta" was her sister, The Good Witch of the North from Frank L. Baum's *Oz* books.

If I ignored the speed limit, I could make it to The Eternal Craft just before closing time.

# CHAPTER 19

I parked next to the Sewickley library again and walked up the street towards Evanora's store. It was five pm and already dusk. The sky had promised rain all day, but none had come. The clouds still laid heavy, reflecting the streetlights and headlights in a sickly yellow color. When I reached The Elemental Craft, Evanora had her back to the door arranging an altar that sat on a table to the left. When she heard the bell, she didn't bother to turn around.

"Good afternoon. Blessed be! What brings you to our shop today?"

"I wanted to ask, are you a good witch or a bad witch, 'Evanora LaCosta'?"

She turned to face me with a smirk that ran across her face.

"Oh, the researcher is so very clever. Used Google, did you?"

"That's right—Evanora is the name of the Wicked Witch of the West, and LaCosta is the Good Witch of the North. So, which witch is it?

"Let's say a little from column A and a little from column B."

"Okay, so then, can I call you Tattypoo?"

"Not if you value your life. And, no Evanora LaCosta isn't my real name."

"So, what is?"

"Me to know, you to wonder. Did you come all the way here to ask me my real name or are you ready to talk about Mohawk and The Marked?"

I shrugged.

"Or, maybe now you want to know about all the weird stuff that's been happening to you?"

"Who said anything weird was happening to me?"

"Well, you didn't look great the first time you were here and you look even worse now. Not sleeping, are we?"

I didn't answer.

"Seeing things too? Maybe thinking you're going a little crazy?"

"A stroke."

"What?"

"I thought that I was having little strokes, TIAs, but..."

"You're not, and you know that you're not. And you're starting to think bigger now. You want to know what's going on with you. You want to know what's real and what isn't."

"I want to know how you knew about these guys. The Marked."

"Mmmmm…" she turned her back to me and began fussing with a display of candles.

"All of those men worked for Mohawk."

"That fact does seem to be more than a coincidence."

"What happened to those men and their families was horrible," I said.

"Say what you will about today's media, they've grown a lot more circumspect in covering murders over the last century. Worried that you're headed down the same path?"

"Who were they? The Marked?"

"You didn't figure that part out? You went to all the trouble to find the facts of their lives, but not the truth?" She looked over her shoulder and shook her head as if disappointed in a lazy, troublesome child.

"The Marked were the ones who done him in." She turned to face me and cocked an eyebrow, waiting for a response. "C'mon? *My Fair Lady*?"

"This isn't funny."

She sighed. "Okay. The Marked are the twelve Institute residents or workers who betrayed Mohawk. Some of them were the ones who got fed up about the lack of explanation about the disappeared children. Others had been flattered when Mohawk chose them to help take part in the rituals," she held up her hand to stop me from speaking. "Yes, the 'sex stuff', but then when they saw what was really going on, they changed their minds and formed a rebellion. They're the ones who knew what was going on. Well, maybe they didn't know exactly, or maybe they didn't really understand or didn't want to understand, but they had seen enough to be scared. So, they hatched a plan to kill Mohawk. Sound familiar?"

I waited for a beat before speaking.

"They were the ones who lynched him."

"They were the ones who decided that it might not be too late to save their souls. Spoiler alert: it was."

"And then they burnt down the Institute? That doesn't make any sense."

"If they had burnt the buildings down, no, it wouldn't have made any sense. But they didn't, so it does."

"I don't even understand what you just said. And how does *this* all affect me?"

She turned back and began to face Santa Muerte candles with the label side out.

"You're being deliberately irritating," I said.

"Irritating?" she said. "Irritating, says the man who walks into a store at closing time and then doesn't buy anything." She clicked her tongue. "The worst type of customer if you ask me."

I kept quiet. She sighed.

"Why don't we get a drink in say, half an hour and talk about our mutual interest?"

"I don't drink."

"Never? You must get very thirsty."

"Booze."

"All right, what about coffee? Or, a glass of lukewarm tap water if that's more your thing?"

"Tea."

"There's a shop called Perk You Up, one block towards downtown and one block to the left. I'll meet you there."

"Deal."

"You're paying."

Good to her word, she showed up forty-five minutes later, ordered a coffee, and sat down.

"I thought we agreed that you were paying," she said.

"You took too long. I couldn't wait any longer."

"Fine."

"So, let's get right to it. How did you…"

"All right, all right. Geez. Give me a sec." She dug through her bag and pulled out a phone and a pair of earbuds. She opened the phone and tapped about for a bit. Her generation, I thought, was the worst.

"Here," she said, "before we talk at all, I want you to see this."

I grimaced at the thought of using someone else's earbuds.

"Don't be a baby," she said. I placed them in my ears and she pressed play on the screen.

The video was dark and a little off-angle. The camera had been placed on a table or something in order to raise it to the line of sight. For the first few minutes, Evanora, with two good arms and a soft face still full with baby fat, drew intricate patterns on the floor. A man her age, tall and handsome, followed her placing candles on top of rough-hewn floorboards. He paused and occasionally looked back at her with puppy-dog eyes. I looked up. Evanora had said something to me, but I had missed it. I pulled out one earbud.

"I said, 'That's the Mill at Institute Farms.' About three years ago."

I returned my attention to the screen. The candles were now lit and she and the man sat crossed legged, holding hands inside a triangle that had been drawn on the floor. Evanora had a book with a cracked and stained leather binding and green marbling on the deckle. The book rested on her lap as she read from it. I couldn't understand the language, but as she spoke, the man would repeat her words in a call and response. This ritual lasted for some time. I was just about to ask her what I was looking for when I started to hear it.

Over Elenora's voice, through the earbuds, was a scratching noise, like something was in the walls of the mill: the same noise that I had heard at my house. A cold sensation formed in the pit of my stomach. I thought, for a moment, that I was going to be sick. Then, there it was: a tiny flash in the middle of the lines she had drawn. The flash became a bright flare that built and built. Smoke began to gather, partially obscuring the video. The man's voice faltered, but Evanora's stayed steady. In fact, her voice grew stronger and steadier as the flame grew and then began moving. The fire pressed itself on the margin of the drawn circle inside of which it was trapped as if testing the boundaries or looking for gaps. On the small screen of the phone, it was hard to tell exactly what was happening, but the scratching grew in volume and pitch until it was the chattering of a thousand insects on the worst hot and humid summer night of your life, when the air seems to close around you and sleep refuses to claim you as its own.

A mass flickered in the fire—a man's face twisted with agony, then a talon, then a mound of guts, oozing and twitching. The worse things looked, the more vile the images the fires put forth, the stronger Evanora's voice became. Her back was to the camera, and I wondered if her eyes were open or closed. Then suddenly, more clearly, the fire transmuted into an image. The flame revealed a middle-aged woman, nude, hanging upside down and being cut open from crotch to neck slowly by a monstrous creature, tall with the head of a horse but with all the fur gone, its skin blistered and oozing and working a mouth full of broken fangs. The woman screamed soundlessly. I didn't want to see this anymore.

"Keep watching," I heard Evanora, the Evanora across from me, say quietly. She was staring down at the table. On the screen, the man beside Evanora stiffened and pulled his hand from hers.

"No!" Evanora shouted clearly this time.

"Mom!" shouted the man, and started to stand unsteadily.

"Alek, no," shouted Evanora, this time with desperation in her voice.

As the man got to his feet and outside of the chalk triangle's boundary, a tentacle tipped with what looked like the stinger of a wasp or ray snapped out of the fire with a whip-crack velocity. The point of it caught the man Evanora had just called Alek in his leg. He screamed. The scratching noise grew louder. In the earbuds, the noise felt like it was filling my brain. My sinuses itched like flies had been caught inside.

The stinger, deeply embedded, pulled him to the ground. He wouldn't stop screaming, shrill notes with little of the human about them. The fire flared up around him, enveloping him in white tongues. He burnt without being consumed. Evanora laid forward on her belly and put her arm out to reach for him as he threw one of his arms out in a seizure. The fire licked up her arm and her face lit up with pain. Now her screams joined his. They were being pulled in, closer to the fire. Evanora reached down into her pocket and threw something into the circle. There was a sudden implosion, like a bonfire suddenly deprived of oxygen and the flame disappeared along with the scratching.

The silence was broken, the sobbing coming from Alek. As he crawled back out of the circle, I could see that his face had become a mass of oozing burnt and blistered skin. One eye laid smeared across his cheek. Evanora tried to push herself up from her belly but fell back down. The arm that had grabbed for Alek was withered. All of the muscle appeared to be gone, the elbow joint was painfully clear through the skin which was now mottled and streaked.

I felt sick. I pulled the other earbud out and closed my eyes for a long minute.

"What? What the hell was that? What's wrong with you? Why would you make something like that? My God, why would you even show me something like that?"

"His foot must have kicked through the salt when he stood up."

"You're telling me that you want me to believe this is real?"

"How the hell did you think my arm got like this?" She hoisted her bad arm off the table and it flopped like the wing of a baby bird.

"I don't know! It isn't any of my business. Birth defect?" I felt terrible as soon as I said it, but I was deeply shaken by what I had seen. "And who was that guy?"

"That was Alek. He was a senior at Carnegie Mellon. A theatre major. He was planning on moving to New York just a few weeks after that video was taken. He ended up not going."

"So, you're telling me he's dead?"

"No, he's very much alive, but I don't know that he, or at least the old Alek, would call it a life."

"What do you mean?"

"He's the Burnt Man."

"What? The urban legend?"

"It's not an urban legend. It's true. Alek is the Burnt Man."

"Start at the beginning."

Her voice was low. "I don't want to talk about this twice. so, don't stop me." She took a long pull of her coffee. "I was a junior at Pitt. Alek, like I said, was a senior at CMU. We had met at an undergrad research conference about depictions of the weird in contemporary culture. I was an anthropology major. He was messed up about the death of his mom the year before. She had struggled with mental illness for decades and eventually, it won. She lost and his dad found her and a bottle of pills beside the pool. Alek had been messing around with Ouija boards and other kid's stuff trying to contact her. I had been researching magic since I was a little goth girl in high school. Some stuff worked, but ninety percent of it was pure, unadulterated bullshit like what I sell in the shop. But I had found some of the true knowledge, just little stuff like making an object unseeable."

"Invisibility…"

"I told you not to interrupt. And no, saying 'invisibility' would mean that no one can see it; unseeable means that one specific person can't see it. Magic is targeted. Anyhow, I met a guy who worked at a rare book shop in the city. He had a sideline in stolen and other unsavory rare books and that's how I ended up with a copy of *Solomon's Seal*. Stupid." She shook her head. "So stupid. So vain. Because I could make a flower age and wither in a matter of seconds or turn fresh milk sour, I thought I was ready for the big leagues. I told Alek that I thought we could summon a spirit, bind it, and make it tell us what had happened to his mom, if she was okay in the next world."

The coffee shop had grown uncomfortably warm. I took off my jacket and Evanora continued to talk. I didn't feel like she was speaking to me anymore; her story had become a recitation or a confession.

"We needed a place with a lot of energy. I had read about Mohawk and what people accused him of..."

"The sex stuff?"

For the first time since she started the story, she looked up and smiled. The smile was sad and pitying.

"Not just 'the sex stuff'. The summonings, the sacrifices, the dead children, that's what the orchards, the orphanage, the mill, what it was all about."

I started to open my mouth.

"Hold your tongue," she said quietly while she made a gesture with her good hand. I couldn't speak. My vocal cords were paralyzed. She smiled. "It's harder with only one hand, but I manage." My eyes grew wide. "Don't panic," she said. "You're fine. I'll lift it as soon as I'm done. I want to get this over with and you're a poor listener.

"So, I thought the Institute would be a hot spot," she continued. "Of course, it was much more than that, basically a Hellmouth, but I was so full of myself, I convinced Alek that we could handle it. We packed up our stuff and snuck into the mill that night. The college had used a cheap chain and padlock on the door and our bolt cutters opened it easily. We practiced the ritual over and over again, and I had told Alek to prepare himself for the chance that we might not get good news. That spirits…"

*Demons*, I mouthed silently. She shrugged her shoulders.

"That's an imprecise word. And it amazes me that you're still interrupting after I pressed your mute button. That spirits enjoy messing with humans, especially when they are angry, and few things anger them more than being summoned. I told Alek that

no matter what happened, he couldn't let go of my hands. And...
he did. The spirit showed him that image of his mom and, true or
not, Alek lost it. He stood up. I've watched that video a million
times, and I'm still not exactly sure what happened. If I drew the
warding wrong or if he kicked through it when he stood up, or
God help us all, if what showed up that night was so powerful that
it was beyond that warding all along and was just playing with us.
Whatever the reason, it got Alek and when I tried to save him, it
got me. Stupid, vain little girl." She moved her hand again,
absently.

Air forced its way out of my throat, and I coughed.

"How…"

"Yes, it's real. Yes, I'm good at it. Better than I was then, at
least."

We sat in silence for a moment until the espresso machine's
steamer hissed and made me jump.

"But you saved him."

"Yeah. I guess. I'm not sure how much of 'him' there still is
though."

"So… why are you still researching it? Why not just move
on?"

"Move on," she snorted and rolled her eyes, tracing the
sugar packet on the table with her hand. "Move on. There is no
moving on. There is no closure. What I want is revenge. Pure and
simple. I want to bind that bastard in a way that he will never get
out. I want him to suffer for all of eternity and always remember
who put him there."

"Can you do that?"

"I'm getting close."

"I… I want to help. I mean. I think it's targeting me, and I
don't know why. So that might be useful, right? You could use that
to help bring him around?"

"I don't need your help."

"I think you do, actually."

"I don't want your help."

"That, I believe. But I want your help. The things that are happening to me. The… weird things… are getting worse, not better. I don't want to die. Not like that." I pointed to the phone.

Evanora regarded the phone's dark screen for a long minute, then sighed deeply.

"Okay, then. Partner. Sometimes it is easier with an extra hand." She stuck out her good hand, and we shook. She took her hand back. She put her phone back in her bag and took out a Sharpie and used it to write on a napkin. "Our first step is recon. Call me tomorrow and we'll set up a day."

She stood to leave.

"I'll walk with you," I said.

"I'll walk with you, I think you mean," she said. I started to say something, but she shook her head at me.

"It's okay to be scared," she said under her breath.

We left the coffee shop and headed back to my car. The streetlights were on and the night was cold. Our breath steamed the air.

"How did you do it, last time? What did you do to make the… thing… leave?"

"I've gone over and over that same question in my mind. I'm still not sure. Like I said, it might have just been messing with us. But I like to think I had something to do with it. What I don't like to think is that it didn't leave at all."

"Okay, but that night," I motioned towards the dark screen of the phone, "at the end, what did you throw at it."

"A rosary. With a first-class Saint Benedict relic."

"A witch with a rosary?"

"I'm ecumenical," she smiled. "I had a Glock 43 in my bag, too. I just couldn't reach it in time. A good witch covers all of her bases."

# CHAPTER 20

By six pm, the sun was already gone. Cars whipped from red light to red light in the city of Butler's downtown like hyperactive toddlers. Alek had already been in the city for an hour, making his way in by foot just as dusk settled in.

The doors to the six-pack store were open 365 days a year, 18 hours a day. Next door was a takeout joint that served hot dogs and fried fish. Over the years, the grease had seeped through the walls so that the floor was always slippery no matter how much the counter people scrubbed. The coolers hummed as air, thick with an ancient fried fish smell, was recycled endlessly. Five booths ran around the perimeter of the store and a sign reading "$1 charge to sit and drink. 1 beer limit" hung on the wall. An old woman sat muttering over a quart of Milwaukee's Best, and two men were talking loudly, one explaining to the other how he was going to beat the charge by getting himself a Pittsburgh lawyer.

Only the woman standing at the register started when Alek walked through the door. Even with his hoodie pulled up and gloves on his hand, the way he slightly dragged his leg and avoided eye contact meant that people noticed him more, not less. Here though, the junkies, the homeless, and the construction workers stopping after a hard day paid no attention to him. They had seen worse or weren't sure he was real or just weren't in the mood to pay any attention to anything other than their drink.

Alek bought a twelve-pack of Natural Ice, really just a case cut in half and bound with packing tape, and brought it to the counter, hugging it to his chest like a lover.

"$13.78, hun," said the woman working the counter. The original shock had worn off. She recognized him now or at least knew who he was from the local legend. He held a crumbled $20 out. She took it and held his change out. He nodded to the counter, and she placed the bills and coins there. He pulled up his sweatshirt to reveal an unzipped red nylon fanny pack. He moved his hips close to the counter and swept the change into the pack with his ruined hands. He pulled the sweatshirt back down as she wrestled the beer into a plastic bag.

"Have a good night, hun," she said as the bell over the door rang him back into the night. Sometimes places like that, places where normal people, or at least people more normal than he, didn't visibly react were worse. He had grown to expect the stares and questions, but when no one said a word or acted like he was unusual, he understood that they had accepted that this is who he was. Times like these he realized that he would never wake up one morning to find himself magically changed back to who he had been.

*Magic. Ha.* The voice inside cackled to life. *Where did magic ever get you? You and your little friend read a couple of books and watch a season of* Buffy *and suddenly you two are experts. Hahaha,* its dry cackle was like dead leaves in the whirlwind sweeping through a filthy parking lot. *Well, that worked out well, didn't it?*

He headed down towards the Connoquenessing Creek with the plastic straps of the bag cutting into his wrist. There was a pull-off under the trestle here, just down the street. Past the trestle, past another railroad bridge, over the tracks, and then on the trail through the woods, eventually he would come across The Jungle.

The Jungle was the place where, by unspoken agreement, the homeless and the addicts had built an encampment and the good people of the city pretended that there was nothing there. Alek had watched them coming and going for years before his accident. The jungle residents clung to the rituals of the straight life without even realizing it. Alek had thought, as a teen, that the homeless just sat around on the street all day waiting for something to happen. Now he knew that even the most rejected of society filled up their day just as they had before they fell from grace. They walked out of the Jungle on errands to the six-pack store, or the Dollar Store, or the Chinese takeout place, but they always ended up at a dealer. Sometimes they didn't make it back without sampling what they purchased and their bodies dotted the sidewalks as they faded into a nod.

Alek had only visited the Jungle once before. After the accident, he thought that maybe here, among other people left behind, he would find friends, company. He found, instead, a vision of hell. Shelters, constructed of tarps and clothes, grew like mushrooms alongside some actual, probably stolen tents. Other residents slept outside in torn sleeping bags or under moldy blankets or on stained mattresses scrounged from curbside and then tossed on the sodden ground. Some people had nodded off with needles still between their toes. Residents had deep sores covering their bodies from infected needle marks or where they had dug and scratched their faces without thinking or noticing. Others looked like they were already dead, strewn upon the ground like battlefield casualties.

Actually, Alek remembered as he walked past the first trestle, they had all looked dead in one way or another. The Jungle was more like a camp of zombies, bodies without souls, than it was a railside collection of friendly movie hobos with bindles and comically patched trousers. Able residents rode the rails in and out, south in the summer or just out of town when the cops bowed to public pressure and rousted them in a show for the media. Trash lay everywhere. Now, as fall receded and winter elbowed its way in, people burnt garbage in old, empty oil and chemical barrels so that a throat constricting stink hung over the camp at all times, mixing with the stench of unwashed bodies, rotting meat, and human feces. Needles were a constant hazard. Someone always seemed to be screaming.

The voice loved every minute of that visit. *All of my work to bring hell to Earth and here you all are making a welcoming party for me. It's like flies building the web for the spider. Glorious! Ah, it's bittersweet really. You work so hard for a goal and then you find your children have already started without you. Working to surpass you. Circle of life, I guess.*

Now, nearing the lower bridge, he saw a couple walk towards him. The woman was petite wearing torn jeans and a grey sweatshirt reading "PINK". Over it, she wore a puffy jacket with a fake fur hood. Her hair was red and matted. She had beads around her neck and open sores across her face. The man with her was taller, but his clothes hung from his bony frame. He wore jeans and untied work boots which made a slapping noise with each step. He wore a heavily lined sweatshirt over his tee. His eyes blinked slowly, looking around but not seeing anything. The two were talking to each other, the woman smiling over something he had just said. They both wore backpacks, and the woman's had something peeking out of the top of hers, showing up from behind her head and bobbing with the rhythm of her steps.

"Hey." They nodded their heads in acknowledgment as he approached. As they passed, the woman did a double-take. "Hey! I know you! The Burning Guy, right?"

*Yes*, the voice said. *These two. They'll do fine.*

The three of them stopped walking in front of a clump of weeds and Alek nodded his head. He concentrated and tried to speak. His voice was hollow; it came from the back of his throat rather than his chest. "I guess that's what they call me, yeah. Something like that."

"Everybody talks about you, man. What are you doing out

here?"

Alek shrugged his shoulders and indicated the beer in his hand. With his free hand, he fished one of the stamp bags he still had left from Antonio's from within his pocket.

"Well, all right," said the man. "We were just headed in to get some beer. Do you think we could borrow one now and then we'll hook you up when we come back?"

Alek pointed down over the bank towards the creek. Under the bridge was a rotting pleather couch and some office chairs were arranged around a firepit with wood still in it.

"I'm Nancy," said the man, "and this is Sluggo," he said indicating the woman.

"Get it?" she said, hooking her thumb over her shoulder and pointing the object sticking out of her backpack, "Because of the bat? Whoosh, whoosh, whoosh." She made swinging motions with her arms. Alek smiled.

An hour later, they had started a fire and seven of the beers were gone. Alek was still nursing his first. Sluggo and Nancy sat with their backs to the creek and talked nonstop. Alek sat silently enjoying the sound of the fire and the flow of the water. The night was otherwise silent down here; the bank shielded them from both the road and the view from the path. They were beneath the bridge itself so that even people walking on the trestle wouldn't be able to see them. Even if someone had seen them, anyone who was back here on the path to The Jungle was here on purpose and knew to mind their own business.

"I mean, don't worry about us. We're doing great. We rode in on the train and we'll ride back out. We still have friends in Florida. I mean we do tai chi like, almost every day, right baby?"

Sluggo nodded her head.

"We could walk right into town and get a straight job anytime we like. We shower, we keep ourselves clean."

Alek stood up.

"What's up, man?" said Nancy, startled out of his story.

"Gotta piss," said Alek and walked towards the creek.

"Oh, cool. S'okay if we grab another beer, right?" Alek heard the top pop before he could answer.

He stood by the creek for a moment listening to the shallow water riffle along the rocks. He arced a long stream into the water.

*Can't get much more polluted, right?*

Alek closed his eyes. The voice kept a steady monologue the whole time Nancy and Sluggo had been talking but not much of it made sense. It sounded like it was talking about the Civil War. He had thought, hoped, that maybe it was weakening. A foolish wish, he knew. The voice had done this before; sometimes it seemed like it was crazy and spoke nothing but nonsense, gibberish really. During these times he couldn't even understand the dense guttural chunks of language that sounded in his head. Sometimes the voice sounded like this own, or like that of a child. But mostly, it sounded cruel. The voice suddenly became clearer, as if it had turned to face him.

*Listen, Boy.* It sounded off as he stood there. *I forgot to tell you the good news. Your mother has whelped a trio of demon pups. You're a big brother! What pride you must feel. Must feel strange, though; I mean, do you even remember what pride is? You haven't had any in so long.*

Blood slipped into Alek's mouth as he chewed through the skin inside his cheek.

*Quite the surprise, we had started to fear she was barren. Har har har. Now don't worry, it was an easy delivery; they just chewed their way right out and she was a champ about the whole thing, screaming and crying tears of blood. The great thing about hell is that she was healed right up by the next day and ready for more action. A real trooper, our mom! Har har har.*

Alek turned back to the campfire. He felt the warmth creep down into his arms again, loosening and limbering his fingers. He grabbed the filet knife out of its sheath in the small of his back.

*I think... Nancy first.*

Butchering took longer this time. Nancy had gone down quickly when the knife went into the side of his neck. He had thrashed and made wet noises, but Sluggo had run. She was scrambling up the mud bank when Alek caught her and began stabbing wildly into her legs and back. The noise of flesh against the blade was like that of thick paper ripping. Alek managed to drag her down and flip her over, but the blade skidded along her ribs and opened a long-jagged slash under her shirt.

*The eye.* whispered the voice, and Sluggo stopped struggling when the long blade pierced her left eye and skewered the brain.

*Oh my.* The voice was gleeful. *That was beautiful. Their squeals. The fear. Do you know, little shrike, that I think I could almost taste the fear she was sweating out? Tasted it right through your mouth. What a wonderful evening. You take us to the nicest places, my boy. But, of course, we're not done yet.*

Alek dragged the bodies back to the fire and cut off their clothes with the filet knife. He wiped the handle and blade of blood and threw it in the fire. He took out the small Xacto knife-tipped tool the voice had led him to in the bushes outside the new City Hall building downtown and went to work, carving the symbols into their flesh.

When he left, still hours before the dawn, he followed the train tracks out of town towards his house. He had taken Sluggo's aluminum bat, and as he walked, he slashed at the dead weeds that crowded between the ties. The creosote smell filled his nose, crowding out the smell of blood and the warm viscera of a human, and he was glad for small mercies that were sometimes still visited upon him.

# CHAPTER 21

A tired-looking servant opened the door and faced Mohawk. The older man's face sagged at the jowls and beneath the red-rimmed eyes. He had missed a patch while saving and white bristles sprang from just below his ear from where more hair crept out. His clothes could have used a pressing and the knees of the pants were shiny where he had spent time absently rubbing his palms in anxiety or boredom or both.

Outside, where Mohawk stood on the spacious wrap-around porch, dusk was beginning to settle. Through the transomed and sidelit double doors, the interior of Judge Pastorius' home was dark and quiet. Gaslights flickered shadows onto the walls and the smell of old books and a sharp cleaning fluid settled in the back of his nose. The judge himself had invited Mohawk here for a talk. Evening clouds gathered as he made his way from the farmland, past the shacks, to the row of large homes that sat on the hill at McKean Street. So goes the story of progress, Mohawk thought to himself, the raw and unspoiled taken over and remade in our own image until it bore only the faintest resemblance to what had been. At which point we fetishize what we destroy and plant shrubs and spacious lawns to prove that the unspoiled could still return, or to torment ourselves with what we had and let slip away.

*You overthink your little world,* the voice chuckled. *The spoilers are the winners. We take. We eat. We thrive. All else are the musings of an idiot drawing in the sand as the tide continues its everlasting consumption.*

"Mr. Samuel Mohawk to see Judge Pastorius."

"Is he expecting you, sir?"

"He is. I am here at his invitation."

"Very good," said the man. "One moment."

The servant walked a short distance down the hall and disappeared through a pair of open pocket doors. His head was bald and liver spots dotted it in a constellation of age. Mohawk saw that the seat of his pants was worn and shiny like the knees. The hem on his left pant leg was beginning to fray. Where, Mohawk wondered silently, had Pastorius found this man?

*It's his uncle,* the voice slithered between his ears. *The old man raised the good judge, and this is how he has repaid him in his dotage. His nephew allows him to answer the door and take the laundry downtown in return for table scraps and an attic room. Oh, I think we'll have some fun tonight, won't we? It's always so nice to find a fellow traveler.*

The old man shuffled back down the hall.

"He'll see you, sir. Please come this way."

The old man left Mohawk standing in the Judge's study and drew the pocket doors behind the two men on the way out. The room was dimly lit by gas lamps and the judge sat in a leather wingback chair. His face was drawn and thin. The circles beneath his eyes were deep and dark. Mohawk could see the features of the servant developing on the face of the master.

*See? Blood will out.*

"Mr. Mohawk."

"Judge Pastorius."

"Forgive me for not standing. Sciatica has me by the back of the neck, and I have just now found a less painful spot."

"Of course. It's a terrible disposition."

"Don't tell me you suffer from this curse, as well, sir?"

"No, no, I don't. But I had in my youth, many the occasion to visit and solicit with those who did. Sciatica and an assortment of likewise pains and aches. I'm sorry to say that in my experience, sometimes only a bit of tincture of opium mixed in brandy with a lash of honey can still the pain."

"Indeed."

"But, of course, you didn't ask me here tonight about medicine for the body, Judge?"

"No, sir, I didn't." The judge moved slightly in his chair and grimaced. "Pull a chair over here closer to me so that I can see your face while we talk."

Mohawk pulled the twin of the chair in which the judge sat closer to the man. Mohawk could see that he was in late middle age. The jaw soft and weak, the hair grey and thinning, and the face florid with a trace of broken blood vessels on the nose.

"I'll get right to the point. My man was at the laundry last week. He tells me that the Chinaman keeps track of all the talk in the town. Victor, my servant, comes home and tells me that Quan Sing told him of a man with power. Power beyond what comes with a robe and a gavel."

*His son was killed at Shiloh. The body was never identified. After the face was pecked away by crows; some dogs dragged him off into the underbrush for a feast that their pups still remember.*

"I see," said Mohawk.

"My son, you see, Mr. Mohawk…"

"Is gone." Mohawk felt a trembling move through his body and a stiffening in his neck as if he needed to stretch. "He disappeared. At Shiloh, I think." Mohawk slipped easily back into his old stage presence. Stringing the mark as if the information was coming slowly from somewhere else. He closed his eyes to concentrate.

"Yes," said the old man with a catch in his voice. "Then it's true."

"Judge, I think that I can help you. But you have to understand. I will need remuneration. Contacting the other side is demanding and will cost me days of work while I rest after."

"Of course, of course," a hint of desperation crept into the judge's voice. "Money is… money is no object. Name your price."

"Let us discuss it after I am successful in reaching your son. May I dim the lights?"

"Certainly, certainly."

Mohawk stood and turned the gas down until the room was filled with shadows. A hurricane lamp on a stand provided most of the illumination, flickering and painting their faces with a yellow glow.

"Take my hands. I need to establish a connection with your son through you. Whatever happens, whatever you may hear, do not let go of my hands. Yes?"

The judge nodded his head and reached out his hand. When they touched, Mohawk snapped upright and his spine straightened with an audible crack. His head was being pulled up, as if by an invisible string, and his shoulders tensed. He had the terrifying feeling of something pushing its way up his spine to the surface of his skull. When he opened his mouth, the voice was not his own. The diction was precise but the sound thick as if his vocal cords had been unused for decades.

"Father?"

The judge jerked his hand, prompting Mohawk's to move of its own volition, clamping the older man's palm tightly.

"Father. Is that you?"

The judge's breath came short and fast. He nodded his head and through a constricted throat said, "Yes."

"Father. Where are you? I can't see you?"

"I'm here. I'm right here, my boy."

"I'm cold." As the voice roiled out of his mouth, Mohawk, still paralyzed inside his own body, felt a wave of cold rise through his body as if he had been dumped in a cold stream. The sensation burnt his skin. The room seemed to close in on the two of them, and the smell of an animal dead in the sun filled the room.

"I think the Rebs got me."

The judge nodded his head and tears began streaming down his face.

"Where are you, James?"

"I don't know Father. I can't see anything. I hear birds. I hear crows."

"Are you all right, son?"

"No. I... I think the Rebs got me."

The dead, de Laurence had taught him, were selfish, stupid things. They pleaded and cajoled, but the trauma of death left them unable to understand where they were or what had happened. They brought some memories with them but were unable to contextualize them. Time vanished for them. They were almost always unbearably lonely. Contacting them was, as a rule, a terrible mistake for the living to make.

"I want to come home."

Sobs wracked the judge's frame. Mohawk's hand clenched even tighter.

"I don't know where to find you, my boy. Tell me where you are."

"It's so dark, and I can't see my men."

"Follow my voice, son. Follow my voice and come to me."

In the shared environment of his skull, Mohawk became aware that the spirit of the boy was trying to make itself corporeal here in the room, and that the voice that lived inside of him was pushing the boy back, blocking his way.

"I'm trying, but something is stopping me, holding me back. Father!"

There was a feeling of being pulled through the eye of a needle and Mohawk realized that the boy was gone. He dropped the judge's grip.

"The voice was your son?"

"Yes, yes, yes." The judge's head was buried in his hands.

Mohawk patted him on the back. "He's a strong boy, but the connection is difficult. We could try again, but…"

"My boy, my boy," sobbed the judge. He looked up at Mohawk with wide eyes. "Whatever it takes. Whatever it costs, I must speak to him again. I must find him."

"I will… I will do my best. But you must understand, if I do this thing for you, you must be willing to help me."

"Yes," the judge sobbed. "Yes. Take what you will. You can have everything: my house, my money. I want to join you, at your camp. I want to follow you."

*No*, said the voice, *use him*.

"No, my brother," Mohawk said as he stood. "At the camp now, we need strong backs and rough hands not quick minds. But you could still be of great service to our mission, Judge."

"How? How? Name it and it's yours."

"Surely young men and women, confused, lost young people must come before you for petty crimes: theft, vagrancy, drunkenness?"

The judge, a sob escaping him, nodded his head.

"Instead of the workhouse, why not send them to me? They would receive a good education, a moral education, and room and board. All at no cost to the state."

"Of course, yes. But how will I know which ones you can help?"

Mohawk opened his mouth to speak and a pain like a fishbone lodged in his throat silenced him. Mohawk slumped in his seat, exhausted. Tears, unbidden rolled down his face. The voice spoke through him again: *I'll tell you.*

# CHAPTER 22

I can remember, once, in the aftermath of my wife leaving me, waking up from a deep sleep. I hadn't slept well in weeks and carried the constant exhaustion between my shoulder blades and behind my eyes all day long. This morning though, I woke and for a moment had no idea where I was. Nothing looked familiar. I knew who I was, and felt safe, but had no concept of how I had gotten there. Beyond that feeling of benign misplacement, there was an incredible lightness. The anxiety that I wore like a too-tight shirt was gone. That feeling only lasted for a few minutes, but I carry that short moment of freedom with me as one of the best times of my life.

I needed that memory on mornings like the one I awoke to after coffee with Evanora. Nick had been sending repeated daily texts, asking for more details. Focusing on writing was impossible as the wreckage of my life snowballed. But that morning, I woke fully planning on driving down to the library and spending my day immersed in old city directories. After just a few minutes of being awake, I realized that trip was not going to happen—not today at least.

I shuffled downstairs, brewed a cup of tea, and made my way back up the stairs to my office. My knees and hips ached as I climbed the stairs. I felt ancient and jumpy. My skin prickled, and I wanted nothing so much as to crawl back in bed. Experience had taught me that if I did, I might be there for days.

Late last night, I had developed an idea that Nick might like. He didn't seem too impressed with notes and reports, so something visual might appeal to him more. I decided to spend the day at home, settling in front of the computer with non-print sources, photos, and artifacts.

I spent the morning combing electronically through a variety of photo archives. I started with the Tennie Harris Photo Archive. Harris had documented Pittsburgh's African-American community in the mid-20th century for the *Pittsburgh Courier*, and all 88,000 photos were stored on the Carnegie Museum of Arts' servers. Then there were 800 photos from the University of Pittsburgh's Historic Photograph Archives, and the digital collection of the Detre Library and Archives at the Heinz History Center. I grabbed about forty of the photos that I thought would work best—street images, public events like sports and parades, night scenes, and images that showed the old industry that defined the times and the environment.

I spent another couple of hours dropping them into a Google map. Nick could click on the pin, see where the image was taken in relation to where his plot points would take place: a nightclub scene in the Hill District where his PI would unwind, the huge St Patrick's Day parade where he would lose the thug tailing him, the views of the city from Polish Hill where his detective could sit on his porch and nurse a drink. It was the sort of stuff a middle-schooler might churn out in a day or two to impress a teacher looking for a book report. I was hoping it would have the same effect on Nick. I wrapped it up and sent him the link.

Thirty minutes later my phone buzzed. I hadn't moved; I was still sitting in the chair staring at the screen. Anyone walking by would have thought I had fallen asleep sitting straight up. I thought about just allowing it to ring and letting Nick go to voicemail, but I knew that he would call back.

"Hello?"

"Aaron? It's Nick."

"Hey, Nick. How are you?"

"I'm great. Listen, I just got this link..."

"Oh, good. I thought that, you know, seeing the images matched up with the locations that we talked about would give you lots to work from—details, faces, mood. I mean, the city is so different than it was 70 years ago, it's really difficult to comprehend unless you can see that overlay on..."

"Right, right. Look, Aaron, I have no fucking clue what I'm supposed to do with this... stuff."

"It's research, Nick."

"It's a bunch of old photos and, I don't know? A map, I guess. What does it have to do with my story? I mean, when I opened it, I thought, well this must be a mistake, why would he be sending this to me?"

"Yeah, well. When Walt was working on a story set somewhere that he had never been..."

"I've been to Pittsburgh."

"You have?"

"Yeah. I was at a conference in a hotel by the airport in... 2012, I think it was."

"Okay, but you have to admit that situation is a little different when you're trying to describe what the actual city looked like in 1947. That's where the photos come in. Use them as a painter would use photos—as references for details."

"Well, why not just write it up for me?"

"Sorry?"

"Look, I told you that I want my guy to live on Polack Hill, right?"

"Polish Hill. Yeah."

"And I'll bet you included a photo of that place, right?

"Yeah, of course."

"So, it would be way easier if you just sent me a couple of paragraphs describing what he would see from his porch, what his neighbors are like, how he fits into the neighborhood, that sort of thing. Okay?"

"Well, I don't want to step on your creative process…"

"You're not. It's just some basic material for me. Just write up a little something for each of these photos, you know, fitting into the plot synopsis and send it off to me. Maybe by Monday?"

Today was Thursday.

"I, uh," I thought about the mortgage. "Yeah, I guess so."

"Great," Nick said. "So, I'm just going to delete this link, pretend it never happened. I'm not going to hold it against you. You're still my guy, right Aaron?"

"Yeah," I said as the phone went silent against my ear.

# CHAPTER 23

Mohawk and his acolyte began building the next week on the farmer's donation of unused bottomland upstream of the city. Mohawk worked feverishly into the night drawing up plans following the dinner. The orphanage was to be built first. The faithful would be housed communally in tents. Mohawk would have his own tent. His private space would be as luxurious as a Mongolian chieftain's yurt. As soon as the thought came to him, he realized that he couldn't remember even hearing the word before.

He had never considered designing a building. He had hired a fine architect in Boston to draw up the plans for the lyceum and had paid little attention to the man's work, only making sure that his specific requests had been incorporated. He had no knowledge of how structures supported themselves or how deeply a foundation should be dug, but night after night, his pencil tore across the paper with measurements, denoting angles and leaving comments for the builders in the margins. Sweat dripped from his face and he lost weight. His eyes burned with a fury, but no matter how much he yearned to rise from his chair, his muscles bound tight and kept him there. The voice rode him hard and carelessly.

During the day, he had a little more control and preached to his congregants whose numbers grew in size every day. His tent and furniture, bedding and lamps, had been ordered and delivered, and he left sleeping rough to take residence there. Followers sold their possessions, gave the money to Mohawk, and came to sleep in simple bunkhouse-style tents on the site of what would be the Institution. When the supplies were delivered, the faithful worked twenty-four-hour shifts building the new bunkhouses, digging the privies, and pulling up the enormous tent from which Mohawk preached to them every day. The nights, even in summer, were cold that year, but as Mohawk had told them, these were the end times and the deprivations they faced now were nothing compared to the pain and suffering those who ignored his word would face in just a short time.

The followers saw wondrous things. Sometimes when he spoke, Mohawk seemed to grow huge and tongues of white flame licked out from his fingertips. When he touched their heads in blessing, they found that they could work long shifts and feel neither hunger nor fatigue. They heard him late at night in angry conversations with someone they couldn't see. It was, they whispered to each other, like Jacob wrestling with the angel.

Mohawk taught them to give up sexual relations and to eat simple meals doled out twice a day. Mohawk himself, however, invited select young women of the Institute to his tent for additional instruction. They left with crusted, sweat-matted hair and a pride that they had been able to restore Mohawk's vital energies. Some of them were even able to keep their visits secret, at least for a while.

No secret worth having is able to be kept for long, however. Even though the acolytes had removed themselves from their old lives, Mohawk still had to send his people into town for supplies or to receive shipments of brick and lumber to keep the building moving apace. Eventually, rumors slipped out and circulated feverishly like the measles among the townspeople.

"Father Mohawk," a voice, young and female, sounded from the flap of the tent.

*It's Clara,* the voice said. *The one with the mole between her teats.*

*I think the next time, we should bite it off. She would be beguiling with a scar.*

Mohawk winced. His week's supply of laudanum had already run out. He was coming up short more and more. The bitter taste and then the release into nothingness was all he could think about. That boy who ran his errands, what was his name, Tobias?

*Thomas,* said the voice, unbidden. The creature was becoming stronger and stronger, coming and going in his mind as it pleased, promising and threatening, amusing itself.

Thomas, Mohawk thought, had better bring that new shipment from the druggist soon.

"Yes, my child," Mohawk said to the sliver of light through the flap. "Please come in. What troubles you?"

"There are men here, Father. Men from the town," she said.

"That's nothing to be upset about, my dear. Just sign for the delivery and have Goodrich direct them as to where to leave the materials."

"No sir. It's not a delivery."

Mohawk sighed, rose from his chair, and left the tent. Across the field, he could see a half-dozen men. They wore clean suits and hats and had impressively groomed beards and mustaches. He saw Judge Pastorius in the back of the group shifting awkwardly from foot to foot and sweating. The town fathers, Mohawk thought to himself, and our inside man.

*Here to welcome the prodigal back,* the voice snickered in a space behind his ear.

"Gentlemen," Mohawk called. "What brings you to the Institute on such a beautiful day? Are you here to join our family?"

One of the men, a round, middle-aged banker with extravagant salt and pepper muttonchops, stepped from the group.

"You would be Sam Mohawk then?"

"I would be, and you are?"

"I, we, are here, representing the good people of Butler. We have brought you this notice." He proffered a sheet of paper. Mohawk took it from his hand. "You have 48 hours to quit your claim on this land and leave the town forever."

Mohawk played his eyes across the face of the paper. He felt his followers form a group behind him, drawn by the strangers and their eagerness to see their leader's reaction.

"A letter of removal?" He shook his head and folded the paper shut. "What century do you think this is gentlemen? Why not just call a charivari, sing some rough music, and then dump me in a horse trough?" He felt a painful stretching along his backbone and a feverish heat sweep through his body. The feeling was identical to what happened when he preached but intensified three-fold.

"Or, why not at least try your hand at it and see the result?" Outside sounds—the birds, the wind, the creaking of the construction site rigging—had vanished. All was silent except for their voices.

"We are approaching you as gentlemen, Mr. Mohawk," Muttonchops said. The men behind him nodded in agreement.

"Ah, but there's the issue. You see, friends, I am not a gentleman, nor am I a peddler to be run out of town on a rail when I become inconvenient." His voice took on an echo and timbre. To those gathered, he seemed to grow in size. Light left the sky as if the crowd was encased in a darkening dome. Fear spread through the men and Mohawk's followers felt a sort of awe. "I am a prophet. I have come to help usher in a new world, a new age. I will not be cowed by the likes of you."

He pushed his arms out in front of him as if shoving a schoolyard bully. Six feet away, Muttonchops flew to the ground as if he had been poleaxed. A wisp of smoke arose from his watch fob, which had suddenly melted against his skin. He brayed in fear and pain. Men lifted him on either side.

"You will leave, sirs." Mohawk had crumpled the notice in

his hand. The paper smoldered. The men tumbled together and headed away from the scene. Pastorius shot Mohawk a backward glance. His eyes were wide with fear like a cow who had seen that it was in line for the killing floor. Mohawk called after them.

"All are welcome here. But should you return, bring hands ready to work and eager to build, not poisoned minds aiming to destroy."

Sound rushed back as the townspeople left the boundary of the camp.

"Back to work, my children," Mohawk said, as the sky filled with light again and his voice returned to normal. "We have much to do and a short time in which to complete our earthly work."

They turned and walked away, murmuring amongst them about what they had seen.

"Clara," Mohawk called after her, "I would like to give you additional instruction this evening. Please come to my tent at eleven."

While far along the eastern sky
I saw the flags of Havoc fly,
As if his forces would assault
The sovereign of the starry vault
And hurl Him back the burning rain
That seared the cities of the plain,

"After the Fire" –Oliver Wendell Holmes

"Give not thyself up, then, to fire, lest it invert thee,
deaden thee, as for the time it did me.
There is a wisdom that is woe;
but there is a woe that is madness."

-*Moby-Dick, or, the Whale,* Herman Melville

# CHAPTER 24

Evanora poured herself another cup of coffee. She had arranged to meet Moody later in the afternoon to recon the mill, but right now the back of her eyes pounded with a headache that stretched into her forehead and down to the back of her neck. She couldn't remember the last time she slept soundly. Sometimes, just after she unlocked and entered the store, she'd have a sudden burst of energy. Oh, she thought at those times, this is how it feels. This is normal. The feeling faded almost immediately, often by the time the first client came in or the first phone call of the day. Certainly, by the time she started sorting through emails and e-orders, she was drained with a deep exhaustion that made even simple tasks herculean. She longed to go back to bed. Her life had been this way for three years now, ever since the summoning.

She had gone over the events of that night endlessly. She could mouth the words along to every terrifying, sickening moment in the video. She knew something bad, something evil, had been released that night, and she had slowly been building a plan against it. She was sure that she knew its name at this point, even though she was loath to write it down, think it, or goddess forbid, speak it.

The woman at the Carnegie had been helpful, leading her to the history of the mill and the man, the thing, who had created it. Urgency drove her. As summer turned to fall and fall to the first chill whispers of winter, the strange events had gotten stronger and more frequent.

Evanora feared sleep now. Before the summoning, she had been someone who could easily spend half of a day in bed. Since that night at the mill, she hadn't had more than a few hours of sleep per night, but they still provided a sweet relief. Then, last year, the sleep paralysis had started. At night, on her back, she would wake, her mind racing, but her body locked. She would attempt to scream and only grunts would issue from her paralyzed larynx. She heard people or things, moving slowly, thumping deliberate footsteps in her store below the apartment. Then a click as they found the door in the back that led to the stairs. Slow dragging footsteps resounded on the stairs. Whatever it was, it was in no hurry. It wasn't threatened. It was in charge. Evanora would try to thrash and try to draw a deep breath in to scream, but only laid there like a piked fish. Then the sound paused before the door. Murmured voices seeped through, too indistinct to recognize or understand what they were saying. Her eyes were open, and she watched from the corners as the knob turned and the door swung open. Something shadowy and wispy slipped in, always staying to the dark corners, never moving to a place where she could see it head-on. Then it was at her bedside. A soft hand whispered across her face, fingertips tracing the hollow of her neck. She struggled and tried to thrash, even to speak. One hand rested on her cheek and the other between her breasts.

*They'll just think your heart stopped when they find you. I'll make sure to tell Alek the truth, but your family, they'll never know.*

The hands pressed hard against her chest, then covered her mouth. The weight was huge and unbearable. Finally, she broke free and screamed, shooting to a sitting position and gasping for breath. The door to the apartment and the one to her bedroom was closed. The scene played out over and over again, several times a week. She was exhausted every single day. She worried about making stupid mistakes, and the more she worried, the more exhausted she felt. She washed the steps with vinegar and hung white heather around the door, but the nighttime visits continued.

After the first two times, she tried to convince herself that the nighttime visits weren't dark magic. Maybe the visitations were just guilt bubbling to the surface from the swamp of her subconscious. But if the Mohawk-thing was strong enough to project like that, and if he knew how far her research had brought her, she needed to move even more quickly.

Like a grown man willfully ignoring the signs of a metastasizing tumor, she might have been able to convince herself that these new horrors were all in her head. If it hadn't been for Alek. She had successfully blocked him from her mind years ago. She avoided him completely. That treatment was unfair, she knew, but she told herself it was for the best. She had seen him only once since the summoning. She walked down from her hospital room. Her arm was in a sling and the skin sang with pain when it touched the bandages, the sling, or even the air itself. A breeze against the ruined limb felt like jamming the arm in boiling water. Tears would spring to her eyes. Over the years she had, with the help of meditation and the occasional gabapentin, been able to come to terms with the pain. She kept a happy, welcoming face when she was in the shop. No one knew how the pain nagged at the back of her head all hours of the day or night, how she had to wrap her arm in plastic in the shower because the pressure of the water drops hitting the flesh would cause her to pass out.

When she entered the room, Alek was laying there with IVs sprouting from his body like morning glories from the dirt. His body was wrapped with gauze and he made tiny moaning noises. She wasn't sure if he was moaning in his sleep or if these were the only noises with which he was able to communicate.

*If I can barely hold it together from the pain in my arm,* she thought, *what must he be going through?*

She turned and left, unaware that he had been awake the

entire time and trying to communicate with her. Evanora prided herself on always moving forward, but there were times when she felt deep shame about the way she had acted that day. The shame festered inside of her, she knew, and she hoped that Alek had long ago forgotten her action and found peace. She knew he hadn't, of course. She saw the notices in the newspaper, read what the foolish and sad people wrote about him on the internet. Saw the photos of him still wearing that Carnegie Mellon hoodie that he had insisted on buying the moment he got his acceptance letter.

When they met at a basement party in a student rental in Oakland, he was bright and shiny; he drew people to him like magpies to coins. He was tall and athletic, strong from years of lacrosse. He had been open and honest, but always kind and sparing of the feelings of others. Evanora had undergone a transformation at college. She came into her own; she was no longer the weird girl in high school, too smart, too loud, too ready to challenge others in hopes of being accepted. At Pitt, she found a place among other smart men and women. For the first time, she realized that her dark hair and eyes helped people notice her. It was her sharp mind and wit that kept them next to her to hear what she would say next.

Alek had been in love with her. That notion was an understood and unstated fact. She couldn't remember if she had told him she was queer, or if she just assumed he knew. Or if she was afraid that if she did tell him that his attention would wain.

He sat in her apartment more nights than not, drinking coffee or wine, sometimes talking, but more often than not, just sitting as Evanora poured over the grimoires that she considered her real course of study. Cultural anthropology was her major, and she genuinely enjoyed the classes, but "Night School" as she and Alek called their evening sessions, was where she found her real challenge. She cultivated sympathetic librarians and shady bookstore employees. She searched the internet and found more chaff than wheat. And then one day, much too soon, she felt that she was ready for a summoning. *Of course*, Alek had said, *of course, I'll come with you. I know you'll do an amazing job, and I want to be there with you when it happens.*

She hadn't seen him in years, but she still lived with him every day. She used the insurance settlement money to set up this store and spent all of her time trying to discover what entity she had summoned and how to avenge Alek's destruction upon it. Her research doubled in intensity. She saw her work before the accident as the pathetic play of a dilettante. Her life had two eras to it: before and after the mill. She was a dogged researcher and had gathered a huge amount of information, but she was terrified. She couldn't face the embarrassment of making the same mistake twice.

She watched the video of the summoning, telling herself it was to analyze where she had gone wrong, but knowing that she was just picking scabs. She kept track of Alek in those newspaper stories, telling herself it was so she could rescue him if he really got into trouble, but knowing that she was refreshing her guilt pool. And when she started seeing him around the house, she convinced herself that it was just her mind reminding her of what she had done to both of them out of ignorance and pride.

He had started appearing in mirrors. The first time she was brushing her teeth, watching the foam drool out, waiting for two minutes to pass when the glass seemed to dim. She blinked hard and as it brightened, she saw him behind her. His face was ruined, the flesh had melted and then hardened like a guttered candle. What was left of his lips tried to shrug themselves into a smile and his arm reached out to touch her shoulder. She spun, and he was gone.

No more than a week later she stood naked after a shower, glaring at the points of her shoulders and hipbones and wondering if she should eat more. He was there again, reaching out to her like a lover. His arm touched, no it passed through, she remembered thinking, her burnt arm. She awoke on the mat in front of the shower. The pain in her arm radiated up her neck and into her head; it stayed with her for two days. The burning consumed her every moment like dry logs on a fire. She couldn't speak or think, much less leave the apartment and open the store. When she could move again, she covered all the mirrors, except for the ones in the shop which she found herself consulting nervously throughout the day. She started drinking her coffee with cream to deaden the reflection of the liquid's surface and kept her phone's face down on the counter relying on the earbuds to answer shop calls.

Alek started calling soon after. But it wasn't his voice on the other end. These calls were mimicry. Alek had a trained actor's baritone. He had used his breath like a trumpeter with his horn. At the end of each murmured obscenity, this voice cracked, hissed and buzzed with exhales that carried the noise of locusts. She had to admit to herself that these things were no longer manifestations of guilt. This was an entity, growing in power, attacking her and forcing her into a corner. The creature was moving all of her resources toward concentrating on avoiding it, dealing with the pain and fear that it caused rather than figuring out the best way to confront and destroy this abomination.

Then Moody showed up. Even if she believed in coincidence, his annoying presence was too strong of a sign to miss. He was still processing all the new knowledge, but he would come around. People like Moody, The Normals, that's how they were. They went on with their lives and thought about the lawn, the bills, new cars, anything so they didn't have to think about the niggling idea in the back of their heads that there was another world, sitting cheek and jowl next to the one in which they wasted their lives. Had Alek ever truly believed she would be able to summon the entity? He had seen her small bits of magic, but those spells were easily brushed off by The Normals as a parlor trick or advanced technology. Thoughts like that kept The Normals happy, Evanora thought. They were so weak that they wouldn't even acknowledge that the internet was a vast tool that kept them focused on each other and the material world and away from thinking what else might be out there, slithering inside their walls and drinking in their hot breath exhaled on nights thick with clouds and rain.

Some of The Normals broke away though, and Moody was one of them. If only he would give up worrying about his damn wall, she sighed. Normals' lives are short and The Others never forget that. They can sit patiently watching, never going away, watching as people build go-cart racing tracks and stuff themselves full of hot fudge sundaes with Spanish peanuts at ice cream stands in the summer. To The Others, this show was an amusement, in the same way The Normals brought their dogs to parks and watched them play together. The big difference, of course, was that sometimes The Others were able to peel a Normal or two away from the pack and convince those sad people to help the beings to cross over. The promised reward was different for everyone, but because of the way The Normals were built, the bait usually came down to what they wanted most: sex and money.

Then the name had come to her last summer. The final piece of the puzzle: Mohawk. The idea of going back to Butler and of going back to the mill was overwhelming. The memories sat heavy and sour in the bottom of her gut. Her people had always been from Butler, going back far before Mohawk's arrival. Her mother and grandmother told her from the time that she was a girl that there was something not right about that city. They told her that strange things happened there again and again. She had never even considered going back. When she left for college, she felt a lightness about herself as if she had been wearing a very heavy but invisible overcoat that she had finally shrugged off.

She packed her bag, used her phone to summon a car to

drive her to Moody's house, and sat outside on the stoop until it arrived. The sun was shining outside, but the flat angle of early December's light did nothing to warm her.

# CHAPTER 25

Before Evanora showed up, I decided to do a little more research. I wanted to know for sure if she was telling the truth. I had Alek's first name, knew that "burns" would be mentioned, and gathered a rough idea of when this all would have taken place.

Finding the information took almost no time at all. The internet had a lot to answer for, but it made my job much easier. There on my screen was an article from the *Trib-Review*. Three years ago, two Pittsburgh college students suffered severe injuries after climbing a utility pole and mistakenly brushing against a power line near the Old Institute Mill in Butler. By all accounts, their survival had been a miracle. Susan Mattson had received extensive damage to her left arm. Alek Tijou had received much worse injuries. Reading between the lines, there was doubt that he would recover. Police suspected drugs or alcohol had been involved.

Her name was Susan, I thought. One accident had changed her from Susan Mattson, college student interested in the occult, to Evanora LaCosta, full-on witch, waist-deep in the sort of things that didn't exist in my nightmares a few weeks ago.

Having their real names meant that the search became much easier. She was right, I thought. Having someone's true name does give you power over them, especially in the age of online information. She and Alek had both received settlements from the power company, although it was a pretty hard-fought civil suit.

The power company insisted that there was no sign that the injuries had been caused by an attractive nuisance on their part. Alek's injuries were so horrific, however, that it seemed that the jury was swayed. The *Sewickley Herald* ran a small article eighteen months later when Susan, now having made her transition to Evanora (although I couldn't find any evidence of a legal name change) opened The Elemental Craft. The story was mostly about the assortment of crystals and tarot readings that the store made available. Evanora's store was strangely absent from the sponsors of Pittsburgh Pagan Day festivities, and the online review places didn't have much to say either. She seemed to keep a low profile, or, I thought, maybe her real customers weren't the types to spend a lot of time on Yelp.

Alek, on the other hand, showed up more frequently. There were follow-up stories in the *Butler Eagle* about his "road to recovery." In the first few months following the incident, spaghetti dinners had been held, complete with raffle baskets donated by local businesses. After the six months, he dropped from sight only to appear a year later in the police reports. It was all small-time stuff, drunk and disorderly and trespassing, and all of it dropped before trial. I got the feeling that the cops and the community didn't want to make his life any worse than it already was.

On the other hand, paranormal blogs had picked up his story. To them, he was The Burnt Man. The writers talked about looking for him late at night along the back roads surrounding the city of Butler. He had been abducted by UFOs or hit by lightning, or he had been a Navy SEAL who had been part of a failed super-soldier experiment. He glowed at night or shot electricity from his fingertips. His touch could fry the wiring in your car beyond repair or set your hair on end like a plasma globe at a children's museum. He lived in a tunnel. He didn't sleep. He appreciated gifts of beer, cigarettes, or weed. One blogger wrote that he was going to find The Burnt Man and talk him into having sex with the writer's girlfriend to see what the effect would be.

I could only find one image of Alek. In the photo, he was wearing a filthy CMU hoodie and tattered jeans. There seemed to be only one that showed his face. In the others, he held his arms up protectively, shielding his face from the camera and revealing the deep scars and angry skin that ran down the back of his hands. There were cracks in his skin in some places, furrows so deep that they looked like knife wounds that had never healed.

These hangers-on and rumor mongers sickened me. For a moment I thought I would have to remember to keep all of this information away from Evanora, then I realized that Alek's story was precisely what was driving her.

My phone vibrated. A text from Evanora. "I'm here."

She was waiting at the back door.

"How'd you get here?" I asked as I let her in, looking for a car in the driveway.

"Uber," she said.

"Long ride," I said. "Was your broom in the shop?"

She gave me a sour look. "I can't decide if I should be disgusted at your joke that reinforces the patriarchy or saddened for you that you have all the dad jokes, but none of the dad."

Her joke stung me more than mine had her, but I let it go. "Bring your bag in here," I said, "We can spread everything out on the dining room table."

"Where's Mr. B?" she asked. When I had suggested using my house as a base for our trip to the Institute, I warned her that the house had a good coating of cat hair. Turned out she loved cats; it seemed hilariously stereotypical to me, but I kept my mouth shut.

"Haven't seen him yet today," I said. "Probably sleeping on a rock in the sun or stalking a squirrel."

"Hmmph," she grunted as she used her hip to swing her bag onto the table and started pulling out books and notes.

"Do you want help?" I asked. She glared at me as she sorted through her bag. "Or I could make tea."

"Tea," she said. "Or coffee would be good."

"Tea it is," I said.

# CHAPTER 26

The cool of the night was sinking into Sam Mohawk's body. The rock outcrop on which he perched drew the heat from his legs and back. Below him, the Institute was an anthill of activity. Guards with rifles stood at the entrance to the Institute. Torches lit the faces of workers as they moved quickly and precisely, laying brick, sawing planks, and setting windows into place. They moved faster and with more strength than would seem possible. Their precision was absolute. An observer on the ground would have been struck by the eeriness of the scene. There was no cross-talk or friendly bantering. The only noise that broke the silence of the night was the sound of hammers and the creaking of wood settling into place. The same observer would have noted that the worker's eyes were rolled back in their heads, the white reflecting the firelight in a sickly way. Thin lines of spittle leaked from the sides of their mouths and mixed with their sweat.

The seat was already part of Institute lore. It sat carved into the rock of the hill that shot up on the far side of the Institute. Mohawk told his followers that it had been made for him by a greater power and that he found it one day while walking the hill seeking solitude and a contemplative retreat. Less charitable followers, gone now, said that he had hired a local stonemason to carve out a comfortable seat where he could sit and spy on the comings and goings of the followers. The stonemason, they said, had disappeared not long after completing the work.

The seat did, in fact, allow a panoramic view of the Institute and its comings and goings. From the perch tonight, Mohawk sat and watched the orphanage construction continue. In a matter of days, the men and women of the Institute had completed what would have taken trained workers months, goaded on by an unseen power, never stopping for food or drink or rest.

"Do we work them too hard, I wonder? Recruits are becoming harder to find."

*When the building is done, we will have more bodies than ever before. Hundreds.*

John Butterfass had drawn the short straw. A follower from the very first weeks of Mohawk's arrival, he had been trusted with the guard duty that night. His replacement didn't show up, and rumor among the other guards, trusted men all, was that Philip Elder had made a run for it. After a long, heated discussion, the men decided that since it was Butterfass' replacement who had gone missing, that Butterfass should be the one to deliver the bad news to Mohawk.

The climb was steep and even now, late in the fall, brambles pulled at his clothes. The last fifty yards were the worst, walking on a narrow ledge to turn the corner to the seat. Watching his footing and grabbing what handholds there were was near impossible in the dark. The final stretch to the turn took every bit of concentration. But what Butterfass noticed the most after making the turn was that the seat sat empty. Sam Mohawk sat in the dirt beside it, looking up and speaking to someone who was not there.

# CHAPTER 27

"This is what we have so far," she said, as we sat over steaming cups of tea. Evanora had brought books with her and they laid strewn on the dining room table. One was titled *The Black Pullet*, another *The Sworn Book of Honorius*, while others had no name on their heavy covers. All were ancient-looking and leather bound. I reached out to page through one, and she slapped my hand away.

"Don't touch," Evanora said. "Not for babies."

"Hmph... Not like the books you sell in the store, eh?"

"Ha. Um... No. Those books have their purpose though."

"Paying the rent?"

"Making sad people who feel like their lives are out of control happy if only for a little while."

"And these?" I swept my arm over the books on the table.

"These," she said slowly as if a weight had settled on her, "these reveal to people who have the eyes to see just how much of the world is so far beyond our knowing let alone our control. I wouldn't sell these in any store to anyone, but I don't think I could just burn them either, not at this point."

"Where did you even buy them?"

"eBay," she said, brushing me aside, her mood shifting.

"That's code for you're not going to tell me."

"That's code for, let's get down to business. And, you don't know for sure that I didn't buy them on eBay. Most of this stuff about dark web occult bazaars is just fodder for silly tv shows. Most of the powerful stuff hides in plain sight just waiting for someone who can see it. Now," she said, "here's what we have so far." She opened her notebook and began to speak.

"Mohawk showed up here in the spring of 1876. Or, at least, I couldn't find any mention of him before; however, there's some indication of a similar fire in Boston in 1875."

"Similar in what way?"

"Well, the Boston fire was, of course, much larger, but accounts from both the Institute Fire and the Boston Fire talk about the fire having an energy of its own, not even needing the fuel of the buildings, but drawing itself into a sort of fire tornado. Accounts from both fires also talk about the odd white color of the flames and a sort of terrifying sound from the center of the disaster. The Massachusetts Historical Society had lots of accounts in journals and letters of people writing to their friends about sleepless nights and terrible dreams following the accident. Some physical manifestations, too." She paged through her notes. "An altar boy reported seeing the holy water in the fonts at the Cathedral of the Holy Cross boiling and then turning slick with algae the day after the fire. No one believed him of course."

"So, you think Mohawk was there for it?" I couldn't think of anything else to say other than to state the obvious. Evanora had proven herself to be a talented researcher in her own right, and I was more than a little embarrassed. She shrugged her shoulders.

"I think Mohawk, or whatever his real name was, caused it. Probably by summoning to this plane for the first time the being that got Alek and is tormenting you."

"Kind of a stretch."

"Yes, but, a few years before the fire, a guy calling himself," she scanned her notebook, "get this, Elias Butler…"

I scoffed, "Could be a coincidence, still…"

She looked up at me. "I think he was from here originally and took the name when he left."

"Go on."

"So, Mohawk/Butler shows up in Boston two years before the fire. People who met him during that time often wrote about the fact that he was missing fingers on his left hand."

"Some kind of accident?"

"More likely, assuming he's our guy, a sacrifice. An early, clumsy attempt at making a blood offering."

"People do that?"

"People do that. People do a lot worse than that. So, he starts calling himself Adhy-apaka, aka the Hellenic Ethnomedon, aka Enphoron, aka the Greco-Tibetan, Ens-movens."

"Geez, he's like a hip-hop producer."

"Right? Guy loves fancy fake names. Anyhow, he starts telling people in Boston high society…"

"How does he end up in Brahmin circles?"

"Spiritualism and the occult are huge at this point in America. The aftermath of the Civil War meant that there were tens of thousands of parents who never knew how their sons died or even got to have a funeral for them. There was a sickness of repressed grief that spread across the nation. And where there's sickness, there's someone who can benefit from it. Basically, all he had to do was show up at some readings and introduce himself, do some dramatic card readings or seances and start worming his way up the social ladder. As I was saying though," she shot me a dirty look, "he starts telling his new best friends that he has just left years of solitary contemplation in a cave in the Pennsylvania forests and has decided to share his knowledge. He wants to build an occult college."

"An Institute."

"Exactly. He even calls it by that name: The Esoteric Institute."

"I mean, it's not 100% convincing, but…"

"It's getting there, right? By the time Mohawk/Butler starts to collect enough donations to build a…" she flipped through her papers again, "'Venetian-inspired palazzo' he's starting to wear out his welcome. He preached extreme celibacy, but…"

"But…"

"Right. Do as I say… He and his boss, a guy named," she flipped through her notes, "de Laurence. He was a real deal necromancer, by the way, did a lot of terrible things that people are still trying to figure out. Anyhow, de Laurence and Mohawk/Butler are gaining fast reputations as womanizers. So, from what I can tell, de Laurence was desperate and decided to go big to restore his follower's belief in him."

"A summoning."

"A summoning that goes bad fast. Whatever he brings here is too big, too powerful for him to control. My guess is that it took him over the moment it appeared and that the fire was a result of that summoning. Thirteen people died."

"Only thirteen? I thought the fire was huge."

"It was, so the low death toll leads me to believe even stronger in an occult origin. Most of the dead were associated with Mohawk/Butler and/or de Laurence."

"And he ends up here?"

"His building is burnt to the ground, his mind is gone, he's possessed by a powerful entity and he's drawn back to the place from whence he came to establish a…"

"Institute," I finished.

"I was going to go a little more baroque with 'a factory of terror', but sure, yours works, too. And, Mohawk is missing fingers, just like Butler. He shows up here, modifies his appeal slightly, goes for the working people rather than the elite and sets up more of a, well, of a factory than a college. But his personality must have still held some sway, because he ended up making the same mistakes over again."

"The sex stuff."

"Again, I was going to say hubris, but sure."

"So, he, Mohawk, he's alive. Back from the dead, like a zombie?

"Ah, no. Or, I guess, yes and no. The demon was never dead, but it took over Mohawk's body."

"Possessed him."

"No, much worse than that," she said. "From what I can tell, this kind of fella takes up a place in its human host and then slowly eats the soul a little at a time, over a period of years until the human soul is completely destroyed and the demon has full residence."

"That's… horrible."

"For the host, undoubtedly. For us, it's kind of positive though. The body, the shell, can be destroyed, and that weakens this type of entity. So, after Mohawk's shell was lynched, the thing was weakened and trapped inside that meat shell. And before the shell rotted away, one of those who know planted the oak. And, as the tree grew, they made sure that apotropaic marks were carved into the trunk."

"You lost me."

She sighed heavily. "Apotropaic marks. Sometimes they were called witches marks? People carved them into their houses to keep witches away. Which is ridiculous, because they work to keep evil in or out of something, and witches aren't evil."

"They could be."

"Yes, of course, but I'm saying, as a profession."

"Isn't it a belief more than a profession?"

"Moving on. So, now that he's free…"

"He?"

"It. Fine. Now that the entity is free, it needs a body to infect in order to exist fully on this plane. It has to be a strong class of evil, because even trapped inside the apotropaic oak, it was able to make contact and exert a little influence. So, we need to move quickly. We need to learn his true name, create a vessel to hold him, and figure out a sacrifice to force him into it. Before it's too late."

"So how do we destroy him?"

"You think I'm right?"

I sighed and let the breath out slowly through my nose before speaking.

"I do, yeah. It's like you said, too many coincidences."

"Well, then, we don't destroy him. Whatever bits of human soul might have existed have long been eaten away. We know he's been gaining power, so it's probably too late to banish him."

"This doesn't sound promising so far."

"We'll do what the old-timers did originally; we'll confine him."

"A demon trap."

"Forced spirit attachment, yeah."

"Can you do that?"

"Yes."

"Have you done it before?"

"No."

"The only tricky thing is…" she paused. "You're not going to like it."

"What?"

"There needs to be an offering of blood. A decent amount."

"You're right. I don't like it. We're not killing someone."

"Of course not. The person doesn't have to die."

"Are you asking me for my blood?"

"No, I wouldn't do that. I'll use mine."

"How's that going to work? You're going to cast the spell and capture the demon, saving the world, while you're bleeding out? That's ridiculous."

"I don't think it will come to that. But if I pass out, I need you there to take care of me."

"I really don't like this."

"And… while I'm weak, there's a really small chance that the entity might hop into my body. In which case, you'll need to let me continue to bleed all the way out."

"Kill you?"

"Not really, just allow me to pass on."

"I can't believe that you would even ask that of me."

Anger flashed in her eyes. "It won't come to that. I won't mess up this time, all right? Besides, we don't really have a choice, do we? We need to move before it's too late." She slipped shut her notebook and took a sip of tea.

As we put on our jackets, I asked, "Just now, when you said 'before it's too late.' What did you mean by that?"

"He's growing in power. Someone is helping him. He'll be looking for a sacrifice or sacrifices of his own to assume his true form on this plain. And he's got to be getting close."

"How close?"

"Close enough that we need to move quickly. He's been able to manipulate me and Alek — people who have a connection to him. Even you, simply because of proximity and sympathy."

"Sympathy? I don't have an ounce of sympathy."

"It means that you're predisposed to seeing and feeling things beyond the day to day."

"I'm really not sure that's true."

"Here's how I see it. You lived next to that tree for so long that whatever tiny, latent sensitivity that you possessed naturally got turned on. Think of it like getting cancer from living under power lines."

"Charming."

"Okay, not the best analogy. What I mean is that there was a lot of energy being thrown off by Mohawk's being trapped in the tree. You were around it so much in such a heightened emotional state that it established a link. Then, once, he was free, he strengthened that link by taking something of yours that you had an attachment to, an object that you had with you at all times: a lucky baseball cap, or a wallet, or..."

"A pocket knife?" My mind flashed to the Gerber tool that had been stolen outside of the courthouse.

"Sure. Anything like that. It's called sympathetic magic. I mean hair or blood works best, but an entity with this level of skill could make lots of things work in a pinch."

Blood. How many times had I cut myself while changing the blade, or opening one of those damnable plastic clamshells? My immortal soul was now in danger because my ShamWow had arrived in an impossible to open package?

"Think about all those crappy voodoo movies you've undoubtedly seen. Steal a little hair, make a doll, and boom, you've got yourself a magic slave. It's all BS of course, and my interests have moved way beyond that into high magic, but there are still a lot of people out there who..." Evanora stopped talking and looked up at me. "I've lost you."

"No, no, I'm listening, you were talking about zombie blood." My phone buzzed in my pocket. There are a limited number of people who call me. Most of them are strangers offering extended warranties on my car or cut-rate cruise ship vacation. And Nick, of course. As I fished the phone from my pants, I was hoping it was that lovely woman who often called to alert me that she had a limited number of spots open in a new health care program.

"Aaron? It's Nick, buddy. What's up?"

"Ah, not much, just um, talking to a friend."

Evanora cut her eyes up from the books that she had been stacking and grimaced.

"No, man. I mean, what's up with *you*?"

"Sorry, I... I'm not sure..."

"Dude. I thought you were going to send me more research this week."

I had blown through my deadline. Admittedly, I had good reason, but...

"Oh, yeah, right. Sorry about that, I just got hung up in some stuff here, and..."

"Yeah, well, I need to get this done, Aaron, and it's a lot more difficult when my team isn't keeping up with me."

*What team?* I was the one doing the work. This situation was a disaster. I needed the money, but this whole project...

"It's just that I'm dealing with some really complicated stuff here."

Evanora looked up at me again disapprovingly.

"Okay, well, your complicated stuff is complicating my stuff. Do you see what I'm saying? I have deadlines, too, Aaron. My editor is breathing down my neck. I want to get this done before my sabbatical, and I don't like to feel rushed."

"Aren't you taking the sabbatical to write the manuscript?"

"Listen, Aaron, I need your input. *Needed* it. Like yesterday."

"Right. Okay. I'll..."

But he had already hung up. I jammed the phone back into my pocket and stared at the wall behind Evanora. I felt my face flush.

Evanora looked at me, unimpressed.

"Trouble?" she asked. She had opened up the top book on her stack and paged through it while I was on the call. She didn't bother to look up as she spoke.

"Yeah," I sighed. "Yeah, this guy I'm working for. It's just. It's just that I'm not doing research, I'm writing the whole damn book. And, yes, Walt and I wrote parts of his books together, but this is different."

"You don't like this guy."

"I don't like this guy. He's a haranguer. And with everything else stressing me out: I mean, this whole thing about trying to get my wall fixed."

Evanora snorted.

"Can we not forget about the demon that could destroy thousands of souls, including our own?

"Right. Yeah, that too. It's just getting all too much…"

Evanora slid a piece of paper into her book to mark it, closed the cover, took a moment to collect herself, and sighed.

"Look, Moody, I don't care about your job. I don't care about this guy from Boston. And I really don't care about your stupid wall. But here's the deal. Assuming all of our work pans out, assuming that we don't die and end up damned to hell, you know what happens then? We go back to our lives. And you'll still have to deal with this guy and whatever else you have going on in that head. I don't know if you're a good writer, and again, I don't really care. But you do seem to be a nice guy, and everything you've said about this guy…"

"Nick."

"Right. Whatever. Everything you've said about Nick leads me to believe that he's a pretty big jerk who you've let get into your head and mess you about. So, and I'm saying this as a…"

She paused for a moment searching for a word.

"Friend?" I added.

"Sure. Yeah. Why not? I'm saying this as a friend, Moody: take credit for what you've accomplished. Take control of your own story."

Her words stung. The pain made me think she was probably right. She held my glance again, then opened her book back to her place and went back to taking notes. I dug my phone back out of my pocket and redialed.

"Yeah?"

"So, here's the deal Nick," I took a deep breath and felt my stomach flip. As a rule, I avoid confrontation as much as possible. And talking on the phone.

"I want credit."

There was a long pause.

"What do you mean? I'll mention you in the acknowledgments. You know that. It's in the contract."

"No, I want real credit. On the cover."

"What? No. No. Screw you. You're getting paid. That's your credit."

"I'm writing the damn book for you, Nick. That's not research."

"Walt told me…"

"Yeah. I have a pretty good idea of what he told you. But that was my deal with him. And you're not him."

"You know what? You can go to hell. I don't need you."

"I'm pretty sure you do."

The line went dead, and I placed the phone down on the table.

"That sounded like it went well," said Evanora, not looking up and with a sly smile.

"Eherm," I grunted and then suddenly remembered. "Wait, before that call, did you just call the entity a demon?"

She threw up her hand. "I'm done talking," she said, "let's recon the mill."

# CHAPTER 28

I felt no great compulsion to show off how out of shape I was, so I decided to drive to our recon. We traveled in silence. As I pulled to a stop in front of the mill, Evanora pressed something that felt like a coin into my hand.

"What's this?"

"A Saint Benedict relic."

"The one that you had when…"

"No. That's a bazooka. This is a club—a second-degree relic, just a scrap of his shirt."

"It's real?"

"Yup."

"How do you know?"

"Because I do."

She used a tone that one would use to address a toddler who was asking too many questions. I could feel my mouth set into a frown that extended up to my eyes. She kept talking, not even looking at me, but staring out at the mill. Dusk had already started to settle in. The light was golden, but deep shadows pocked the ground and the far side of the mill.

"It should work enough to keep the bad juju from knocking you back into never-neverland."

"Is 'bad juju' a technical metaphysical term?"

She opened the door and stepped out. I looked into my palm. The relic was laid on a piece of metal the size of a nickel.

On the back, protected by resin was a tiny scrap piece of grey fabric backed with red silk. I tucked the relic into the coin pocket of my jeans and followed her to the mill.

Evanora was breathing as heavily as I was by the time we reached the door.

"Are you okay?" I asked under my breath.

"Yeah. I'm fine." She was irritated. "I just haven't been back here since…"

"Do you want to go back to the car?" She opened the mill door and entered before I could finish the question.

"Hi, and welcome to the… Hey! It's you!" Kara greeted us.

"Yeah, I decided to come back."

"And you brought a friend! Great! How are you feeling?"

"Much better, thanks." I reached into my pocket and fingered the relic.

"Oh, that's great. Listen, I don't want to be a downer, but we're only open for another hour…"

"Oh, that's no problem," Evanora said. "I've been here before myself. We just happened to be in the neighborhood and thought that it would be fun to stop and see the old place."

"Oh! Cool," Kara said. "Listen, since you've been here before, I mean, did you want the tour?"

"No," we both said at the same time.

"Then would it okay if I just kind of did the side work, so I can be ready to go at six?"

"Sure," Evanora said.

Kara went upstairs and we could hear file drawers opening and closing.

"I feel sick," I said.

"Me too, but it's just our nerves; we would know if the crazy stuff had started. Here. Make yourself useful." She dug in her bag and pulled out a black hardback journal and a felt-tip pen and handed it to me. She walked to the far wall and began stepping it off. "I'll give you the measurements and you write them down."

"Can't we switch? I have really bad handwriting?"

"Yeah, sure, just heal my arm and we can get right to it."

I was sure that I was blushing. "Sorry."

She moved quickly and quietly calling out the measurements in feet. When she had made her way all around, she came back.

"Let me see," she said. I held the book open to her so she could check the figures. "Yeah, that'll work. Here, give it to me." She put the book back into her bag.

"Shouldn't we be more accurate?"

"No, I just need the rough area so I know how much chalk to bring. It's going to be a bigger circle. I'm not going to mess it up this time."

I couldn't tell if she was talking to herself or to me.

I slid the book in, and she turned away digging in her bag again. "Here," she said and handed me her phone. She returned to the bag and pulled out a silver rectangle the size of a business card and the thickness of a pack of gum with a plug sticking out the top. She plugged it into the bottom of her phone and then took the phone back. I looked over her shoulder as she started taking photos of the space inside the mill.

"What is…"

"Infrared. Those ghost hunter jackasses aren't always wrong. Even a blind pig finds a walnut once in a while, I guess. We can see where any odd warm or cold spots are and then…"

"Hey!" We hadn't heard Kara come down the stairs. "I knew it!"

"Sorry?" Evanora said, dropping her phone into her bag smoothly.

"You two. I knew it. You're ghost hunters, aren't you?"

"Ah, Kara…"

"You got us, Kara, is it?" Evanora stepped over my words.

"I knew you weren't just here for the mill."

Evanora walked towards her and talked in a low voice.

"Do you ever see things here, Kara? Weird things? Or feel like someone's watching you. Do you think one of your departed is trying to contact you?" This confidant, hypnotic persona was the same role I had seen her play in the store.

"Well… you know, sometimes I'll come in and things will be moved around or, there will be a cold gust, like even in the summer."

"Mmm-hmmm… That's very significant. Moody!" she barked at me. "Write that down!" I patted my pockets until I found a crumpled receipt. I still had her pen. Evanora rolled her eyes and looked back at Kara. "These psychics. Not at all interested in the day to day."

"He's a psychic? Oh my God. That's why he passed out."

Evanora nodded her head. "But here's the thing, Kara. No one knows we're here investigating. You're the only one. And we want to keep it that way."

Kara was nodding her head in synch with Evanora. "I've seen the shows on TV. It's a highly competitive field."

"Exactly. But you could help us."

Kara's face changed. "I don't know. The semester is almost over, and I really need to get credit for this internship."

"Look, Kara," I said. "It's no different from me keeping my mouth shut about passing out. You know that we can keep a secret."

"That's right," Evanora said, looking straight into the young woman's face. The muscles in Kara's forehead relaxed, and she cocked her head like a dog who sees someone she loves.

"What do I have to do?" she asked.

"Two weeks from today," Evanora started, "when you leave at night. Don't lock the door or arm the security system."

"There's a security system?" I asked. Kara nodded her head and mouthed "yes"; Evanora ignored me.

"Then," Evanora continued, "we'll come in, make our recordings and we'll lock up on our way out. You'll come in the next morning and no one will be the wiser. What do you say?"

"But when the story comes out, they'll know I did it."

"Not at all. We already have an official permission request in, but you know how long paperwork takes and we need to move fast. Once the permission comes in, we'll come back and get some B-roll, mix it with the stuff we get in two weeks and it will all look seamless. The only way people will know that you're involved will be when they see your name in the credits."

"Can I stay? In two weeks? I could help."

"No," Evanora said. "Too dangerous."

I could see Kara reconsidering.

"Okay. You can stay when we come back with official permission. I mean think about it. If we, for some reason, get caught, we can just say we broke in and you're blameless, but if you're here…"

"I'd lose my internship."

"Right. And possibly go to jail. But we're used to this sort of thing."

"We've done it hundreds of times."

Evanora glared at me.

"Well, dozens. I just mean it's not our first paranormal rodeo."

Evanora returned looking at Kara. She had the look of a snake eyeing its prey, and I noticed for the first time that she was holding her good hand in an odd gesture.

"What do you think, Kara? Will you help us out?"

"Yes. Sure," she said. "Why not?"

I breathed a heavy sigh.

"That's so good of you," Evanora said, "I'm so proud of you," and she reached up and cupped Kara's cheek in her hand, then turned to move back beside me.

"Thank you, Kara." She turned and pulled at my arm. "C'mon."

"Wait," Kara called after us. "I'm supposed to ask if you'd be interested in anything from our gift store."

"Oh," said Evanora as she walked over. "Yes, yes, I think I would. How about… this." She picked up a cheaply made die-cast model of the mill no bigger than a tennis ball. She turned to me.

"Really?" I asked.

She turned it over, weighing it in her hand. "I love it. In fact, maybe I'll start a collection," she dropped it in her bag. "Would you pay Kara and I'll get the money back to you?"

"Oh… sure." I handed over bills.

As Kara made change, she looked up at us. "I just realized that I'm helping you guys out, and I don't even know your names."

"Oh! Right," I said. I decided to needle Evanora. I wasn't particularly happy about her using her power on that woman. "I'm Moody and this is Susan."

She stiffened beside me and didn't speak until we got to the car. She slammed her door, and I sat heavily in the driver's seat for a moment before digging for my seat belt.

"Well, that went well," I said, looking at her while I reached to click the buckle. "I'm not super happy about you bewitching that woman. Something like that seems to fall a little heavily on the black side of magic, but I guess we got what we wanted. Do you need to stop at my place before I drive you home?"

She looked straight ahead. Her fist was clenched and her face was flushed.

"Tatty?" I said, unwilling to let it go just yet.

"What…? What the…? What the hell were you thinking?" She yelled from a place deep inside her chest.

"Geez! It was just a little joke."

"My name, to you and to everyone else, is Evanora. Not Tatty and certainly not the other…"

"C'mon I was just busting your chops. You were getting really David Copperfield in there."

"You used my name, part of my *real name* in a place of power. A place where I have already been attacked and suffered. Now, if anything was in there, it might know who I am and that I'm coming back. And now it has the upper hand, all because *you* couldn't keep your goddamn mouth shut! All because you had to chime in. We are not equal partners here, Moody."

"I said that I was sorry!"

"Just keep my name out of your godforsaken mouth. Forget what you found. The woman with that name is dead. She died, along with her friend, Alek," she stabbed her finger back at the mill, "in that place. She was a vainglorious little girl who thought that she had all the power she needed. And she didn't. And so, she paid. So, don't ever bring her up to me again. Questions?"

Without answering, I turned the key and eased down the rocky, rutted drive.

# CHAPTER 29

As she watched the taillights shrink into the distance, Kara sighed and felt a certain lightness. The day had felt endless. The mill was often empty with nothing for her to do but file the few bits of paperwork that came by and answer the occasional call. School trips were scheduled weeks in advance and one of the professional docents, retired men and women obsessed with local history and numb to the whispered annoyances of bored elementary children, took care of those responsibilities. Sometimes a week would pass at work and she wouldn't see another soul. Cell reception was terrible here, so she spent a lot of time watching downloaded movies and re-reading the few ancient magazines upstairs in the office. During her first week here she had considered leaving, but she had procrastinated past the add/drop date and she needed these credits badly. Not to mention the tuition money she had already paid.

There was a pretty simple closing up protocol. She was supposed to sweep every night, but only did about once a week. Then, she put the money from the register in the cash box and carried it up the old, open wooden stairs to the second floor where the small office had been carved out among the huge pieces of machinery, cogs, and gears. She made sure the computer was off and unplugged the power strip—the wiring made everyone a little nervous. Her supervising professor had mentioned it during training. It was old, had been poorly installed, and was almost always overtaxed. Sometimes she thought she caught a whiff of ozone or even a deep burning smell like a trash fire and her heart would race, but as she had been told, she had an active imagination.

Next, she turned off the office lights and locked the door. Locking the door always seemed like an exercise in magical thinking. It was hollowcore and cheap. She could have put her foot through it easily. Even if it had been sturdy, the office was just thin drywall on studs that had been thrown together over a weekend. Tape on the floor would have been just as effective in creating a secure environment. She flicked off the upstairs lights and headed back down the stairs. Then it was simply a matter of turning off the downstairs lights and making sure the lock on the main door was secure. Every time they found evidence of kids nosing around, the board would talk about installing a security system or CCTV. Money, however, was always a problem.

Watching her steps, Kara started down the steps to the main floor. Making the last descent of the night was always tricky. The stairs were uneven and without the lights from upstairs, she had to place her feet carefully as she went. This attention to detail was probably why she didn't notice the apparitions on the first floor until she was almost completely down.

She raised her head when she heard the smokehouse door slam from outside. The outbuilding sat twenty feet from the mill, but the door was old and poorly hung. The wind often caught the outbuilding's door and slammed it against the small building's frame. The initial noise jolted her and stopped her dead on the steps. She turned towards the window behind her, now dark, that looked out towards the smokehouse. The wet, squelching noises, arrhythmic and drawing closer, locked her knees in fear.

She turned back around. The first floor was lit with a silvery light that had no definite source. Men, women, and children dressed in simple homespun clothing bustled about like ants at a spilled bag of sugar. They were hammering, sawing, mortaring, building the very structure in which Kara now stood. They worked without pause. To Kara's eyes, it seemed as if their hands were moving of their own will. Their heads sat stiffly on their necks staring straight ahead, not focused on the work or even acknowledging each other. The noise outside drew closer, but only Kara seemed to notice. She could hear it becoming louder now, drawing closer against the outside wall.

Suddenly the mill door exploded open and a powerful gust of wind flowed in. The doorway glowed even brighter than the first floor, but the ghostly workers paid no mind, continuing at their task. Still frozen in place, Kara could see the sickly silver light coming from a mound outside the door, like a huge jellyfish thrown on the beach. It was at least eight feet tall and almost as wide. Its flesh was greasy and pale. The skin pulsed and stretched as if something was trapped underneath. A face would boil up, stretching the skin almost translucent and then be pulled back down, an arm, then a leg. The mound had tentacles that flailed and paused like a snake's tongue testing the air. It moved closer to the door, and the light grew brighter and dazzling. It hurt Kara's eyes, but she couldn't look away. The pain reached into the back of her head, and then, as if fighting her way from a nightmare, she managed to pull her head away and close her eyes. She felt her knees buckle.

As she fell, she slid backward on her tailbone landing on the next-to-last step like a child playing on a staircase. A short, sharp shock of pain traveled up her spine and tears flooded her eyes. When she wiped them away, the first floor was empty. The lights hanging from open electrical boxes revealed nothing but the weathered floorboards, the driveshaft, and the belts that were always there. She took a deep breath and rubbed her eyes. There was nothing there. She had, she thought, gotten dizzy and fallen on the stairs. The strange hallucination must have visited her while she lay there. She needed more sleep. Maybe, she thought, her mom was right and she should start taking vitamins. She stood and rubbed the base of her spine ruefully. *This is what happens when you talk to ghost hunters*, she thought, and limped to the door.

# CHAPTER 30

The day of the orphanage dedication festival was one of rest at the Institute. The devotees had collapsed after the last day of cleaning and decorating. For all their work, the place hardly seemed like the church socials from their old lives. There was no bunting above hastily constructed tables, no area marked off for baseball games, no dais built for a speaker to engage in a stemwinder of a speech in the hot sun.

The doorways of the orphanage opened into a grand hall. The interior was sparkling and clean. Gaslight chandeliers hung from the high ceilings and burned with a flickering glow. Although while they were building, the workers had been told to envision long trestle tables filled with the unfortunate children eating simple nourishing food and gathering to sing morning and evening songs, even this room was still empty. At the moment, however, only the sound of footsteps rang hollow against the bare walls and floor.

The children arrived the day before by wagon. Just thirteen to start, mostly from towns to the north where the oil boom had busted and left an inordinate number of families who could no longer take care of their children. These were children who had been born to oil patch whores or to mothers who struggled for years after their husbands died in the rough work of the field until they finally had to acknowledge the truth that they couldn't care for their children anymore.

The boys and girls arrived dazed from the long overnight

trip. They were hungry and crawling with lice and fleas; some were wearing clothes that even a poor man would have thrown away rather than use as rags. The female devotees hovered and cooed over them while the men smiled reassuringly and offered them words of welcome and encouragement. The children were gathered and washed by the women who threw the filthy clothes in a pile, doused them with kerosene and let them burn. The children were fed their meal as they sat in new robes that looked like shifts. Then they were led to one of the large tents, filled with cots and newly washed bedding still crisp from the line. Time to take a nap, they were told. There was going to be a grand celebration that night and they were going to be the guests of honor.

Mohawk sat in his tent. His permanent residence had been completed the day before, but he held off moving until after the orphanage dedication. He had come to enjoy his home here in the grand yurt, with the creaking and splashing noises of the mill as it powered the grindstones leaking through the canvas walls. The mill was a fine building. He had heard locals while he was in town, whispering that the creek didn't have enough power to spin stones that large, but Mohawk had paid them no mind. Soon, harvest time would be here and then the locals and their cash would flock to the institute to use his mill, closer and better made than the McConnell's, nearly to 15 miles away. The town would come to him and, slowly, slowly, he would take it all.

*Sad little mouse,* the voice growled in the back of his head, *the time is coming. Make our preparations. I will be strong enough to be free of your body by the end of the harvest. But only if I am fed.*

There was a whisper against the tent flap.

"Yes," he said.

"Father Mohawk?"

"Come in, my child."

A young woman entered. What was her name, Mohawk

thought? Anna? Annamae?

*Emma,* said the voice. *The one who cries the entire time and smells like piss. A delightful young woman.*

Mohawk put his hands over his eyes for a moment and worked hard to push the voice back into his head again. A tiny drop of blood spilled from his left eye.

"Father!" Emma said.

"It's nothing, my dear. The stress of... planning the festival." He sighed and composed himself. "What can I do for you?"

The young woman held out her cupped hands. Curled inside like a nest of baby birds was a collection of locks of hair: blonde, black, brown, all light, soft, and clean.

"Their hair, Father. For the memory book. It's such a wonderful idea. They will be thankful when they are grown and are able to look back on this time."

The voice's laughter thundered in his head like the resonance from a bass drum. The pain made his knees weaken a little. Emma rushed to his side, and he steadied himself with a hand on her shoulder.

"Should I call someone?" her voice was anxious and frightened. He could feel the voice luxuriating in the fear; a shiver went down his spine and his scrotum constricted.

"No, no, I'm fine dear. Let me sit."

She led him to the chair by his desk and he slumped down.

"Here," he patted the desk. "Leave the hair here." She looked at him with concern. "I'm fine," he said. "I'm just tired."

"You should rest."

"There will be time for rest soon enough. Thank you, Emma."

She beamed at his knowing her name. "Of course," she murmured and turned to walk out. She reached the flap when he called her name again. A wisp of fear ran through her as she feared that he would ask her to stay for instruction.

"Yes?" Her voice was small again.

"You were able to gather the mementos without waking them?"

She breathed easier.

"Yes. We put the laudanum in the soup, just as you suggested. They were so hungry; they didn't even taste it. They fell to their beds like babes."

*Share and share alike, eh? I told you. Finally, all of your hokum medical experience is working out for us, eh?*

"Thank you, Emma. I won't forget what you've done."

Emma smiled as she left the tent, but the gesture didn't reach her eyes. She was unsure whether Mohawk's last words to her had been praise or a threat.

After she left, Mohawk turned the hair in his hand. The locks were soft, clean, and smelling of soap. The children had been bathed and deloused as soon as they arrived. The hair felt light in his hand as if it would float away if he didn't hold it tightly.

*This is no time for weakness,* the voice whispered somewhere behind his eyes, then swimming behind his forehead. *The die is cast. This is what you wanted. These children are the first steps; they are the end of the beginning. They are my bridge to my walking in your sad little world.*

"What happens to me then? After you're gone."

*When the steed is given free rein, the rider no longer chooses the path.*

"Will I still have magic?"

*I knew a man once. He was a bit like you. A simple sort, spending his time thinking under trees. He thirsted for knowledge; he studied the temple that we built for Solomon, but he spent long nights looking for something more—the Angelical Stone.*

"The stone of Moses? You speak of Newton, the first scientist?" The comingling of science and magic had been a favorite topic for Randolph. Mohawk had spent long evenings surrounded by acrid smoke as the man held forth, practicing for the marks.

*Scientist?* The voice chuckled with a noise like sandpaper against skin. *That little creature wasn't the first scientist, he was the last of the old kind of magician.*

"Newton? One like me?"

*Like you!* The laughter roared this time and the blood in Mohawk's eyes pulsed. *Is a house cat like a lion? Oh, no, you're just a little tabby with cans tied to its tail. There will be others like Newton, but you aren't one of them. Oh. Human vanity. I never tire of it. I must remember to tell Artiphus of this conversation. Hmmm...* The voice made a sound of satisfaction like a fat man being served an especially generous helping of cobbler. *I came to Newton and offered him what we have. We talked long nights of alchemy and of the pebble for which he searched the great beach of knowledge. But in the end, I really only taught him one bit of truth about magic. For everything that you take, you must give. The ledger stays balanced. Always. So, little tabby, what have you taken and how much must you pay?*

Mohawk had a good idea of what the voice meant. The voice's goal the entire time had been to build strength: enough strength to leave Mohawk and hunt and stalk the Earth on its own, in shapes of its choosing. Mohawk would be left behind. He had read stories like his own in de Laurence's books. The magician in Prague who had failed in his attempt to make Azaeal his slave. Mohawk knew how this story ended. He would be an empty husk, unless he, himself, was able to find a body to ride, someone to carry the small amount of his soul that the voice hadn't consumed. He had read the ritual in de Laurence's books and had the incantations among the notes he had been able to spirit away from Boston. But he wondered if he would have the ability when the time came. And the time was coming, soon.

The voice had done its work upon him so slowly, so subtly, that Mohawk had barely noticed. Now he imagined the being curled like a trilobite deep in the mud of Mohawk's body, nibbling bit by bit on Mohawk's soul, hoarding the little that was left like a miserly child with Christmas candy. Eventually, though, even the most careful of child was left with an empty wrapper and a stained mouth.

Already the sun dipped towards the horizon. Mohawk had been preparing since the night before, but he felt not the slightest fatigued. He gathered his bowls and candles, his chalk and books, and made his way to the orphanage. There was much work to be done.

Only twelve of the devotees had been invited to the consecration of the orphanage. Mohawk had told them that they, the most faithful and favored, would witness the children's consecration ceremony. They arrived that night to find the hall dimly lit. On the floor, in a space big enough for a hay wagon to be parked, was an enormous circle within a circle. Between the outlines of the shapes, intricate glyphs and wards had been drawn and the outer circle had been over-lined with salt. Four pentagrams had been drawn at the corners of the room. To the east of the circles, between two of the pentagrams, a triangle had been drawn with a circle and runes inside. It was large enough for a man to sit inside and placed within were two brass bowls, a curved knife, and a candle.

The children were led into the large circle, holding hands. One balked, afraid, but was soothed and led forward by one of the women. They had been warned to step carefully and to avoid treading on the lines or the salt. Their eyes were still glazed with sleep and opium. When they had formed a circle within the innermost chalk circle, the devotees removed themselves to the corners and Mohawk began the incantation. He placed the manikin that Benjamin Balmer had carved for him inside the larger of two brass bowls. The wooden doll was a hideous thing: an octopus shape but with four tentacles, two of which ended in greedy sucker-tipped fingers and two of which ended in stingers.

A mouth sat within another mouth lined with sharp teeth. Too many eyes were set in the wrong places. Balmer had suffered nightmares for a week after finishing the carving. He had left the Institute one night and disappeared. Devotees returning from town whispered that police had found him with his head caved in after he jumped in front of a trolley.

Mohawk's murmuring continued nonstop. The devotees who had brought in the children sought each other's eyes and looked confused—where was the band, the speeches? Mohawk dropped the children's hair into the bowl on top of the doll, followed by a handful of dried plants. The children stiffened. He gripped the sickle-like blade of the knife and dark blood poured from his palm and boiled on top of the mixture.

A great noise was heard like the rushing of the wind or the noise of a waterfall. The acolyte's eyes grew wide with fear as they covered their ears seeking some relief from the cacophony that seemed to bury itself inside their heads. Mohawk felt the top of his head rise as if he was being pulled up by a string, and then a feeling like a splinter being drawn from the skin. His body fell into a pile like loose rags when flame burst from the bowl spilling out foul-smelling smoke.

From his position on the floor, fear gripped him deeply. He could see the bright white fire: it was the same flame that he had seen in Boston. Some of the older children fought through the opium and began to scream. The younger ones cowered, but still they all held hands. The flame writhed and moved among them while their faces contorted in pain. The fire solidified into shapes—a horde of cicadas finding mouths and ears, the cephalopod creature wildly whipping its stingered tentacles, then, for a moment, inside the circle, the creature became Mohawk himself. The human Mohawk felt bile rise in his throat. The demon Mohawk threw back its head. Its jaw unlocked and grew to a monstrous size with razor-sharp teeth. It bit off a little boy's arm and howled victoriously as blood spilled. The noise was like a lion now, deep and resonate, and constant. Two of the devotees passed out while the others stood rigid, unbelieving, and paralyzed with fear. The circle of children began to draw itself tight like a knot around a neck. Mohawk realized that the children's bodies were being melted and shrunken into each other, the way a piece of bacon shrinks on a hot griddle. Their screams turned into wet noises and then diminished completely. He heard one of the devotees vomiting and crying behind him. He closed his eyes against it all and felt the wetness of tears of blood seeping from the corners.

Then the ordeal was over. He felt something like a hypodermic being inserted into his flesh and then the presence of the voice again—no words, but a buzzing chattering noise of a million insects. There was a lump of flesh left in the circle like a wet glistening boulder. A few body parts could still be recognized protruding from the moist surface.

Mohawk stood. He felt full and exhausted as after a great feast. The exhaustion that he had ignored for the past days came flooding in. He needed to rest and to digest like a snake or a lion. Without a glance towards the others, he made his way back to his tent. Women were waiting there who would take care of him and watch over him while he slept.

The devotees stood shell shocked at what they had seen. They filed out soundlessly and back to the bunkhouses. No one spoke a word and the thickness of the fog that came in from the creek obscured them from each other's sight.

# CHAPTER 31

Evanora and I drove in silence back to my house. Finally, when I had unlocked the back door and she was gathering up the last of her things from the dining room table, I spoke.

"I'm sorry," I said.

"I don't have anything more to say on the subject. It's over."

"But..."

"It's over, Moody. I don't want to talk about it."

"Okay. Fine."

"Look, as a peace offering, I'll let you drive me home," she said.

"Oh, wow," I said. "You really are a good and magnanimous witch. Your sister, Glinda, must be jealous."

"Oh, she is, and Momba's green with envy." She smiled at me as she cracked the joke.

I laughed. "That's even worse than one of mine."

"Besides, that drive up was more expensive than I had thought. Metaphysics doesn't pay that well, you know."

"I guess that's why my high school guidance counselor kept trying to steer me towards the military."

"Before we go, I'd like to take a look at this stump."

"Good idea," I said. "It's around front."

We shrugged on our jackets. She grabbed her bag, as I locked the front door behind us. I turned to see Mr. B standing at chest level on the railing of the deck.

"B!" I said, "What a pleasant surprise, buddy." He jumped into my arms and rubbed his head against my chest. "Wow, you must have missed me." I turned to Evanora. "He never does that. In fact, he's usually not even thrilled about me picking him up."

She scratched his head and looked him over.

"He certainly is an unusual cat," she said.

"Don't you get started too. My neighbor claims that he's an exotic jungle cat from the wilds of the Amazon or something…"

"No," she said, scratching him under his chin. "I don't think that, but he is… different."

"The stump," I said, pointing with my chin, my arms full of cat. We walked down the steps from the porch, to the yard, to street level. "You can see what a mess my wall still is. Can you believe it? And here's the thing," I continued as we crossed the street to stand by the stump. "As far as I can tell, that wall, the wall that runs the length of the whole block, that wall was built the same time as the house which means that it's like 120 years old, so I want it restored, not just rebuilt. I don't want a bunch of cinderblocks thrown up…"

"Moody," she said as we stopped in front of the stump.

"Yeah?"

"Save it for city hall."

The streetlights had snapped on while we were talking inside. Still. the stump was easy to see. Piles of sawdust still sat moldering on the sidewalk as if an extremely aggressive termite infestation had taken place. The stump itself was a ring of wood, hollow inside; the actual living wood had been nothing more than a thin shell.

"You say this was hollow all the way up like a chimney?"

"No, not all the way from what I could tell. There was a space inside, like a raccoon den."

She looked at me, puzzled.

"Okay. Maybe a weird metaphor. There was a space almost

big enough for a man to stand, but not big enough for him to lie down. Like if I were in it, I'd have to hunch over and it's not like I'm super tall. C'mon, B! Quit it!" Mr. B had started squirming in my arms.

"The Little Ease," Evanora said as she bent down to get a closer look.

"Hmm?"

"The Little Ease. That's what a cell like this is called. The 'good people' used to put witches in them. Pitch black and proportioned so that the prisoner can't fully stand or fully sit. The pain is unbearable. People went crazy in a matter of days."

"But if he, it, was a demon?" Mr. B pushed against my face with his paws. I knew that he wanted me to put him down, but I didn't want him to get in Evanora's way.

Evanora looked up at me from her crouch. "They can feel pain too, Moody. And loneliness. They crave attention and power. Imagine being here for over a century, awake, conscious the whole time, in agony, knowing and hearing the world going on without you and being ignored the whole... Hello. What are you then?"

"What is it?"

"Looks like a glyph or a sigil of some kind. Maybe to keep him in."

"But if it's on the inside, wouldn't that mean..."

I was too late. She had reached out and touched the symbol to brush dirt and soot from it. The stump lit up with blue fire that burned without consuming. Evanora's body stiffened and her eyes rolled back in her head. She thrashed and groaned, but her two fingers were stuck on the sigil as if they had been welded to it. Her moans of pain were unearthly, like nothing I had ever heard before. The noise drove me to panic, and I reached out to help her. I juggled the cat as my movement made him dig his claws into my arm for purchase.

"Don't..." she moaned.

"Evanora!" I shouted. Mr. B leaped from my arms and slammed broadside into Evanora's face. The weight and force of the collision knocked her over and her hand pulled free with an audible gristly snap like removing the leg of a roast chicken. I ran to her side.

"Oh, my God. Evanora are you…"

Evanora leaned to the side and vomited a thin yellow stream. She took a deep breath and pushed herself up with her good arm.

Mr. B sat on the sidewalk and cleaned his paws.

"Yeah. I'm… fine. It's a good thing; I can't really lose another arm," she smiled sadly.

"Let's go inside." I helped her to her feet.

"No. I want to go home, Moody. I'm tired."

Mr. B followed us across the street to my garage behind the house. He hopped up onto the deck steps.

"You stay here, buddy. I'll be back." Evanora was leaning on me. Her breath was sour, and she carried a sharp smell of sweat. "Good thing he was here, huh? He's like, the hero of the day."

"Yeah," said Evanora. "Thanks, Mr. B. Sure was a coincidence."

It was going to take at least 45 minutes to get her back to her apartment above the store. For the first ten minutes, we drove in silence. Finally, I couldn't take it anymore.

"So… you're okay?"

"Yeah. I think so. Sore. My mouth tastes like a monkey cage, but okay overall, I guess."

"What was it? Some sort of magic thing?"

"It was stupid of me to touch it. I don't know what I was thinking. I just wanted to see it more clearly, I guess, but, yeah, a sigil."

"Which is…?"

"Which is actually kind of helpful. A sigil is an icon…"

"Like an emoji."

"No. Not really like that at all. A sigil is a shorthand the old-timers discovered. It's a pictorial representation of an entity, like a signature. A pictogram. It must have left it inside while it was captured in an attempt to magic its way out. I should be able to find it in *The Key of Solomon* or one of the other old texts. Then I should be able to figure out who we are dealing with. And if I can do that, match the sigil to the..."

"- demon."

"- entity. Then we can bind it."

"So, it was kind of lucky after all."

"I appreciate your optimism, but no, it was awful. I could hear its voice in my head again. Even for those few short seconds and I was back in the mill with... Stop!"

I slammed on the brakes, the anti-lock kicking and thrumming against my foot. We sat for a moment. The radio, which was turned off, suddenly began blaring the hissing white noise of static through the speakers.

"It was Alek!" she said. Her eyes were racing to the flood of headlights and out the side windows. "I saw Alek!" She threw open the door and stepped out. "Alek?"

"Evanora," I said, "C'mon. What are you doing?" I punched on the four ways and stepped outside.

"I saw him. Walking up the berm and then he went into the woods."

"It couldn't have been." She leaned back in and rummaged through her bag, returning with a flashlight. The light illuminated the forest on the side of the road. The static on the car radio changed. It was a scratching now. It was the same scratching I had heard in the house and in my head.

"Evanora?"

"Alek?" she yelled. "Come out. I want to see you. I want to talk to you. Something bad is happening. You need to be safe."

Gooseflesh shivered up my back and my head pounded. She

was right. There was someone out there. I could feel their eyes on my back. I could hear the cracking of twigs in the woods. A snorting like a whitetail buck asserting dominance snapped through the silent night air.

"Evanora?"

"You stay here," she said. "I'm going to find him."

"No!" I shouted.

"I need to find him," she yelled back at me.

"No! Don't leave me here."

The scratching noise was deafening. It no longer seemed to be from the car's speaker. It seemed to be all around us, like a thousand cicadas chittering on the last summer night before the apocalypse. I got back into the car and reached over, grabbing the back of her jacket. I pulled hard, and she tumbled back into the seat.

I punched the radio off, but the sound continued.

"Come back! Shut the door! Shut the door!" I yelled.

"He needs me! I can help him." She threw herself out of the car and fell on her injured side. The arm couldn't catch her and she hit the tar and chipped surface of the road with a heavy thud. I jumped from my side of the car and ran to her.

"We have to go!"

"I can help him!"

I grabbed her up from the roadside by her jacket and half carried and half pushed her back to the car. I shoved her into her seat and she fought me, crying and yelling. When she was in, I slammed her door and ran around to my side. Throwing myself into the seat, I pulled my door shut with my left hand. She had managed to get her door open again, but I kept my right hand firmly grabbing her jacket as she struggled to get back outside. I pulled her closer to the driver's side, shifted into drive, and took off. Her door swung shut but before it did, I swear I saw her flashlight catch a pair of glowing yellow reflective eyes eight feet off the ground.

Ten miles down the road, the scratching was gone, replaced by classic rock. I pulled over, still breathing deeply and reshut my door, which had been whistling from not being shut the whole way. Evanora did the same on her side.

"You okay?" I asked.

She nodded her head yes. "I'm sorry," she said. "It's been such a long day," she turned to face me. "I swear it was him."

"There was something there, I don't doubt that for a second."

"I just wanted to help him. What if he's going through this, too?"

"Look, let's worry about that in the morning, okay?"

"Yeah," she said, "That's smart."

She only said one more thing to me that night. When we got to her apartment, she pulled herself out of the car and began walking away. Then she turned, came back, and opened the door. "Take the interstate home," she said. "And take Mr. B inside if he's waiting for you."

# CHAPTER 32

Four days later, I was still on edge. I had some Xanax and Ambien left from the rough spot right after my wife left, and I had been relying on them to get to sleep more than I was comfortable with. Tonight, I thought, I would just be still and try to clear my head of everything that I had seen, everything that had happened. I would try to be quiet and remember what life had been like before I started passing out in my kitchen.

Nick waited several days after my ultimatum but had finally called back. When I saw his number flash on my phone, my heart pounded, and I thought that I would vomit. When I answered, we were cordial. He agreed that the work that I was doing was more than just research. The pay would stay the same but I would get a "with Aaron Moody" on the cover. In a small font. With no co-author bio on the leaf. It felt like a huge victory for me. I spent the day in the sort of joyful numbness that I hadn't enjoyed in a very long time.

I settled down by eight that night. Mr. B decided that he had more important work to do than sit with me and stood at the door mewing until I let him out. As I sat back down on the couch, my phone vibrated again. I didn't even bother to check the number this time. What could go wrong on a day as fine as this one?

"Hello?"

"Mr. Moody? This is Ruby."

"I'm sorry, who?"

"Ruby? From City Hall. The receptionist?"

"Oh! Right! I'm sorry. Hi, Ruby. What can I do for you?"

"I told you I would call, Mr. Moody."

"Okay."

"They're here tonight, Mr. Moody. The Basement Department is open."

"Tonight? Now? It's after eight."

"I told you, Mr. Moody, they don't keep regular hours. If you want to talk to them, now's your chance."

I sighed. "Okay. Thanks, Ruby. I'll be right down."

This is ridiculous, I thought to myself as I stooped to put on my shoes. All I wanted was to get my wall fixed. After weeks of the run-around, I end up going to Old City Hall at night to meet some strange division of city government because an old lady sitting at a card table told me they might be able to help? My life really was spiraling out of control. On the other hand, I thought, palming my key fob, I was on a roll. What did I have to lose?

The streetlight outside of Old City Hall was out. A glow came from inside the front doors. Would the doors even be unlocked at this time of night, I wondered, then shrugged as the knob turned and the door clicked open.

Ruby sat at her post. It was the first time I had ever seen her alone. She smiled as she recognized me coming down the hall.

"Mr. Moody," she said in a stage whisper. "You made it."

"Yeah, ah, thanks for calling me. You really think they can help?"

"I think so, Mr. Moody, I really do. They're one of the oldest departments here and they really know how to get things done. They know just the right people to ask."

"Where all the bodies are buried," I said trying to joke and immediately regretting it.

"Something like that," she said. "You better get going."

"Okay, so just down the stairs?"

"No. You have to take the elevator," she said, pointing to the black iron birdcage.

"No. Really? I didn't think that still worked. In fact, I swear there was a Do Not Use sign on it the last time I was here."

"It's the best way," she said, shrugging.

"Okay, okay," I said. I really wanted that wall fixed. December had been mild so far, but I had worked with enough contractors to know that once the real winter ice and snow came, they would say we had to wait until spring. Once spring arrived, they would say they were all booked up with projects. Or worse, they would show up one day, yellow tape everything off, make a mess, and then disappear for several months. I wanted to deal with that scenario even less than I wanted to ride the death trap birdcage.

I stepped in and pulled the gate behind me. There were no buttons, but just as I was trying to figure out how to make the elevator move, the machine jerked hard and then descended to two floors below. A subbasement? How did a building this old even have a subbasement? I pulled the cage back open and walked to the only door at the end of a short hall.

I reached the door. It was unlabeled. Did no one in this building think of nameplates or stencils? Why was every door I needed to open a blank door?

Grasp the nettle, I thought as I reached out. The dry winter air built a static charge and a tiny spark shot into my hand. I jumped and muttered under my breath, then twisted the doorknob, opened the door, and stepped inside. The room was small and claustrophobic. Green shaded lights, the kind that might appear over a pool table in an old movie, dimly lit the space. In front of me, seven men and women shuffled and stamped and dropped papers into pneumatic tubes with an efficiency that seemed like a pantomime. No one registered my presence. I took a step forward and stood at the counter. Still, no one acknowledged that I was there.

"Ahem…" I cleared my throat and the man closest to me stopped collating and looked at me.

"Yes?"

"Hi. I, ah, Ruby sent me?"

"Because?"

"Oh, I… have a problem, or a request actually."

"Which is?"

"So, a few weeks ago, a tree fell on the wall in front of my house. It's part of the wall that runs in front of all the houses in the neighborhood."

"Which neighborhood?"

"Institute Hill."

"Was it an oak?"

"Ah… yes. Yes, it was. How did you…"

"And a man was killed."

"Yes, that's right. You do know what I'm talking about."

"So why are you here?"

"I want the city to repair my wall. Because it was a city crew."

"That brought down the tree without the proper paperwork."

"Yes! That… that's right." For the first time in weeks, I felt like someone was actually listening to me. For the first time, I felt like something might be accomplished.

"Well, Mr..."

"Moody. Aaron Moody."

"Well, Mr. Moody. We could help you…"

"Are you serious? This is wonderful. But look, I don't think that I should have to pay to have…"

"But these things don't just happen, Mr. Moody. Wheels must be greased, tribute must be paid, if you understand what I'm saying."

"A bribe? You're flat out asking for me to pay a bribe to get my wall fixed that the city destroyed in the first place?"

The man shrugged his shoulders. "Nothing is free in this world Mr. Moody. We all make sacrifices."

"I… uh… fine." I was sick of it all. "How much is this going to cost me? Above and beyond the taxes I already pay faithfully. Like an honest citizen."

"I think… meat."

"I'm sorry. Meat?"

"Seven nice thick porterhouses. Well-marbled. No less than 18 ounces each. And no wet-aged detritus. Nothing from a big box store. Quality meat from a local farm."

"You're asking for a bribe. In beef?"

He shrugged again and went back to collating. I waited a moment for more, but it was, once again, as if I were invisible. I walked back to the elevator and rode up, slowly this time, as if an elderly fisherman was reeling me up.

"Well," Ruby asked. She was all smiles and wafts of overly strong rose perfume.

"They asked for a bribe."

"Oh good!"

"Good?"

"Well, that means that things will move ahead. You can leave the tribute with me. I'll make sure it gets to them." She lowered her voice. "Was it meat or wine?"

"Meat," I said, thoroughly confused.

"Oh, that *is* a good sign. Congratulations, Mr. Moody. Have a good night."

I drove home in a fog of confusion.

I should report them, I thought. But then I realized I had failed to get anyone's name. And I didn't know to whom I could report them without going through the entire bureaucratic snafu again. So, I decided to text Evanora instead.

-You're not going to believe what happened.

-What? Are you okay? Do you need help?

-It's my wall. I went to talk to some people about getting my wall fixed.

- Ugh. I don't want to hear about your stupid wall. I'm researching wards.

-It was super odd.

-Don't you have your own research to be doing? I'll talk to you tomorrow, Moody.

She was right. Upon checking my email, I found that Nick had politely asked for more "tidbits" as he put it. I went home and wrote until midnight and then poured myself into bed where I stayed until 7:00, my dreams filled with men and women in green eyeshades sitting at a card table digging into bloody steaks.

# CHAPTER 33

Two days later, I drove to Cranberry Township. When I first moved to Butler, there were still trailer parks and farms in this area in the south of the county. In the short span of time, the region had become the fastest-growing suburb of Pittsburgh and one of the most rapid growth areas in the overall United States. Housing developments sprang up like poisonous mushrooms after the rain, and the state was investing millions of dollars to widen what had been a pleasantly winding country lane. Gentrification had some benefits though. I had read an article in *Pittsburgh* magazine about a butcher shop that had opened here that catered in all organic, grass-fed, local beef cut to order.

The store was located on the second floor of what had once been a beautiful old barn. The former space for parked tractors and a small granary was now white and sleek with industrial lighting that might have been original, but more likely had been distressed by a kid in Indonesia before being sold at 1,000% markup. A guy with a flamboyant beard greeted me at the counter. His look would have fit in perfectly with Mohawk's group.

"What can I get you today?"

"I need seven porterhouses. They are to be well-marbled..."

"All of our meat is well-marbled. It's grass-fed...."

"... and each one should be no less than 18 ounces. 18-20 ounces would be great."

"I can do that," he said and busied himself with the crinkle of white paper and tape. I took a look over the meat in the counter. This was a head-to-tail place with every cut and offal imaginable offered in trays or advertised with cards. I remembered how my grandmother would buy beef heart for her cats and mince it finely as a special splurge for them. Mr. B, I thought, might enjoy that sort of treat.

"Anything else?" the counterman asked, thumping the packages down on the scale.

"Yeah," I said as I opened the cooler I had brought with me. "How about a beef heart?"

I drove right to the Old City Hall. It was lunchtime, and I thought there might be fewer people. Sure enough, Ruby sat alone, looking off into the distance with a thousand-yard stare.

"Hey, Ruby," I said, approaching her desk.

"Oh! Mr. Moody! What a pleasant surprise." I put the Styrofoam cooler on her table which flexed under the weight in a disturbing manner. "What have we here?"

"It's the ummm… meat for…"

"Say no more," she smiled. This was the most lively I had ever seen her. "I will take care of it." She cracked the cooler open and looked inside. "Oh, ho ho ho ho," she chortled. "That," she said, "is a nice touch. I'll make sure our friends get your gift." She put her finger by the side of her nose like a gangster in an old movie.

Nice touch? I thought. What was she talking about? I was all the way to my car when I realized that I had left the heart for Mr. B in the cooler by mistake. I wasn't about to go and ask for it back.

*Who holds the devil, let him hold him well,*
*He hardly will be caught a second time.*
-*Faust*, Johann Wolfgang von Goethe

# CHAPTER 34

A minivan pulled into my driveway and I watched from the kitchen window as Evanora got out. She struggled for a moment, juggling a large tote bag as she tried to shift enough weight and build the momentum to close the door. The driver started to get out, and she angrily waved him away, finally slamming the door for good measure.

"You know, I would have picked you up and saved you the money," I said when she got to the back door.

"The way I see it, in a few hours, it may be the case that neither of us has any use for money."

She smiled as she spoke, but my stomach flipped over. I didn't want to do this thing tonight. It was all beyond me. I kept trying to convince myself it was the right thing, that we had to stop the creature, but I really just wanted to crawl into bed and hope that everything worked out for the best.

"Where am I going?" she asked.

"Oh. Sorry, through to the dining room." She followed me and sat her bag down on one of the chairs.

"Okay. First things first. If I die tonight and there are remains…"

"What?" A jolt of fear and adrenaline shot through my body.

"I like to be prepared," she said, a little softer. "So, if the worst happens tonight. Well, I guess if my body's still here and not in pieces then it's probably like the second or third worst, but if I die tonight, please call this number and tell them." She handed over an index card to me with a local number.

"Who is it?"

She waved my question away.

"Doesn't matter. Just call and tell them that I am dead and where my body is. They'll take care of everything. You don't have to get involved. Oh! If I do die tonight, you probably shouldn't touch my body. Like try to move it or anything."

"I… guess… okay."

"What about you?"

"What about me what?"

"If you die tonight? Who should I contact?"

"I… I don't know… My ex-wife I guess, but… I haven't talked to her in…"

There was a long silence between us. My throat constricted.

She spoke softly, "Moody. There isn't anybody who would need to know if you die?"

Tears started filling my eyes.

"It's ah…" I wiped them away and cleared my throat. "This is just stress, that's all…" I wiped my eyes and nose on the back of my hand. "Ah, no… I mean. I never thought of it. I don't have a will. My parents are dead. I'm an only child." My voice started to break again.

"It's okay," she said. She moved closer and squeezed my hand. "It was a stupid question, and it doesn't matter because we're going to be fine. Okay?"

I nodded my head.

"Really, I mean it."

"Hmmph," I cleared my throat. "I'm going to make some tea. Do you want any?"

"No. Thank you," she said. "I'm fasting for a clear mind. And, I don't want a full bladder while I'm sitting in a chalk circle for a couple of hours."

"Good point," I said. "I guess I'll skip it too. I'm just going to go splash some water on my face."

When I returned, she was rummaging through her bag. She stopped and looked up at me.

"All right," she said. "I should have everything that we need."

"Should? Why does that make me nervous?"

Evanora glared at me. "I have everything we need for an evocation."

"I thought we were doing a summoning?"

"*I* am performing an evocation which you are free to call a summoning if that helps get you through the night."

She pulled out a finely woven folded cloth from her bag, unfurled it, and spread it out on the kitchen table.

"Take this," she said, passing me a list on the back of an envelope.

"Was this your gas bill?"

"It was the envelope to my gas bill. Now it's an occult checklist. I transmogrified it with a magic ballpoint pen. Check off the items as I call them out: chalk, salt, sigil, candles, notes from *The Key of Solomon*, knife, Abramelin Oil."

The items sat on the table. The chalk, salt, and candles were in small drawstring muslin bags. The knife had a worked leather sheath and a wooden handle, smoothed and stained with use. Evanora's notes were loose leaf, bound together with a staple in the left-hand corner and the oil was murky inside a glass swing-top bottle.

She looked up at me. "Well?"

"Check," I said, "that's everything on the list, but there's still stuff in the bag. You forgot something on your list."

"Hmmm?" she looked at me.

"What's that?" I asked pointing to a box peeking out of her bag.

"Granola bars. I told you—I'm fasting. We might be there for a while and I might want a snack when we're done."

"You really do have ice water in your veins."

"Let's hope not—the incantation will never work."

Evanora looked at all the items on the table and sighed.

"You have the relic I gave you?" she asked me.

"Yup," I said, patting my jeans pocket.

"Okay. So, here's what will happen. We're going to drive over there. Hopefully, Kara is holding up here end of the deal and has left the door unlocked. We anoint ourselves with this oil before we open the door."

"Anoint?"

"We rub the oil on our hands and face before we go in."

I wrinkled my nose. "What's in it?"

"The rendered fat of unbaptized babies who I stole from their mothers on Walpurgisnacht."

I must have started, because she rolled her eyes. She swung the top of the bottle off and waved it under my nose.

"Oh! Cinnamon-y!"

She smirked back at me. "It's plants, herbs, and olive oil. Entities hate it. Try not to get it in your mouth. Your tongue will go numb. So, then, we go in. I draw the circle and the triangle in chalk. Then, I outline the binding area in salt. The entity won't be able to get through as long as those lines stay intact."

"That's what went wrong before," I said and then instantly regretted it.

Evanora took a deep breath, then continued. "The entity is going to be using all sorts of tricks against us. Hallucinations, visual and aural. Remember lying is what these things do, so don't fall for anything that comes out of its mouth… or… wherever."

"Wherever?"

"It can take different forms. It can even split itself. This is big time."

I felt sick.

"But it can't hurt us?"

"It can't, no, as long as the lines stay intact. Something or someone that it has taken over and controls could, but we're moving fast and for it to have seen that far ahead on this plane means that it's stronger than we think."

"And when you say stronger…"

"I mean that it's been harvesting souls. It's preparing to leave its host."

"Alek."

"Yes," she said and took a deep breath.

"And the host?"

"Nothing left. Like the shell of a cicada at the end of summer."

"I'm really feeling sick."

"Focus on the task, not your fear. And especially not on the entity and what it says or does or what it looks or smells like."

"Smells?"

"Stay with me, okay." Her eyes drilled into mine. "I don't want to joke about this. We have to get this; we have to make this right. It's too late to back out."

I looked back at her but couldn't speak. My mouth has too dry.

"Okay," she continued. "When the incantation is complete, the entity will be bound to the vessel. I will gather the vessel. Do not touch anything until I tell you to. Understand?"

I nodded.

"We'll clean up. We'll go home and have a big breakfast."

"So, basically, I just do whatever you tell me. Like wait for your directions? Why do I even have to be there?"

"I can't leave the triangle once I start. If someone nosy calls the cops or a neighbor decides to walk their dog, you'll have to deal with it. Stall them until I complete everything. You'll have to keep me safe."

"I'll do whatever you tell me."

"No! Dammit. Have you not been listening at all?" Her eyes flared, and she slapped the table with her hand. "I'll be focusing all of my energy on the spell. I won't be able to have a conversation with you. You'll know what to do when. Just keeping us safe will be your biggest job."

I nodded and watched as she began to repack her bag.

"What's it like?" I asked.

"What is what like?" She kept adjusting items in her bag.

"When you cast a spell." She wrinkled her nose in distaste at my *Charmed*-level knowledge of magical terms. "Do you feel... I don't know? Invincible? Powerful?"

Evanora stopped what she was doing, sighed, and looked up at me.

"It's not about power. I mean, it was, and that was the problem. Susan wanted magic for power. To show people how strong she was and how wrong they were about her. She tried to take possession of power that she hadn't earned. And that's why we all ended up in this mess."

I kept my mouth shut.

"Okay, but that doesn't really answer my question."

Evanora looked at me, hesitated, and then started again.

"What's it like inside the circle? During an evocation like this one? I'm not trying to control the entity; I'm trying to control myself. Before you start any magic, but especially magic this big, you have to know who you are, where your center is. That was one of many things I ignored last time. I have to forget that I'm sitting inside a chalk circle of ancient design, forget that the only thing keeping me from being lost forever are some runes and salt. I have to focus on my real power, my true weapon: knowledge. If I forget who I am or if I step into that circle without knowing, it's all over before it begins. The entity will use that; I'll have opened up a conduit for it to enter and that will be that. Game over."

She paused and took a breath.

"Is that what happened… before? I'm not trying to be a jerk, but I feel like I should have some idea since I'm basically setting myself up as Alek 2.0."

She shrugged her shoulders.

"I… ah… yeah, I think so. Neither of us belonged there."

"Why did Mohawk end up inside Alek instead of you?"

"I wish I knew. I mean, he was closer and proximity is important, but… Look, Alek was a fantastic actor. He could have, would have been a big star on stage or film; whatever he wanted he could have had. One of the reasons he was so good was that he could let a role take him over because he was, I don't know. It sounds cruel or dismissive and that's not what I'm trying to do here. I loved, I love Alek, like a brother, but his gift was being empty. He didn't have to be someone because he could be anyone, and multiple anyones. He could pick up a persona and wear it like a jacket. And… I think… it saw that empty space and slid right into it."

She shook her head and pinched the bridge of her nose.

"You know, for a long time after, I was even a little miffed. I mean, why didn't it take me over, I'm the special one with all the power right?" A brittle laugh shot from her mouth.

"Maybe if I had just stayed here and studied the craft for another year, instead of trying to teach myself, maybe just one more year, I could have figured out more, but…"

"This," she said hoisting her bad arm. "This is just collateral damage from my pride. Susan knew who she wanted to be but not who she was. If she had, she never would have tried to do something so far beyond her."

"You can't get down on yourself like that," I started, "you have to…"

She raised her hand. "Stop. We're done with this

conversation. The last thing any of us need is me doing too much thinking. It will ruin the intention and sour the spell. Susan wanted magic for power. Now, I'll use magic to set it all back right."

Evanora made a final adjustment in her bag and then looked up at me.

"Ready?" she asked.

"I guess. Are you going to change here? I don't know if there's anywhere at the mill."

"Change? Into what?"

"You know… your… clothes."

"I'm wearing clothes, Moody. It's something I often do."

"I mean, your witch clothes."

She looked at me in a state of astonishment.

"Witch clothes? Like what? A robe? A pointy hat? Maybe attach a magical wart?"

"No. I just mean. You're just wearing jeans and a tee-shirt. Don't you have special clothes for this sort of thing?"

"Yeah. Jeans and a tee-shirt. I have a fleece jacket in my bag in case it gets chilly. Did you put together a special outfit for tonight? As my lovely assistant, by any chance do you have a tuxedo jacket and a leotard? Some fishnets? Because I'd really like to see that. No, I'd really like to film that ensemble."

"Forget it," I muttered. "I was just asking."

"Witch clothes," she snorted under her breath and hoisted her bag on her shoulder.

"Let's just pretend I didn't say anything."

Outside, the air was cold and stung my lungs. A waning moon dimly lit the city. I walked around the front of the car and opened my door. Out of the corner of my eye, I saw something moving fast and low, coming right towards me.

"Ahhhhhhhhhh!" I jumped back and fumbled in my pocket for the relic Evanora had given me. Before I could even get my hand in my pocket, the dark blur was on the driver's seat, turning to face me.

"Mrrrrrro?"

"I took a deep gasping breath.

"Mr. B? My God. You almost gave me a heart attack, buddy."

I could hear Evanora snickering as she walked towards the passenger side of the door.

"Looks like I don't have a thing to worry about tonight. And to I think I was worried about you being a liability."

"He just ... came out of nowhere and... Hey! A liability?"

"Joke. Let's go."

"C'mon, Mr. B," I said and reached for him. He jumped into the back seat. I sighed. "C'mon, buddy. We have stuff to do." I leaned in and reached back. He stayed just out of my reach. I stood up and moved to the rear driver's side door. Evanora stood looking at me and shaking her head.

"Stumped by a cat."

"Well, he is a wild exotic cat..."

"Just leave him. We have to get going."

"But..." I stood up to face her over the car. "Will he be safe?"

"More so than we most likely."

"Okay, buddy," I said to the backseat. "Looks like you win again. Don't tell your owner, okay?"

"Moody?" I looked over the car roof at her. "We're all going to be fine," Evanora said then stopped before she opened her door.

"Did you bring a flashlight like I told you?"

"Yeah," I said. "Fresh batteries and everything. I don't think we'll need it though. The mill has lights."

"You'll need it," she said to me as she slid into the passenger seat and closed the door. "Things are going to get dark tonight."

# CHAPTER 35

True to her word, Kara had left the lock hanging on the chain but unfastened. While Evanora began setting up the area, I shuttled back and forth with her bag and supplies. For over an hour now, I stood against the wall watching her work.

"Gah. I'm going crazy. I wish there something more I could do."

"Go take a walk while I finish up," Evanora said. "Get some fresh air. It's going to be a long night."

"Are you sure?" I said. "It looks like you're almost ready."

"No, no. Not even close," she said, inscribing shapes onto the floor with chalk. "You go ahead. Check on Mr. B. I'll bet he's lonely."

I made my way back out, gently closing and latching the door behind me. There was some light flickering in the windows, but Kara had told us that there were lamps on timers inside the mill to deter trespassers, so I wasn't worried about drawing attention.

Mr. B, on the other hand, seemed determined to make sure that someone knew he was here. I could hear him meowing, long and pitiful, from twenty feet away from the car, even with the windows rolled up.

"Ah, c'mon, buddy," I said to him through the glass. "It's okay. This situation is all just such a mess. I told you not to come anyhow." I placed my hand on the glass where he had braced his paw. He started meowing more and faster. He was furious. He started butting his head against the glass. I had never seen him do anything like that.

"Hey, hey, hey. Careful. C'mon, little brother." He was a small animal, but there was a resounding thud each time he butted his head. "You can't do that; you're going to hurt yourself."

I reached for the handle and cracked the door to try to slide into the seat and comfort him while still depriving him of an escape route. The space between the car door and the jamb must have been as large as a garage door to him and he took off at a dead run across the long lawn.

"Dammit, B!" I muttered and took off after him. The moon glowed down giving me just enough illumination to catch occasional glimpses of the white at the tip of his tail and the grass parting as he bound through it. He ran past the cemetery wall, then doglegged away from the mill and came to a rest at the smokehouse door. He turned around and watched me run with a vague interest and what seemed to be amusement.

"Damn… it…" I wheezed when I caught up to him. The blood was thumping in my ears and my knee had already begun to ache. When this adventure was over, I swore that I would join the YMCA. Being this out of shape was ridiculous. I stood bent over with my hands on my thighs until I could breathe again. B waited for me to recover. I stood up, leaned back, stretching my back, and took a deep breath. Then I smelled it.

My lungs filled with a deep smell of filth and fresh blood. As a boy, I hunted with my father for whitetail deer in the Pennsylvania woods. When I was 13, he gut-shot a big doe. She squealed and drummed her legs until he shot her in the head at close range, out of panic more than anything, I think. The only thing worse than that deer's exploded and collapsed head was the smell when we ran the knife down the skin of the belly and the blood and ruined guts spilled out. Mr. B looked at me and then the door as if to say, *You know you have to look. You know that's why we're here.*

I turned on the flashlight that I had stuffed in my pocket before we left the house. With my left hand, I pulled open the door. Mr. B growled low beside me and sat in front of my feet.

Kara hung upside down from a chain in the center of the smokehouse. She was nude and had been cut open from crotch to throat. Her mouth hung open in a last scream and her eyes were wide, the whites filled with blood. Her guts hung from her body looping and piling on the floor. Symbols had been carved into her arms and legs. I stumbled back outside, turned toward the mill, and heaved. There was nothing in my system to vomit, but I stood there, bent over as my stomach violently spasmed.

*My God,* I thought. *Poor Kara. She had nothing to do with all this. Who would have...?*

Light flared through the windows from inside the mill.

*She had started.* Evanora had tricked me into leaving, and I had taken the bait. She was all alone, and the thing would be stronger than we thought with this last sacrifice.

Mr. B was already running towards the mill and I followed him right up to the door and unlatched it. He scampered in, and I threw myself through the doorway, only to bounce back as if I had fallen into a trampoline. I tried again, throwing punches, but there was what felt like an invisible elastic membrane blocking my way. Evanora sat cross-legged in one of the circles she had drawn with her eyes closed and her mouth moving. In the bigger circle, in the center of the room, a white flame three feet across and eight feet high twisted like a tornado. She had lied to me when she said there were still hours of preparation. Not only was she done preparing, but she was also almost done summoning.

"Alone and unbound, I address Abaddon. I command the shadow claiming now its power. By that of this name and this flame..."

The air shimmered in my vision as if I was looking across a parking lot on a summer's day. The shimmers danced and then began to take shape in a monochromatic silvery tone. A young man in a Civil War uniform sobbed as he cradled another soldier whose head had been cracked like a hard-boiled egg, the brains spilling out. Bodies writhed and were devoured by flames inside a vast marble hall. Townspeople stood around a man hanging from a tree, the body bloated before my eyes and then burst viscera. Men and women copulated with various and changing partners in front of a vast mound made up of what had once been human flesh. I couldn't move my head or tear my eyes away. A deep terror filled me along with a despair so bleak that I couldn't see or remember why I was standing there or why I even bothered to live. One of the women in the orgy turned and locked eyes on me and then suddenly she was my ex-wife, looking at me and laughing. I tried to scream but all that would leave my throat was a gurgle like I was drowning in a mud puddle, the grit settling into my lungs. Then, at last, I saw Susan and Alek as they had been that night, screaming and thrashing in pain, their flesh bubbling and sloughing. I was finally able to look away. I turned my head and thought for a moment that the hallucination had followed me.

In the sickening pale firelight, to the right, standing in front of the massive old millstones was Alek. His pants were soaked in blood and he was bare-chested. Tears of crimson ran from the corners of his eyes. He had finger-painted glyphs across his chest and ruined face in Kara's blood. The lines of the symbols following the whorls of scars and long-ago melted flesh. He held a baseball bat in his hand.

# CHAPTER 36

My arm started to burn. The bad arm, I mean. That was the first sign that the spell was working. I pushed the pain away and concentrated on the words. Moody was out there somewhere. For a moment, fear for him flashed up into the back of my head, but I shoved it down. He was okay, or he wasn't. I couldn't get distracted this time. Then, a great deafening roar flooded through my head. I felt that if I had touched the side of my jaw that I would find blood flowing from my ears. Panic crept up from my stomach, and I feared that the wind would sweep me away, out of the circle that I had drawn. The circle that protected me. I centered myself again. My mouth recited the words that I had memorized, but my mind was running through my matronage. The women and a few men of power who had come before me, who had raised me and taught me, and who had led me to this point in time.

In front of me, inside the triangle, the silver fire started to appear and move of its own volition into violent, vulgar tableaus. But I was no longer seeing. I had moved deep inside myself to a vast universe of lights and stars where I floated and moved as if slipping through my own bloodstream. I could reach out and reorder the lights, moving them as I saw fit with great skill and power. I saw the women, my aunties, and grandmothers smiling as I did so, restoring the order inside myself and then, as a result, to this wicked space. I felt my body, my flesh, stretch, and old muscles reawaken as if I had just come out of a long deep sleep. I opened my eyes which had been clenched for long minutes and saw the creature in front of me. Just for one moment, I could see the whole room as if I had left my body for a moment. Moody was there, fighting to break the perimeter spell that I had laid to keep him out. The Mohawk thing was there blustering and raging, but I also saw something like fear or concern for itself betrayed in its eyes. And I saw someone else, moving behind me in the shadows.

# CHAPTER 37

Evanora's body shuddered as I watched, and I had a sudden panic that the demon had been able to attack her even within her circle. She righted herself and stretched her neck like a wrestler warming up, but with her eyes still closed and her lips still moving.

"Ah," the monstrosity spoke from inside the circle. The voice boomed and echoed against the mill's ceiling. "The little apprentice who believes herself to be a master. When we're done here, I'll be taking you with me to be a whore in hell. After all, I'll need a replacement. This one," he pointed to Alek, "this one wants his mommy back. Isn't that right, little burnt songbird?"

While the demon spoke, Alek had been working his way behind Evanora as she continued the incantation with her eyes closed.

"No shelter but that of my making..."

Alek reared back and brought the baseball bat across Evanora's back. The air *woof*ed out of her and I heard ribs crack. The membrane that she had warded the room with and which I had been leaning on disappeared, and I fell flat on my face.

The thing's laughter rang off the mill's ceiling. A wheezing groan that might have been a laugh or a sob escaped Alek, and he brought the bat down again, this time on Evanora's knee.

"Finish the little songbird witch. I tire of all of this half-life here and there. I crave new amusement and the screams of your mother have become boring."

Alek made the sound again and drew back his bat.

And then his face was obscured by a writhing grey mass of fur and teeth. With a low growl and a hiss, Mr. B had launched himself from a stack of pamphlet boxes onto Alek's face with a wild ferocity. Alek made a high-pitched noise like an injured rabbit, dropped the bat, and reached with both hands to pry the cat off his face. Blood streamed down where Mr. B had opened up deep cuts on his forehead and around his eyes. One deep cut had opened up the hole in his face that served as a nostril and another cut extended the fold at the corner of his eye into a dripping bloody furrow. As he threw Mr. B to the wooden floor, Alek's feet became tangled in the bat and he fell hard without catching himself. I could hear a bone break from where I was. As he fell, he crossed into the triangle. When he hit, his blood sprayed up and into the white flame that surrounded the monstrosity. The fire flared up suddenly and a tentacle with a stingered-end sunk itself into the meat of Alek's shoulder. The monstrosity drew him in closer and as the flame grew, the thing drew Alex against it, and then it was sliding inside of the man. It inhabited him. Alek's skin stretched and bulged in impossible ways like a fat man trying on a too-small suit. There was the cracking noise of bones heaving themselves out of joints. Alek made hideous gurgling noises and screamed gibberish. The smell of burning garbage filled the mill. His eyes rolled back in his head. It seemed to go on forever. And then a great silence.

I heard Evanora in my head: *chalk*. I still don't know how I managed to break the fear that had frozen me to my spot. In the almost nightly nightmares I have about that evening, I never do. Instead in my dream, I stand stock-still in fear as the Alek Thing steps from the warding triangle and kills us all slowly.

I ran forward, and, careful not to cross the line myself and filled in the line of the triangle that had been broken when Alek had crossed. The Alek Thing waved its hand just as I finished and a diminished shock blow sent me skittering across the floor, filling my palms with splinters. I pulled myself back onto my elbows. A knife sat in front of Evanora within the circle. She had been planning to sacrifice herself to get the required blood. She had lied to me. Now she dug in her bag frenzied and then pulled out something small enough to fit into the palm of her hand.

The Alek Thing raged. The noise caused me actual physical pain. It was the sound of a thousand bulls bellowing at once in fear and pain. I watched as Alek, the demon now fully inside of him and heedless of preserving the shell that it no longer needed, slammed its fists against the invisible walls that the restored triangle had created. Bones cracked in its hands. Bloody foam flew from its mouth and snot ran from its nose. Its eyes bulged and had turned completely black. When it opened its mouth to bellow, I could see rows of jagged crooked teeth like the mouth of a shark and a deeply split tongue. The two sides moving independently of each other. It met my eyes and bellowed again. I felt my bladder begin to loosen. I couldn't look away.

Evanora closed her eyes again.

"By flame and blood, by stone and will, shall you hear me. By the thousand sacred names and the sigils drawn, I command you. I bind you."

She looked at the object, one last time, kissed it, and then with her good arm, sent it arching into the triangle, to land at the Alek Thing's feet.

"You bitch. You…"

The flame came up again, a blue color this time, swirling around the Alek Thing which screamed and pounded its hands against an invisible barrier. A great noise of a whirlwind or a train passing too close, filled the space, replacing the bellows of the monster until I lost all sense of where or who I was and the edges of my vision tunneled.

No more than a few minutes could have passed before I

came to. Mr. B was licking my hair. The room stunk like a wet campfire. Smoke filled the lower six inches of the room and flickering light illuminated the mill's walls. The mill was on fire.

"Oh God. Evanora." I hauled myself up painfully and went to her. She still lay inside the circle.

"Evanora!" I yelled and shook her.

"Ahhhh… my ribs. You idiot."

"Oh my God. You're alive. We have to get out of here."

"O, help me up." The fire had begun to intensify. "My bag," she motioned to the floor. I grabbed the bag and looped it across my body, then grabbed Mr. B and stuck him in the bag. He looked annoyed but stayed. "Get the vessel," she said, pointing to the triangle.

"But if I cross…"

"It's over now. Just get it. I can barely walk. I think he broke my leg."

Fear rose up in the back of my throat like vomit again. I took a deep breath through my nostrils and strode over. I stopped at the chalk.

"Moody! C'mon!" Evanora shouted.

*Grasp the nettle*, I thought, and I stepped across the lines. Nothing happened. I grabbed the object off the floor and ran back to Evanora. My heart was pounding.

"Lean on me," I said, and we limped towards the door. The first floor was filled with smoke, but he felt our way out coughing and gagging down the front steps and away from the mill. The short trip to the car felt like climbing Kilimanjaro. When we were there, we rested our backs against the cool of the car hood and watched the mill burn.

"He killed Kara."

Evanora didn't answer. She looked at the ground and then back at the flames.

"You need a hospital," I said. Her leg was at an odd angle

and was almost surely broken. Lord only knew what her back looked like or what kind of internal damage the blow might have caused.

"I do. I certainly do." She laughed, and I realized that she was in shock. "We did it, Moody."

"I guess we did. C'mon," I moved to help her to the passenger side door.

"Wait," she said, "give me the vessel."

I still had it wrapped in my fist, so tightly, that she had to peel my fingers back, laughing as she did so.

"The mill!" I said, realizing for the first time what the vessel had been. It was the small, shoddy die-cast mill she had bought during our first visit there.

"I told you I was thinking of starting a collection," she smiled and let me guide her into the seat.

# CHAPTER 38

The mill was a complete loss, according to the paper, burnt to the ground with an odd ferocity for a building with nothing really in it. The fire marshal declared the cause to be faulty wiring. Kara's body, or what was left of it, was found during the investigation. The heat and ferocity of the fire had reduced her to bones. Any evidence of the trauma had been burnt away. The investigation settled on the idea that she had been working late and become trapped in the smokehouse when the fire started. Sparks shot up from the mill and onto the shake shingles of the smokehouse. The marshal said that the blaze would have been incredibly hot and inescapably fast. Her school held a memorial service for her with a candlelit vigil two days after the fire. I drove there, then sat shaking in the parking lot. My chest constricted and all I could see was her body hanging there. I drove home and went straight to bed.

I managed to pull myself together long enough to go back to the mill to look for Mr. B. The site was still taped off. The ground was churned into mud from the firefighters' boots. The mill was nothing more than a hole in the ground filled with debris. The smokehouse had been reduced to a four-foot-high blackened square of stones that had been the foundation and partial walls. A few flowers and balloons were placed in front of where the smokehouse door had been. Kara had been odd, but that hadn't stopped people from loving her.

I kicked through the weeds calling for Mr. B. I took a stick and poked dissolutely at the wreckage that had been the mill. There had been so much smoke that I hadn't been able to see if he had managed to escape. When I had bundled Evanora in the car, Mr. B hadn't even crossed my mind. The idea of him dying horribly in the fire began to invade my thoughts every moment of every day. I drove back home, put a bowl of kibble on the deck, and stared out of the window at it, willing him to show up, until the sky grew dark and I could feel the cold on the other side of the window.

Evanora was in the hospital for a week. She had suffered a broken leg and two cracked ribs. I visited her every day. Some days, I didn't speak. Sometimes I would read to her from the newspaper. Sometimes she would tell me old stories about the city that her mother and grandmother had told her. On the last day of her stay, when I walked in, she was propped up on pillows. Her face flushed with color and the deep dark circle under eyes had largely dissipated. Inside a tote bag, I smuggled Mr. B in with me. The night before, around 11, I heard a cry outside. When I opened the door, there he sat. A little worse for wear; he was missing a few singed whiskers and there was a cut on his haunch. But he was alive. I opened a celebratory can of tuna and slept soundly for the first time with him curled into a crescent against my belly. He barely fussed when I swept him into the tote bag before entering the hospital. Now, he hopped onto the bed with her.

"Mr. B!" she said. "The hero returns!" She looked up at me and smiled. I told her that I was falling apart—obsessing over abandoning him at the mill. She scratched under his chin and he extended his neck and shaped his mouth so that he looked like he was grinning at us.

"I really want to take him home with me," she said.

A sick feeling hit the bottom of my stomach. Of course, she did. And B would probably love it. A witch and her familiar.

"Oh, but I won't," she said scratching him under his chin. He moved his face so that he looked like he was smiling in pleasure. "I think you two need each other. It wouldn't be fair."

"Yeah," I said. I was still jumping at any sound and the nightmares had kept me from sleeping since the fire. I was already looking for PTSD support groups.

"But there is something you could do for me," she said looking up at me.

"Yeah? I mean, of course, name it."

"Drive me home. They said they're going to discharge me at noon."

"Of course, no problem. I'll be here and help you get settled at your place. I can even stay if you need me to…"

She held up her hand. "Just the ride. I just conquered an evil entity. I don't need help getting to the bathroom."

"We."

"What?"

"We conquered an evil entity."

"Yeah. That's right," she said, "*we.*"

I smiled.

"And you said *entity* instead of *demon.*"

Mr. B purred and curled himself into a tight ball next to her arm.

The last of the day's light was thin but bright as I drove home after dropping her off at her apartment. Coming around the corner I could see a white van emblazoned on the side panel with "Mattson Brothers—Stone Masonry and Historical Renovation" parked in front of my house and a dump truck parked in front of it. As I turned into the alley to go to my garage, I nodded hello to the crew. A man my age, but tall and thin with a shock of black hair going grey and steely, stood chewing on a smoldering cigar while two solidly built young men in their twenties cleaned the broken stones from my wall and threw the debris into the back of the dump truck as the winter's late sun shone down and warmed the muscles of their backs.

# CHAPTER 39

On the second night after Mohawk was hanged, a wagon with a single mule moved soundlessly down the street. A waxing moon fought against the clouds in the cold air. A woman with hair the color of steel sat with the reins in her hands. Beside her sat her younger sister, and in the wagon bed, her two nephews, grown men thick with muscle, who steadied a young oak tree with its roots wrapped in burlap. Shovels sat at their feet.

The group pulled up beside the hanging body of Mohawk. Crows had enjoyed their way with the body. The eyes and the tongue were gone. The blood caked blackly on the corpse which had not yet begun to swell. One of the men stood up from his seat on the wagon and with his Barlow knife, sliced through the rope. The body hit the ground with the sound of a full feed sack being tossed onto a granary floor. The woman with steel-colored hair stepped down from the wagon and stood over the body. She spat on the ground and nodded at her sister. Her lips moved quickly and soundlessly while her hands danced in the air. A drunkard coming home late would have not have seen or heard anything. If he had looked towards the activity, a chill might have walked up his spine and he might have stepped a little quicker, but in the morning, he would rub his burning eyes and not even remember passing.

The woman stepped back and nodded to her nephews. They took up their shovels and began spading into the ground, making a neat pile of dirt to the side. The digging was easy. The two women laid a cloth on the ground and from a satchel brought forth a book, needle and silvery thread, and slim, finely made knives and chisels. More words were spoken over the tools and the objects caught and held the available moonlight.

The men completed their task in a short time and motioned to the women with a nod of their heads. They picked up the body by the shoulders and feet and heaved it into the hole. Joining them at the graveside, the women looked down at the rictus of Mohawk's face. His eyes were still open with bits of dirt clinging to the whites. The younger of the two women stepped into the grave, and, taking up the needle and thread, skillfully sewed together Mohawk's mouth and eyes. There was a low keening, like an old house shifting on its foundation in a storm. The sisters looked at each other.

"Just in time," whispered the taller of the men and earned a withering glance of reproach from his aunt. He offered his mother an arm to help her step out of the grave. She ignored it, hiking up her skirt and stepping out with grace. She placed the needle back on the cloth as her sister picked up one of the knives. She nodded at the men, who cut away the burlap that protected the oak's roots. Together they lifted the tree which crowned a little taller than they stood and placed it atop of Mohawk's chest. The groaning noise laced through the night air again.

The woman with steel-colored hair stepped down into the grave and her sister dragged the cloth and its implements to within arm's reach. With nimble fingers, the elder cut symbols into the bark of the oak, low on the trunk. The images glowed with blue light and then, like water soaking into a cloth, were absorbed into the tree. Her mouth and that of her sister worked soundlessly the entire time. Thirty minutes of incantations and carving went by. Finally, the two women stopped speaking at the same time. The older woman stepped nimbly out of the grave and nodded at her sister. She picked up a small vial and splashed the contents on the branches and trunks. The tree seemed to lurch like someone awaking from a deep sleep, shrugging its shoulders and stretching its feet. There was a noise like a child kicking her feet through fallen leaves as the tree's roots grew visibly. With a final crack, the growth was done. The roots had fastened themselves into something like a rib cage around Mohawk's body and had already begun to break the flesh down, drawing it with root tendrils the size of hairs to the center trunk.

The witches, pleased, nodded and motioned to the men. They stepped up and filled the dirt back over the body and the tree roots. As the sisters gathered their tools and cloth back into the satchel, the men tamped the dirt down gently as if patting the back of an old friend. They paused for a moment as a keening noise like a faraway cat in heat echoed through the night. When there was no more of the noise, they returned to their work.

After the men were done, the women spoke a few last words and then all four gathered themselves back into the wagon. The mule walked on with the smallest touch of the reins. In the morning, if a newcomer to town had asked, the locals would have said that the oak had been there as long as anyone could remember.

*About the Author*

Michael Dittman is a professor of English and Creative Writing who lives and writes near Pittsburgh, Pennsylvania surrounded by the palimpsest of the Appalachian Rust Belt. He is the author of *Jack Kerouac; A Biography*, *Masterpieces of the Beat Generation*, and *Small Brutal Incidents*. Contact him at michaeldittman.com

CPSIA information can be obtained
at www.ICGtesting.com
Printed in the USA
BVHW051624160523
664249BV00020B/193